JAWS OF DEATH

Before Lannigan got to his partner's side, Slim had knocked the wolf away. The animal lay at his feet, kicking convulsively. Lannigan grabbed Slim's arm and pulled him back. Slim's hand was streaming blood.

"I never saw a wolf act like that before," said Lannigan.

"I have." China Slim's voice was low and sober. "I seen 'em come on you after they was shot dead. Not just wolves, either. Dogs, coons, skunks. That wolf had rabies. Lobo, you're looking at a dead man standing here."

Other Exciting Western Adventures From Dell Books

LANNIGAN'S REVENGE

Mel Marshall

A DELL BOOK

Published by
Dell Publishing Co., Inc.
1 Dag Hammarskjold Plaza
New York, New York 10017

Dell ® TM 681510, Dell Publishing Co., Inc.

ISBN: 0-440-15014-0

Printed in the United States of America

First printing—June 1980

*To Dona Horine in gratitude for her
invaluable assistance*

CHAPTER 1

Anybody taking a quick glance at the fracas going on in the S Bar T bunkhouse would have sworn that more than two men were fighting.

Lannigan had toppled Harris with a belly-punch, and before the bigger man could get up from the floor, had jumped on him astraddle. Harris had been more surprised than hurt by Lannigan's looping blow and was ready when the little man landed on him. He grabbed Lannigan in a bear hug that took one arm out of action and seriously hampered Lannigan's ability to swing his free arm effectively.

For a minute or so the two men thrashed around on the floor, first Lannigan on top, then Harris. The other hands were standing back to give the fighters room, watching the struggle with the critical, knowing eyes of men who'd not only seen plenty of similar fights, but who'd taken part in their share of them.

"Damn you, runt, leggo my ear!" Harris's voice rose sharply out of the farrago of flailing arms and legs, and there was pain in it.

One of the onlookers asked, "You think we oughta make 'em break it up?"

"Ah, let 'em finish," another said. "The little fella come real close to taking Hardcase last week, when they tangled at the saloon in Chispos. Let's see how they finish up this time."

Harris yelled again, but Lannigan was silent. His mouth was full of ear and his jaws were clamped tight. He'd been in enough rough-and-tumble fights to know that Marquis of Queensberry rules didn't apply on Texas cattle ranches any more than they did in saloons in the cattle country. Neither man expected a stand-up-and-box-clean scrap, and neither was being disappointed.

Hardcase Harris brought a knee up, but the two men were so close together that the knee scraped the floor before it reached Lannigan's crotch. Harris let up on the bear hug and held on with one arm while he looped the other and pounded on the small man's neck with a horn-hard fist. Lannigan opened his mouth to breathe and lost his clamp on the ear he'd been bulldogging. The fighters rolled, their boots thudding on the floor, and upset a chair. Prod Seeton heard the ruckus as he was passing by on his way to the corral and rushed into the bunkhouse ready for action. He shoved through the cluster of cowhands arced just inside the door and dived into the fight.

Prod was almost as big as Lannigan and Harris put together, and stronger than either of them. He'd earned his job as foreman of the S Bar T because he could handle men and cattle equally well, and because he was big and tough enough to settle disputes between the hands even when the disputes had erupted into a flurry of swinging fists, like the one between Lannigan and Harris. Seeton pulled the combatants apart and yanked them to their feet, then stood between them while the two men swayed briefly. After they'd found their balance they were just angry and groggy enough to try to get at one another and continue fighting, but Prod held them apart with one of his big hands pressed against each man's chest.

He waited while the pair leaned on his hands, panting, too winded to say anything. Prod wanted to grin when he looked at Lannigan, but was wise enough not to. The little man was barely an inch over five feet tall, and was proportionately slight in build. He was hatless, but the fracas hadn't ruffled his short, tight-curled hair, which was red, as befitted his Irish name. It was neither brick-red nor Hereford red, but more the dark russet of a good roan cutting horse. Lannigan's eyes were the deep blue of a pair of unfaded jeans. Set deep in his head, they gave him an old-man's look that contrasted strangely with his youthful, almost unlined face and deeply tanned cheeks. A few beads of sweat were trickling down his cheeks and dripping off his square-cut chin, and he brushed them off with his sleeve.

Seeton said, "All right, now. You two roosters back off and tell me how this started out."

Harris and Lannigan began talking at the same time, and Prod shut them up. He jabbed a thick finger at Harris. "You talk first, Hardcase," he commanded. "Lannigan, you button up your mouth till he's finished, then I'll listen to you."

"Ah, this feisty little runt can't take a joke," Harris growled.

He was as tall as Seeton, but not as heavily built, and towered over Lannigan by a foot. Harris's body had the lean wiriness that comes from hard work starting at daybreak and ending after sundown, and his hands moved in the quick, sure fashion of men who use them every minute of the long hours they work. His face explained his nickname. It was lean and stony-hard, with bumps of muscle bunched at the jaw points. His eyes were as sleety-gray as a bad winter sky; his thin lips disappeared almost completely when pressed together. On cheeks that bore the pits of old smallpox scars, a two-day stubble of heavy beard showed blue-black.

"I wasn't trying to rile him," Harris went on, putting a hand up to feel the ear from which a small trickle of blood was dripping and running down his neck. "I just come in from my morning line-ride and said hello to him, and the damned little runt sailed into me."

"That right, Lannigan?" Seeton asked.

Glowering at Harris across the foreman's burly chest, the small man nodded. "I guess I hit him first, all right. But he didn't tell you the whole story, about how I beat him up last week when he called me a runt before."

"Wait a minute." Seeton frowned at Lannigan. "You just begun working here yesterday evening."

"Aw, the peewee's talking about another run-in we had, at the saloon over to Chispos," Harris put in.

Prod and Lannigan started to talk at the same time, and Harris still hadn't finished what he was trying to say, so for a moment their voices filled the bunkhouse. Seeton finally shouted the other two into silence. Looking from Harris to Lannigan, he asked, "Now, what's this about a fracas you two had last week? It's the first I heard about it."

Again the two fighters tried to answer at the same time, until the foreman shouted them down. He turned to the other ranch hands who were still crowding into the corner of the door. "Any of you men with Harris when him and Lannigan tangled over to Chispos?"

"Me and Jug was along," one of them volunteered.

"You tell me what happened, then," Seeton ordered.

"It wasn't such a much, Prod. We went over to pick up that load of freight, you remember? Got it all in

the wagon, and stepped in at the Dixie for a beer before we started back. Lannigan was there when we
went in, and we commenced talking. He'd just asked
us did we know any spreads around here that needed
hands, and Hardcase piped up. He said something
about Lannigan not being big enough to deck a cow-
pony, told him a runt his size oughta go south of the
Concho and get a job on a sheep ranch. Lannigan
sailed into him, and had him down on the floor before
me and Jug could pull 'em apart."

"You didn't say anything about all that to me,"
Prod told the man. He turned to Lannigan and
jabbed a finger in his chest. "And you didn't tell me
you had a grudge going with one of my S Bar T
hands, either. I'd've known about it, I never would've
hired you on."

"I wasn't chasing this bigmouth here," Lannigan
protested. "I settled him up when we had that brush
in the saloon. And if any of them mentioned being
from the S Bar T, I don't recall it."

"He's telling it straight, Prod," Jug interrupted from
the group near the door. "Didn't none of us tell him
where we was from. Hell, we hadn't been talking
more'n a minute before they started to fight. Then me
and Sam got Harris outa the saloon right away."

Seeton was still dissatisfied. "How'd you two happen to stay peaceful last night?" he asked Harris and
Lannigan. "Why'd you have to wait until Sunday
morning to act up?"

"They didn't know each other was here last night,"
Sam volunteered. "Lannigan didn't come in the bunkhouse till after we'd all turned in."

"That's the way it was," Lannigan agreed. "By the
time I got my pony settled in the corral and had some
supper, it was dark. So when I got in the bunkhouse
here, I just lighted the lamp long enough to fix up a

place to sleep. I don't even remember who it was told me which bunk to take or anything else."

"It was me," one of the men by the door said.

"Me and Pecos had the early line-ride today," Harris told the foreman. "We got outa the bunkhouse before it was light enough to see anything much. And I'd just come in, a few minutes ago, when the runt jumped me again."

"Now, stop calling me a runt, damn it!" Lannigan ducked under Seeton's arm and closed with Harris once more. Before the foreman could move, he bounced a fist off Harris's jaw and the big man hit the floor.

Seeton grabbed Lannigan's shirttail and pulled him back from his stance over Harris. "You cool down," he commanded. Anger crept into his voice for the first time. "Hardcase didn't call you a fighting name; you didn't have any call to hit him."

"Runt's a fighting word in my book," Lannigan retorted. "So's peewee and shorty and any other kind of name that makes fun of me because I'm not the size of a Brahma bull, like most of these fellows."

Lannigan's protests ended in a grunting sigh as Harris rose to his knees and started throwing punches into the small man's midsection. Seeton kicked out to stop Harris, and the kneeling man grabbed the foreman's booted foot, twisted it, and toppled Seeton to the floor.

For a few seconds there was a three-way fracas going: Harris, Lannigan, and Prod swinging indiscriminately, none of them able to pick a target in the interweaving of swaying bodies and flailing arms. Seeton was the first to recover; he was fresher than the other two. He got a hand on Lannigan's chest and pushed him across the floor, backward, into the knot of men at the door. They grabbed and held him while

Seeton backhanded Harris, knocking him to the floor again. The foreman got to his feet, his face welted from the punches he'd taken.

"That's all she wrote," he announced. "Hardcase, Lannigan, you're both fired. Get your hotrolls together and come on over to the office for your time."

"Now, damn it, Prod, this wasn't my fault," Harris protested from his seat on the floor. "That little sawed-off saddle tramp hit me first. I didn't start it."

"Hell he didn't!" Lannigan called. He was still struggling to break away from the hands that were restraining him. "He knew better'n to call me what he did!"

Seeton looked with hard eyes at both Lannigan and Harris. He told them, "This's Sunday, and I don't hold with doing any kind of business on the Lord's day, but I don't aim to have you two on my hands overnight. Both of you know the Major's rules, and both of you know you broke 'em. So you keep apart till you're off the S Bar T range, you hear me? Or I'll handle you unmerciful, and both of you know I can do it." He stamped out of the bunkhouse, the high heels of his boots thudding on the floor to echo the anger he carried with him.

For a moment, Harris and Lannigan glared at one another, then Lannigan said, "Well, flapjaw, you got us fired. Might not make much nevermind to you, but like I told you and them others at the saloon last week, it's been a spell since I held a steady job. Ever time I ask a foreman for work, he looks at me and says I ain't big enough to pull my weight. When I hired on here last night, I aimed to stay a while."

"You go to hell, ru——" Harris saw Lannigan's hands clenching to fists and changed in mid-word. "Lannigan. I don't like it any more'n you do." He turned away before the small man could reply, and walked back to his bunk where he began throwing the odds and ends of his personal gear into a set of scuffed saddlebags.

Lannigan followed Harris's example. The other hands stood and watched silently. Their faces showed sympathy, but both Lannigan and Hardcase were too edgy to encourage any expressions of condolence. Packing was a matter of only a few minutes for the newly unemployed cowhands. Lannigan finished first; having just arrived the night before, he hadn't yet strung out any belongings around his bunk. The other men stepped away from the door to open a passage as he came toward them, but none of them were able to find any words. Lannigan opened the door, turned back and raised a hand in farewell salute, and headed for the main house, where Seeton's office was located.

Sam, the hand who'd been at Chispos, said, "You hadn't oughta riled him again, Hardcase. Way the little fellow was talking to us the other day, he must've needed this job pretty bad."

"Damn it, I need my job, too!" Harris snapped. "The way I feel, I owed him for decking me in the saloon. He jumped me before I was ready, or I'd've cleaned up on him then." He took his pistol belt from the nail on which it hung above his bunk and strapped it on. He went on: "If I was his size, I'd take two looks at whoever said something I didn't like. I'll tell you this right now: I got two things to settle with Mr. Runt Lannigan. I won't forget him, you can put up money on that." He shouldered his bedroll and started for the door. "Well, maybe I'll see you men at roundup or on the trail somewheres. And if I don't run into you before, we'll all get together in hell."

Ambling over to the main house with the spraddling gait of one who spends most of his time in the saddle, Harris dropped his soogans at the door and went in. As he walked along the short hallway to the foreman's office, he heard Seeton saying to Lannigan, "It might've been different if I hadn't give you the rules last night. The Major's an easy man to work for, but there's two things he won't overlook, and I warned you about both of 'em. No gambling or fighting in the bunkhouse, you recall I said. If you and Hardcase had been smart enough to save your scrap for someplace like back of the corral, I might feel different. Since you didn't, and all the men seen you, I got no choice."

"You don't hear me bellyaching," Lannigan replied. "I done what I had to do, you're doing what you got to do now."

"Wish you had some more time in the books." There was genuine regret in Seeton's voice. "I'd like to give you enough to stake you till you get took on someplace else, but all I can figure to do is pay you for yesterday and today. Two dollars."

"I don't want charity or nothing I didn't earn," Lannigan snapped. "Keep your damn money. I didn't do any work for you."

"You better take it," Seeton urged. "And stop by the cook shack before you go, tell Salty I said give you some grub, enough to tide you over while you're traveling."

"I don't need that, either," Lannigan shot back. He turned away from the foreman's desk, saw Harris standing in the doorway, and said, "You write this down, Hardcase—if you're smart enough to write at all. Any time we rub up against one another again, remember all the name I answer to is Lannigan. You forget that, and you'll be wearing a tooth tattoo on your other ear."

"Whenever you think you've growed bigger'n a button, you're welcome to try putting one on me," Harris growled. "I hope we do meet up again. You gettin' me fired off this job's not something I'm about to forget."

Seeton broke up the fresh dispute before it could get started. He told them, "Both of you shut up. I don't give a damn what you do to each other after you get off the S Bar T range, but I don't trust either one of you if you was to ride away together. Lannigan, you wait up a minute until I get Harris paid off." He bent to the squat safe beside his desk and pulled out a canvas money-sack, counted silver dollars onto the top of the desk, and shoved them over to Harris. "This is the eighteenth of the month, so here's your eighteen dollars." He watched while Harris trickled the money into the pocket of his jeans, then asked, "Where you two boys figuring to head for?"

Lannigan replied, "I got no place in particular in mind."

"Me neither," Harris said. "Just drift till I find a place where I'm welcomed to stop."

"Then it don't matter which way either one of you travels, does it?" Seeton asked. He fished another dollar out of the moneybag. "I don't see it'll be hard whichever way you go. It's just about gather-time, so most spreads'll be looking for extra hands to work through that and roundup and trailing. This Texas range ain't as wide open as it used to be. There's new brands on up north now, along the Trinity, even between it and the Red, clear up to the Canadian. Whichever of you rides south has got the old spreads down from the Forks of the Brazos. Either way you go, you'll have about an equal shot at picking up a new job. That sound reasonable?"

"If I got a choice, I'll go north," Harris said. "Lannigan, he belongs down south of the Concho, in sheep country."

"You ain't got a choice," the foreman told him curtly. "I aim to be fair to both ot you men." He held up the dollar. "Now, I'm going to flip this, and you'll go whichever way you call. That strike you as fair?"

Lannigan nodded. "Sounds all right to me."

"Hardcase?" Seeton asked.

"You made up your mind already, Prod. Go ahead."

Seeton thumbed the dollar into the air. It landed on his desk, whirled, spinning briefly on edge. Before it stopped, the foreman slapped his big hand over it. He said, "You call, Lannigan."

"Tails is as good as anything," the small man shrugged.

Lifting his hand, Seeton exposed the coin. It lay heads up. He said, "Well, you got your pick, Harris. You'll head north, I guess?"

"That's the way I want to go."

"You'll ride south, then, Lannigan." Seeton's voice hardened. "And don't either one of you try to circle back and meet up until you're off the S Bar T, if you got anything like that in mind." He looked pointedly at Harris's gunbelt and then turned his eyes to Lannigan, who wore no pistol. "I got no time burying one of you and hanging the other one. Now, get saddled up and ride."

Under the foreman's watchful eye the two men saddled silently, not even exchanging angry glances. Seeton forked his own mustang and rode out with them from the cluster of corrals and buildings that formed the headquarters of the S Bar T. After the trio had covered three or four miles in silence, the foreman waved Lannigan and Harris off in the directions they'd won by the coin toss.

Harris rode without looking back. Lannigan turned in his saddle two or three times to look over his shoulder, but each time he glanced back he saw Harris

forging steadily northward and Seeton still keeping
vigil at the spot where they'd separated.

"Well, pony," the small man said, "looks like we'll
be on the trail a while again. But we'll stop someplace, sooner or later."

Lannigan rode south through the crisp, clean air of
the afternoon. It was only half past February, but
spring was already hinted in the rolling fresh-greened
plain that lay in a gently westerly rise. The plains—as
distinguished from the prairie that swept in a broad
semicircle to the north and west of them—stretched in
a belt two hundred miles wide from the Red River on
the north, a belt four hundred miles long, ending
when the land dropped abruptly at the Balcones Escarpment. South of the escarpment, coastal llanos
took over for the hundred miles that was left of Texas
before it stopped at the Gulf of Mexico. On the east,
the plains belt stopped at the edge of the farmlands,
rich bottom-soiled earth between the Colorado and
the Sabine rivers.

Bottomland and llanos were Old Texas, where settlement had begun during the 1830s and had crept
north between the rivers and west over the coastal
llanos in broad vees that came together at the state's
eastern border, where the Sabine poured into the
Gulf. The plains had not really been settled until the
late 1860s, when Confederate soldiers who'd lost their
homes to war poured into Texas to build new lives.
They'd helped the Rangers push the Comanches
north, above the Red River. Then, after MacKenzie
broke the tribe at Palo Duro, the ranches had trickled
up toward the Canadian River, fanning out across the
prairie, taking over the shortgrass country from the
pastores who'd brought their sheep east from New
Mexico a century earlier. By the middle of the 1870s,

sheepherding had been pushed down south to the Concho.

Riding south from the S Bar T, Lannigan traversed the plains from their center, above the Forks of the Brazos, and every few miles saw them present a different aspect. He rode first through sparsely wooded country marked by only a few scattered mottes of trees: pinoak, hackberry, mesquite, cottonwood. Then he entered a stretch where only prickly pear and rocks flourished amid vast expanses of barely grassed red soil. He saw no signs of settlement, and expected to see none. Ranches between the Brazos and the Concho measured their size not in acres, but in sections, each section a square mile. On the scant-grassed plains fifty to a hundred acres were required to provide a year of grazing for a single steer. It was still country across which a man might ride for two or three days without seeing a house or another human.

Before bedding down for the night beside one of the isolated, nameless creeks that flowed willy-nilly, now north to the Brazos, now south to the Concho, Lannigan was regretting his stiff-necked refusal of Prod Seeton's offer to provide him with travel rations. The S Bar T followed the custom that was universal on Texas ranches; Sunday was a short working day. Unless it was during roundup, or there was a storm or other kind of emergency, the hands did only the most necessary routine jobs between an early breakfast and midmorning. They began drifting into the bunkhouse, as Hardcase had, shortly before noon. Instead of dinner at noon and supper at night, the cook set out an especially elaborate meal early in the afternoon. The fight had started before the Sunday meal had been served.

By the time Lannigan staked his pony and spread his hotroll under a pinoak a dozen yards from the creek, his stomach was growling unhappily. Scrounging in his saddlebags, he found two or three thumb-sized scraps of jerky. Squatting beside the creek, he ate the hard jerky slowly and methodically, peeling off tissue-thin shavings from the scraps with his knife and chewing them with a mouthful of creek water for a long time before swallowing. The jerky and water stopped his stomach's growls, but didn't go far toward filling it. When he crawled into his soogans and settled down for the night, he was still conscious of a vacant feeling in his midsection. In the manner of men alone since the beginning of time, Lannigan talked himself to sleep.

"Shut up, belly," he commanded. "It ain't your fault you're empty, I know that. I jawed when I oughta kept my fool mouth shut. But you settle down now and let me go to sleep, and I'll see can't I fill you up, tomorrow."

CHAPTER 2

A breakfast of water, even the sweet, clear water of a spring-fed creek, isn't a meal that gives an already-hungry jobless cowhand an exhilarating start at daybreak. Lannigan rode away from the creek just before sunup, knowing he had a day in the saddle ahead of him. His stomach kept telling him it was empty and unhappy, which pretty well matched his general disposition. As the day wore on, his stomach grew progressively emptier and Lannigan progressively unhappier.

From start to late afternoon he crossed no trails that indicated the existence of a ranch on either side of the vaguely defined north-to-south trace he was riding. Early in the day he stopped moving in a straight line and began swinging in wide arcs to left and right of the trace, hoping to pick up some kind of track that would lead him to a ranch or town. Late afternoon arrived and he still had seen no promising trail; the few that marked the plain were all old and obviously unused. His constant scanning of the horizon had brought no sight of a single thread of smoke staining the brilliant unclouded sky.

Dusk was settling in when Lannigan saw the campfire, a dot of brightness below the fast-vanishing line of the horizon. Fire meant a camp and a camp meant food. Lannigan could have sat down to a meal with

Hardcase Harris by the time he saw the flickering glow that beckoned him. He was, he judged, at least six miles from the campfire, a half hour or so if he kept his horse to the same steady walk the tiring animal had maintained all day. Even though he knew his pony was muscle-weary, he urged it to a lope to eat up the distance faster.

Steadily, the dot of brightness came closer as the mustang's hooves thudded over the plain. Lannigan kept swallowing the saliva that flowed into his mouth at the thought of eating. When he got close to the fire, he saw a wagon silhouetted by the flames and the black outline of a man holding a rifle standing between the fire and the wagon.

Lannigan reined in at a polite distance and called, "Mind if I ride on in? It's just me by myself."

"Come along," the stranger invited. "Be glad to have company."

Walking his horse into the circle of firelight, Lannigan let the man with the rifle take a good look at him before dismounting. He tossed the pony's reins to the ground and walked slowly toward the fire. A yard away from the stranger, he stopped. In the moment of silence that passed while he was being inspected, Lannigan grew aware of a strange odor, the unpleasant smell of old sun-ripened meat, that hung in the air.

"Name of Lannigan," he said, when he judged it was time to break the silence. "Seen your fire a ways off and headed for it. Haven't had only my pony to talk to the past two days."

"Yip, a man can get right lonesome on a long trip. Well, come on over to the fire and set. You had supper?"

"No. I was hoping I'd find a place where I could stop before dark, but didn't see any trails. I—" Lannigan hesitated before making the confession. "I run clear outa grub."

"I got stew and coffee boiling," the stranger said. "Such as it is, you're welcome to share it."

Neither man offered to shake hands; handshakes were reserved for ceremonious occasions or were exchanged between close friends on a reunion after a long separation. Prairie-wise travelers in Texas kept both hands free on meeting strangers.

Lannigan followed his involuntary host up to the fire and they got their first good look at one another as they stood facing in front of the blazing buffalo chips. The stranger was a tall, thin half-bearded individual. Like Lannigan, he wore no pistol belt, and had on the hickory shirt and well-washed faded denim jeans and jacket that were worn by most men in rural Texas from spring to autumn. The man's face was tanned to a saddle-leather brown above his short-cut grizzled beard that showed more white than dark hairs. His head, uncovered in the warm evening air, was bald except for a sparse white side-fringe, and his eyes were needle-sharp as he squinted at Lannigan in the red-glowing firelight.

"My name's Washburn," he said. It was less an introduction than the admission of his visitor to some inner secret. "Nobody calls me that, acourse, and sometimes I just about forget to answer to it. Be obliged if you'll call me China Slim, or just plain Slim."

"Glad to know you," Lannigan said. He was having trouble keeping his eyes off the covered iron pot that sat on a mound of coals that had been raked up at one edge of the campfire. A coffeepot sat on a smaller mound at one side, steam beginning to rise from its spout.

"Set," Slim invited. He jackknifed his own long legs

and settled down near the stew-pot. "Be a few minutes before supper's fit to eat. I didn't stop for the night until later than most days. It won't be much when it's ready, just plain meat with cornmeal thickening. The only game I seen since I run outa beef was a stringy old buck antelope moseying north up to his summer range. Et his chops last night, and they was a'most too tough t'chew."

"Whatever it is, it'll taste right good to me. It's been a while since I ate." Lannigan sat on the ground beside his host. He was conscious again of the odor of old meat, and looked around, trying to discover its source. All that he could see was the wagon, barely visible in the dimness at the edge of the firelight; then his eyes adjusted to the gloom beyond and he could make out the dim moving figures of a span of mules past the wagon. He decided it was time to settle any questions Slim might have about his reason for being there; he knew that courtesy wouldn't allow any questions. He said, "I'm drifting south, looking for work. Just got off the S Bar T. Punching."

"Little bit late, if you're looking for a roundup or a trail herd to join. Most of the spreads this far south's hired on all the extra hands they'll be needing."

"Oh, I'll run into something," the small man replied confidently. "Always have before, when I need a job."

"A man does, mostly, when he really looks. Right now, seems like there's more outfits than men to work 'em." Slim took the lid off a stewpot and stirred its contents with a long-handled iron spoon that had been resting on a flat rock beside the fire. He noticed how eagerly Lannigan leaned forward, and let the pot-lid stay on the stone where he'd placed it. "Smells like it's ready, I guess we might just as well eat." He walked the few steps to the wagon and came back carrying two tin plates, two spoons, and two tin cups.

Handing one of each to Lannigan, he invited, "Dig in, while it's hot."

Slim had told the truth, Lannigan discovered with his first mouthful of the stew. The old antelope buck's flesh was tough and stringy and took a lot of chewing, but Lannigan didn't mind that at all. He chomped heartily and gulped the pieces of meat distributed through the thin cornmeal gruel with as much enjoyment as he'd have taken from a prime beefsteak at any other time. The two men ate in silence that was broken only when Slim urged his guest to take a second helping. No urging was really required. The second plate of stew filled Lannigan's empty stomach, and he felt comfortable for the first time since he'd gotten up from breakfast at the S Bar T the morning before.

China Slim's hunger was not great. He cleaned his plate, eating with a slow deliberation. He waited for Lannigan to finish his second plate of stew before pouring fragrantly steaming ink-black coffee into their cups.

"So you're a cowhand," he said reflectively, after he'd taken a few sips of the strong brew.

Lannigan nodded. "Since I was sixteen, and that's going on six years ago. Oh, sure, times between jobs I've turned a hand to other things, but cowpunching's mainly what I work at."

"Started kinda young, didn't you?"

"Had to. When I got to Texas from Missouri, I needed to get to work right quick. But the ranches was beginning to spread out about that time, and jobs were easy to come by."

"Missouri, now," Slim said thoughtfully. The light of reminiscence was in his eyes. "Last time I was in Missouri was forty-three, and I was about the age you was when you hit Texas. Some mighty pretty country, back there in Missouri."

"I guess so. I never saw much of it, though. They kept me shut up in an orphan's home, next to the county poor farm. That was the only Missouri country I seen before I run away."

"Ma and pa both dead, eh?"

"Must be, or I wouldn't've wound up that way, in the orphans' home. Nobody ever told me who they was or what happened to 'em. About all I ever found out was my name. Don't know where they got it."

"Pity. Things like that happens, though." Slim stared briefly into the firelight. "Cowhanding, now. Don't that get pretty salty sometimes? A man's got to keep hold of his nerves when he rides into a bunch of milling steers, or he ropes a yearling and has to jump off of his horse and bulldog it down to the ground, things like that. I don't see—" Whatever Slim had been about to say didn't come out.

Lannigan took up the conversation. "I never thought much about it being risky. Just part of the job. You go ahead and do it, is all."

"Um-hmm." Obviously, Slim was thinking about something else. Lannigan sat silently, waiting, until his host said, "Since you got no job to go to, I don't suppose you're in a real big hurry."

"Well, I can't just drift, I need to hire on some-wheres. Trouble is, I haven't been up this far north before. Before I hired on at the S Bar T, I was punching for the King Ranch, down along the coast. Time I located at the S Bar T, I was busted, and that job blowed up before I put anything by."

"Which I take to mean you got to have a job pretty sudden?"

"That's the way it sizes up. You know if there's a spread close around here that might hire on a hand?"

"Lazy S-X main house is about eight miles south-west. If you go straight south, you'll run into the Double B in maybe fifteen miles. They're the nearest, but I don't know how they're fixed for hands."

"That's the best news I've had all day. I haven't seen a thing since I left the S Bar T range yesterday."

"Spreads are spaced out pretty good around here. They're a lot thinner further north, where the Canadian country's opening up."

"I wouldn't know about that. Haven't been up there, yet."

China Slim waited a while before picking up the conversation. He refilled their coffee cups and studied Lannigan's firelit face before saying, "Look here, I ain't just being nosy, Lannigan, but I get the feeling you might not turn away from a job of work, even if it wasn't right in your regular line."

"No. I guess I'm ready to take about anything that comes along." Now, courtesy demanded that Lannigan let Slim carry the talk forward. He waited, hiding his curiosity.

"I got a job that calls for a man who don't spook easy, one that wouldn't be put off by a little chancy work."

"Like you said, I'm ready to listen."

"Well." Slim rubbed his beard. "I got a bitch-wolf and her whelps in a den about a mile from here. It's worth twenty dollars to me if you got the nerve to crawl in that den and clean it out."

Lannigan stared wide-eyed at Slim. Dragging out his words very slowly, he asked, "You mean you want somebody to go in and bulldog a she-wolf in her own cave?"

"Now, I didn't say it that way," Slim replied quickly. "You'd shoot the wolf-bitch. The whelps won't be bigger'n your foot. They wouldn't give you any worry."

"Why don't you do it yourself?"

"Can't squeeze through to the back of the den is why. I tried to this evening, but there's a narrow place a man big as me can't get past. I don't mean to be personal, but you're little enough to make it."

Lannigan sat silently, thinking about the offer. He judged people by the way they reacted to his size when he first met them. Anybody making a joking or slighting reference to his diminutive stature got a black mark at the onset, and sometimes, as with Hardcase Harris, the mark got bigger and blacker as time went on. China Slim had passed his test. Not until now, when there was a valid reason to mention it, had he appeared to notice that Lannigan was small. He said slowly, "I'm not real sure I'm fast enough on the trigger or even a good enough shot to come out of a job like that."

"You don't have to worry about the shooting," Slim assured him. "I got an old fuke in the wagon that'll start a load of shot to spreading about six inches from the barrel. You wouldn't need to do any aiming, and the fuke's short—easy to handle in a tight spot."

"It sounds like I'd be in a real tight spot, too, if I took you up. Maybe I'd better hear a little bit more before I say yes or no."

"Well, hell, there ain't much else to tell you about it," Slim replied. "If you're wondering, I'm a wolfer, so I know what I'm talking about. Lazy S-X is hiring me to clear their range, and I just about got the job done, but I got to clean out that den before I can call it quits. If I leave the bitch and her whelps, she'll mate with the first dog-wolf that comes along and there'll be a new pack started. Then, I get a bad name because I didn't do a good job."

Lannigan had heard about wolfers, professional exterminators of the big gray predator lobos and the smaller but equally destructive Texas red wolves. Both breeds killed cattle and sheep not only for food, but for the sheer pleasure of killing. Slim was the first wolfer he'd ever met, though. He said, "I think maybe I want to know a lot more about what that job's going to call for."

"You say you've punched cattle six years or so. Must've been times when you've shot wolves. That's all the job is."

"I've shot wolves while I was riding herd, not closed up in a cave. That's to say, I've shot at wolves. Can't recall ever knocking one down. Coyotes, sure. I've killed a bunch of them, but wolves are a lot cagier."

"You said it right, Lannigan. Most anybody that's reasonably good with a rifle can kill a coyote. Wolves, though, they got a way of learning how far a .45-70 carries. They stay clear."

"Unless they're cornered in a den, like this she-wolf you're talking about," Lannigan said. There was no expression in his voice.

"Well, now, I'll admit it ain't a job you'd be likely to run into every day," Slim admitted. "But it ain't as tricky as you're making it out to be. Look here, I'll boost the ante to thirty dollars. That's as much as you'd draw down for a month, punching cattle."

What the wolfer said was true, Lannigan knew, but he was in no hurry to agree. He asked, "You're sure I can get off a shot with that fancy gun—what'd you call it? Fuke?—before the she-wolf jumps me?"

"Sure you can. And a fuke's not a fancy gun. It's just a ten-gauge sawed-off shotgun, what the old-time buffalo hunters used before they got hold of Sharps and Henrys. They'd run the buffalo on horseback, swing in close enough to a running critter to shoot it in the neck. A fuke ain't much for pretty, but it sure is a killer. Put a double load of powder and a handful of number ought buckshot in both barrels, and you'll just about tear the head off any kind of beast if you're inside of twenty or thirty feet from it."

"It'd be dark in the cave, though. How'd I see to aim?"

"You'd carry a torch, the bitch won't jump you if you've got live fire in your hand. And you don't need to aim, just hold the fuke in her general direction and let her have both barrels."

"Yes. I can see how that'd work," Lannigan agreed, frowning as he tried to separate the reality of the job from the cloak of easiness he felt sure Slim was draping over it. "If it's all that easy, why don't you just stake yourself out in front of the cave and shoot the wolf when she comes out?"

"If it was that easy, you think I'd be offering you good money to take the job on?" Slim demanded. "I been sitting in front of that den day and night for three days. The minute she gets close to the mouth, she smells me and won't come out. I got her so cagey now that she likely won't try to come into the open for a week. That answer your question?"

"I guess. Yes, I can see why you'd have to kill her in the den."

"Maybe if I wanted to wait around until she was near starved, I'd get her outside. Thing is, that denned bitch is all I need to clean up on before my job's done, and I've got another job waiting that I want to get to."

"I guess you've already tried trapping that she-wolf," Lannigan suggested.

"Traps!" Slim exploded. "Why, I been trying them for a month! One time, I had eight traps around that den opening, and she slipped by every one of 'em. Damn it, Lannigan, I know wolfing; it's my trade. If I tell you somebody's got to go in after that bitch and her whelps, that's the way it is."

"Even if it puts you in a bind."

"Now, if you figure to jack up the price I offered you to go the job, you just forget it. It's worth thirty dollars to me, but not a penny more."

"Oh, I'm not one to dicker you up, Slim. But I was just thinking, wolfing must pay you pretty good."

"Like anything else, you work at it steady, and it pays out. I guess I took about a hundred fifty lobos and maybe half that many red wolves this past three months. If I wasn't set on doing an A-number-one bang-up job, I'd wind up right now, but a range only stays clear about two or three years, and I aim to come back."

"It ain't my business," Lannigan said carefully, "but do they pay you by the job? Or is it piecework?"

"You'd call it piecework, I guess. Five dollars bounty from the ranch for every skin. Acourse, I just give them the scalp, and then I got the skin to sell for myself. There's a fur dealer down to Fredericksburg buys off of me, three, sometimes four, dollars a skin. Real prime winter pelt, maybe five or six."

Lannigan whistled. He didn't have to carry out the addition to realize that Slim was making more in a month than a thirty-dollar cowboy could earn in a year. He asked, "You don't figure to make anything off the deal you're offering me, then? Just doing it for good will?"

"About like that. It's worth it to me to clean up the job."

Lannigan knew it was up to him to say "yes" or "no" to the wolfer's offer, but couldn't force himself to a decision. There was something unnerving about the idea of facing a full-grown wolf in a den where she was guarding her offspring. To gain a little more time, he asked, "I guess you trap, mostly? You said wolves are hard to shoot."

"Damned hard." Slim looked at the small man obliquely, as though he understood the thoughts passing through Lannigan's mind. He added, "Once in a while, I'll set up a tree-stand, but that's more trouble than trapping."

"What got you started wolfing, anyhow?"

"Got too old and stiff to sail any longer. I told you I was through Missouri back in forty-three. I was heading for New Orleans. I had it in my mind since I was about five years old to be a sailor."

"And you made it?"

"Sure. Fifteen years afore the mast. That's where I got to be called China Slim."

"You mean you sailed to China?"

"Sailed, hell. I jumped ship there, in Canton. Spent more'n three years up and down the China coast. Learned their lingo; took on some of their ways, too, I guess. Had me a lot of pretty little yellow-skinned women—you could buy a fourteen-year-old girl for a dollar, back then. Finally got a hankering to come home; signed on a California frigate. That was in forty-nine, and the big gold rush was on. All of us jumped ship in Frisco when we heard about it. Headed for the diggin's to pan for gold.

"Did you get any?"

"Nope. Gold wasn't as easy to find as it was made it out to be. I tried my hand a while as too tough titty. Went back to sailing, come , put in at every port from Panama clear north to mada. Ship I was on foundered off the Washington coast, I stayed ashore a spell there, that's where I learned wolf trapping. There was lots of new settlers m.

They couldn't keep a cow or horse or sheep or goat, the damned wolves was so thick."

"That's still a long way from Texas."

"Oh, I didn't stay there; weather's too miserable. I signed on again; come around the Horn to the Gulf. But I tell you something, Lannigan. Seafaring's a young man's trade. I shipped up the Gulf coast to the Atlantic ports, Galveston, Biloxi, Mobile, Baltimore, New York, Boston; but climbing ratlines in ice-cold rain got too much for me after a while. I shored for keeps when I wound up in Galveston at the end of a hitch. Tried punching cattle for a spell, but that was rougher'n seafaring. So, I took up wolfing." Slim fell silent, his mind exploring the past in greater detail than he'd recounted.

Lannigan did not break in on the older man's reverie. He still had thinking of his own to do, not about the past, but about the future. Common sense told him he'd be a fool to go into the wolf's den. He knew nothing about wolves; had never handled the kind of gun China Slim had described as a fuke. His empty pockets told a different story. Thirty dollars was a month's wages for a half-hour's risk.

He might waste a month looking for a new job. Lannigan had little stomach for following the example of saddle tramps who toured ranches between jobs, staying a few days at each one as a nonpaying guest. His pride wouldn't let him do that. But unless he earned Slim's thirty dollars, he'd have little choice but to put pride aside for the immediate future. He became aware that Slim was staring at him in the dimmed light of the dying fire.

The wolfer said, "Well, Lannigan, you wanted time to think about it. Reckon you've had enough?"

"You make it sound like an easy job."

"It is. Take twenty minutes, maybe half an hour."

"In the dark, with a gun I don't know anything about. How big did you say a full-grown she-wolf gets to be, Slim?"

"Oh, a hundred, hundred ten or fifteen. Stands high as my hips. On you, she'd stand about to your belly-button."

"Well, I told you I'm looking for a job, and you hit me with the first offer I've had," Lannigan found himself saying, much to his surprise. He kept talking to hide his nervousness, his mind telling him all the while that Slim made the job sound too simple. "All right. For thirty dollars I'll go in and shoot that she-wolf for you."

CHAPTER 3

A thin streak of rosy-purple dawn was showing when the fragrance of boiling coffee brought Lannigan out of his soogans. China Slim was hunkered down beside the rekindled fire, stirring the stew, and the coffeepot was gurgling in the beginning of a boil. Slim turned his head when he heard the susurrus of the canvas unfolding and watched Lannigan crawl out of the blankets, but said nothing until the small man joined him at the fire.

"Well, you had a chance to sleep on our deal," Slim said. "You feel like changing your mind?"

"Nope. But I don't feel like crawling into a wolf cave before I eat some breakfast."

In a subtle way the relationship between the two men had altered overnight. Had Lannigan refused the job he'd been offered, he would not have mentioned breakfast but would have waited for Slim to invite him to stay for the meal. As the wolfer's employee, it was now Slim's obligation to provide breakfast.

Slim said, "Oh, we got lots of time. It's way too early to hit out for the den. We don't want to get there before the sun's pretty high. You got to learn what to look out for when you crawl into that hole, so we'll have to talk a while. And there's chores to do, too."

After being reminded of what he'd be doing later in

the morning, the antelope stew didn't taste quite as good to Lannigan as it had the night before. He ate a plateful, though, and when the two had emptied their coffee cups, helped Slim to wash the dishes from supper and breakfast in the outfall of the little spring that gushed up a few paces from the fire.

They worked together silently, giving their attention to the job at hand, saving conversation for their second cup of coffee. The clean plates and spoons were stowed away in the necessary box that was bolted to the off-side of the wagon, and from the box Slim took a battered coffee grinder into which he poured a double handful of beans. Lannigan sat down to grind while Slim rinsed out the pot and filled it with fresh spring water. The ground coffee having been added to the water and the pot set on the fire, Slim folded his long legs and settled to the ground near Lannigan.

"We'll talk while it boils up," he said. "I been seeing the questions on your face ever since you got outa your hotroll. Time we talked out the answers and give your mind a rest."

Lannigan's smile was thin. "You're right about the questions. I woke up two or three times last night, and every time I thought about something else I wanted to know about."

"Such as what?"

"Such as how we'll be sure that she-wolf's in her den before I crawl in after her. I'd hate to go in it wondering if she was there or not."

"I took care of that yesterday—you'll see when we get there. And if she's not inside, we'll just come back here and wait a spell."

"I'm not sure I'd be much good if we waited too long. All I can think about now is getting it over with."

"You'll be all right when the time comes," Slim said reassuringly. "That is, if I figured you right. Just don't think about it too much beforehand. It's sorta like having a tooth that gives you fits and you put off having it pulled. The longer you wait, the worse it's going to look."

"How in hell can I not think about it?"

"Best way I know is to keep busy. Maybe we best let the coffee to boil and go pick up chips so we'll have plenty for later on. And we'll water our animals while we're doing that. There's water standing in an old buffalo wallow just past that rise, and that's where the chips are thickest. If we still got time to kill, I got a few pelts that's on stretchers and needs to come off. Or we can go look for a jackrabbit or a young coon to fry up for supper."

"I guess I'd feel better if we moved around a little bit and save talking until later," Lannigan agreed. "Whatever chores you want to do first, it's all right with me."

"We'll tend the animals, then," Slim decided. He got up and pulled the scant coals that remained from the dying breakfast fire around the coffeepot, using the green limb that was his fire tool. "Lots of time to do the rest later on."

Lannigan followed the wolfer to the wagon. Now, in the daylight, he could see what he had been smelling. Invisible last night, a half-dozen wolfskins on oval wooden stretching-frames stood propped in the wagon bed. He asked, "The trader that buys your wolf-hides, what does he do with them? Who does he sell them to?"

"Skins," Slim corrected. "Cattle and buffalo's got hides, wolves got skins. Pelts, they're called in the fur trade.

"Old Georg Helmut, the trader that buys mine, says

he ships most of 'em to Russia, to make coats for their soldiers. And he says a thin-tanned wolfskin makes the best drumhead going. Hell, I don't care where he gets rid of 'em, as long as I got my money out of 'em."

Carrying the gunnysacks that Slim produced from the wagon and leading the mustang and mules, they walked over the rise to the old buffalo wallow, a saucerlike depression filled with water at its center. On the flat land around it, bleached skeletons of buffalo lay thick, in places one piled atop another. After they'd staked the animals beside the water the two men walked among the skeletons and filled their sacks with the hard rounds of dry manure that lay everywhere on the ground. In less than an hour of slow, steady walking and bending, the gunnysacks were full, the stock watered, and they were on their way back to camp.

Lannigan said thoughtfully, "Buffalo've thinned out a lot, I guess. From what I heard when I first came up here to this part of Texas, they used to be thick as fleas, but all I've seen are little herds, a hundred or two."

"There was lots of 'em when I come here," Slim agreed. "Men couldn't get anyplace where he didn't hear them big Sharps and Henrys booming. Come to think of it, I ain't seen a big herd myself the last couple of years."

"What happened? Have the hunters killed them off?"

"Not a chance. There's so damn many buffalo, we'll never see the last of 'em. Like wolves. I trap over a range, and three, four years later there's as many wolves as ever on it when I come back." He frowned and added thoughtfully, "Acourse, wolves breeds a lot faster than buffalo does."

"How much faster? Aren't buffalo about like a cow?"

"About. I don't rightly remember, but I guess ten months. A wolf-bitch, now, she'll drop her whelps in nine weeks and breed two or three times a year. That's why I got to get the one you're going in for before I wind this job up. She's got maybe eight or nine whelps in that den now, and if I leave her alive, she'll breed again in two, three weeks."

"I guess you've learned a lot about wolves," Lannigan suggested.

"Quite considerable," Slim replied. "And you better start to learn a few things, too, soon as we get these animals staked. Coffee ought've boiled by now and be near cool. I'm ready for another cup, and I bet you are, too."

They dumped the chips out of their sack near the fire. Slim stepped to the spring and came back with a cup of cold water to pour into the coffee and settle its grounds to the bottom. He filled cups for himself and Lannigan and motioned for the small man to sit down.

"Now, then," he began. "If it'll ease your mind, you'll have a rope tied around your belly when you go in that den, and I'll have hold of the other end of it. If you get in trouble, pull on it twice and I'll drag you out."

"That makes me feel better. I was wondering what to do if something went wrong beyond that narrow place you said you couldn't pass through."

"Nothing won't go wrong if you do just what I tell you to," Slim replied emphatically. "That narrow place, now, you'll run into it about thirty feet inside the cave. The floor starts slanting up just afore you get to it. You can smell the den from there, so I'd guess you'll have another twenty feet to go after you squeeze through."

"You're sure it's wide enough for me?"

"Yes, damn it! You're a lot littler than me, and I didn't miss making it by much. If it comes to me having to drag you through it ass-backwards, though, you better be able to help me a little bit."

Lannigan successfully suppressed the shiver that started around his ankles and ran all the way up his spine. He said, "One thing that worries me, Slim. I've got the torch in one hand, the what-you-call-it, fuke, in the other one. How'm I going to shoulder the gun, then?"

"You ain't. Shoot it like a pistol, the barrel's only about a foot long and the grip's cut down. Don't bother to aim, either. Once you see the bitch's eyes, let go with both barrels."

"Should I try a shot or two first, before I go in?"

"No need. Just be careful while you're carrying it. That old fuke's got a hair trigger, and it'll be cocked."

"All right," the small man agreed. There was doubt in his voice.

Slim looked at Lannigan narrowly. "You want to back out?"

"No, damn it!" Slim's question rubbed the raw spot on Lannigan's pride, the spot that became especially sensitive any time somebody suggested that his diminutive size kept him from doing things a bigger man would take in stride. "I told you I'd do the job, and I don't go back on my word. Not ever. You remember that, Slim."

"All right. Don't get all hottened up." Slim glanced at the sun, climbing now toward its zenith in the cloudless sky. "If you're all ready, let's get the gear together and go."

❋   ❋   ❋

A half hour later the two men got off the wagon a hundred yards from the bluff into which the wolf's tunnel ran. Slim pointed out the cave mouth to Lannigan, a slit created by some long-ago earth movement in the crystalline schist that lay a few yards under the soil's surface.

"You wait here," the wolfer said. "I'll go make sure the bitch is in the den. There'll be tracks, if she's come out."

"How can you tell? There'd be old tracks, too, wouldn't there?"

"I smoothed the dirt around the opening before I come away last night. She was inside then, I heard her growling."

Reaching under the wagon seat, Slim produced a heavy holstered Navy Colt on a pistol-belt. He strapped the gun on and walked over to the bluff. After a brief glance, he returned to the wagon.

"She's inside, all right," he told Lannigan. "Let's go."

Carrying the sawed-off shotgun, loaded and primed, a hundred feet of half-inch rope, and the torch Slim had made by wrapping strips cut from a gunnysack around a length of tree limb and dipping the porous cloth in kerosene, they approached the cave. As the opening loomed bigger and blacker, Lannigan's throat began to dry up. He swallowed hard as he walked, trying to hide his frequent gulpings from his companion. If China Slim noticed, he was careful not to show it. A few feet from the den mouth, Slim put out an arm to stop Lannigan. He pointed to the soil around the opening, the area he'd brushed smooth.

"See her tracks?" he asked. "You can tell where she come out after I left yesterday and went back in sometime this morning, I'd guess. Prob'ly hunted most of the night. A nursing bitch needs plenty of food and water."

Lannigan did not reply. He was studying the cave mouth. This close, it had a definitely sinister look. He wondered how he'd feel after he got inside, into the darkness.

"Well?" Slim asked. "Ready to rig up?"

"Ready as I'll ever be." Lannigan took a deep breath, as though he was preparing to plunge head-first into an icy river. "I sure as hell won't get much braver than I feel now, so let's get on with it."

They coiled the rope near the den mouth, Slim using a sailor's skill to lay a neat, flat circle from which the rope would pay out freely. He was about to tie the end around Lannigan's waist when he looked down and said, "Better go in there on sock-feet. That rock's real slick underfoot."

"I'm not wearing any socks," Lannigan confessed. "But barefoot oughta be real good." He pulled off his boots. "Now, then."

Slim looped the rope twice around Lannigan's waist, knotting each turn separately. He handed the little man the torch and the fuke and asked, "You ain't forgot what I told you, now?"

"Not hardly. Fuke's cocked. Rope's set. All that's left is to light the torch."

Slim pulled a stick off a match block and rubbed its head on the striking pad glued to the underside of the block. He held the matchstick carefully while its impregnated tip fizzled and spat and at last flamed up, then touched it to the oily cloth of the torch.

"Guess you can go in," he announced.

Lannigan walked the few steps to the cave-mouth, the cool earth soft under his tender feet. Concealing his nervousness, he slipped into the cleft. It was, he thought, the hardest half-dozen steps he'd taken since he'd run away from the orphanage. Both times, he was setting out into the unknown. That time ten years ago had taken place during a stormy night of pitch darkness, and he'd felt fear, but less fear than now, while he was taking those first few running steps to the fence that surrounded the home. Then, after he'd gotten over the fence and known he was free, fear had left him as soon as he'd begun to think of his need to put distance between himself and the orphanage. He hoped the same thing would happen now, as he started into the cave.

Inside, the tunnel was not as black as Lannigan had feared it would be, but the light faded quickly as he moved along the slick stone floor. Light vanished completely after he'd maneuvered around a bend in the cave. The air here was still, and smoke pouring from the torch hung in wreaths around him. It irritated his throat, and he began to cough, his eyes started watering.

From the darkness ahead a cough answered Lannigan's. This cough, though, grew into a growl, then a rumbling snarl. Lannigan hesitated. His feet were cold, pressing on the smooth rock floor, but sweat was springing out everywhere else on his body. He took a few steps forward, straining to see through the swirls that his movements created in the clouding smoke. Another series of growls and snarls brought him to a halt.

When he stopped, the smoke seemed to envelop him; it did not flow behind him and out of the cave, as he'd assumed it would. He moved ahead to keep from choking, and walked steadily until he reached the narrow place China Slim had described. Getting through was a tight squeeze, even for a man as small as Lannigan. He had to twist sidewise and compress his chest while he lifted one leg, then the other, through the opening that ended a foot above the tunnel's floor.

Past the bottleneck, a rank feral odor struck through the smoke. It hit him like an invisible wall, and caused him to halt once more. There were no growls coming from the blackness ahead now, so Lannigan moved on. Now, though, the roof of the cave was slanting down and the floor was sloping up. He could not stand erect after he'd moved ahead a short distance, but had to drop to his knees and waddle, his bare toes scraping painfully on the hard rock floor.

Again the growls started echoing off the low roof and narrow walls, rumbling and echoing, amplified and resonating in the confined space through which Lannigan was now inching. The smoke was denser in the restricted space. Lannigan began to gag when it hit him, mixed with rank animal odors, old blood and carrion, urine and feces, dog magnified by a thousand.

He tried holding the torch behind him, but his shadow blocked the light, and he bumped his head on a ledge that stuck out from the otherwise smooth cavern wall. The sweat was no longer beaded on his body and face, but was rolling off him in rivulets; he could feel it soaking into his clothing.

Ahead, the growls continued. They stopped for a moment, then an angry howl sounded, an ululating blast that filled the constricted space and rang in Lannigan's ears for what seemed to him to be an eternity. When the howling died away, the growls resumed, interspersed with strings of angry yelping barks.

Lannigan by now was both choking and quivering, but the quivers were from muscle-strain rather than fear. He was so uncomfortable in the posture he'd been forced to use that he'd forgotten to be afraid. His knees felt as though they'd been pounded with steel hammers for several hours, and each time he moved his feet, every toe was a separate pulsing ache when it touched down on the stone floor. The torch in his left hand and the fuke in his right each seemed to weigh a ton. His lungs were filled with smoke, his throat parched, and his eyes were watering copiously.

Keeping the torch ahead of him, Lannigan moved on. He slipped once, his knees sliding on a glassy-smooth spot on the floor, and when he tried to hold himself erect he brought the shotgun down with a clatter on the rock. A delayed reaction set him trembling harder than usual when he realized that the gun might have gone off; had it fired, the buckshot ricocheting off the cave's walls would have riddled him. In spite of his stinging eyes and the burning acrid smoke that filled his lungs and forced coughs that scraped like sand along his throat, Lannigan stopped, kneeling dead-still, until the shakes left him.

Belatedly, he realized that the smoke filling the tunnel so thickly was making breathing difficult. It came to him for the first time that unless he kept moving as fast as possible he could suffocate before he got to the end of the den and killed the wolf that was waiting there. Lannigan tried to move faster, but his trembling legs, their muscles overstrained by his crouching posture, responded slowly. He could only inch along, as he'd been doing.

Abruptly, the narrow tunnel widened into a chamber. Through the smoke, Lannigan saw the gleaming phosphorescent green eyes of the wolf. She was on her hindquarters, staring at the opening to the den. Here in the chamber, the smoke and smell were so overwhelming that Lannigan knew he must get out quickly to escape collapse. Almost without thinking, he pushed the fuke's muzzle toward the wolf and fired. If he aimed at all, he was not conscious of doing so. He pulled each of the gun's triggers in quick succession. The double load of buckshot took the wolf in the chest and neck. Blood spurted over the animal's light-gray fur. The green glow of its eyes faded and died away as the wolf crumpled slowly to the floor of the den, its fangs still exposed in the fearsome snarl it had displayed when alive.

Now powder-smoke began expanding to fill the den. Before its roiling yellowish swirls thickened, Lannigan could see the squirming whelps behind the wolf's body. He tried to count them, but they were all moving, tumbling over one another, crowding up to the body of their dam. His own lungs were smarting and burning and dizziness was growing in his head. He began backing out, but kept bumping into the stone walls of the narrow tunnel. His legs were trembling and almost out of his control as their muscles began to turn rubbery under the strain to which they'd been put.

Lannigan lay down on his face and tried to crawl backward over the stone floor, but his legs kept getting entangled with the rope. He kicked out, trying to free them, and felt the rope tighten. Then he was suddenly being dragged backward over the hard floor. The hauling turned his body sideways and his head struck the tunnel wall; he dropped both the torch and the fuke. For a quick frightened moment his body was pulled across the tunnel, and Lannigan was stuck. The rope cut into his belly, jamming him in place, unable to go forward or back, unable to free himself from the narrow walls. He grabbed the rope and pulled as hard as he could. The pressure slackened and he could now squirm around to face the exit. He groped behind himself for gun and torch, somehow managed to grab them. He tugged at the rope again and it tightened, this time slowly and carefully.

Aided by the rope, Lannigan could move forward at a crawl, but he moved in almost total blackness, for he could not bring the torch past his body in the narrow tunnel, and with it behind him his own torso cut off its light. There was a bad moment or two when he got to the bottleneck and could not squirm through it, could not lift himself on weakened legs to squeeze between the sharp edges of the gap, which were—to him at that moment—high above the tunnel floor. Then, somehow, fingers, toes, legs, and torso combined in a single convulsive effort, and he popped through the gap.

It was clear going after that. The tunnel widened, the pinched roof slanted up from the floor, and Lannigan could walk erect. The smoke had cleared here, too, and he could breathe again. The rope kept its smooth tension, helping him to move ahead. He tried to go faster, to run, but his legs would not obey his commands to speed up. He was tottering when he saw daylight ahead and took the final few steps that brought him to the open air.

Never had such commonplace, everyday things as sunshine and fresh, untainted air been such blessed boons. Lannigan's legs gave way, and he almost fell, but Slim rushed up to grab him. Between gasping and coughing and fighting the nausea that was making his stomach turn in flip-flops, he gasped, "Well, I got your damned wolf. She's laying at the end of that tunnel. And there's a bunch of little ones back there, too. I'll go after 'em soon as I've had a breather."

Then Lannigan blacked out.

CHAPTER 4

Lannigan's lapse into unconsciousness lasted only a few moments. He swam back to awareness to the accompaniment of drops of water landing on his face and opened his eyes to see Slim splashing him from the canteen they'd brought. He shook his head and the wolfer stopped, offered him the canteen to drink from. The water went down his throat cool and sweet, and the scratchiness eased but did not quite go away. The tears were clearing from his eyes, and he was surprised that the sun had moved so little in its arc while he'd been in the den. He'd thought it must be close to sunset.

"How long was I in there?" he asked the wolfer.

"Fifteen, maybe twenty, minutes."

"It seemed to me more like fifteen or twenty hours. The hell of it is, I've got to go back now and get the wolf's body and the whelps."

"You sure she's dead?"

"I'm sure. There was blood spurting out of her neck, and her eyes started to fade when she fell over. They didn't shine green any longer."

"She's dead, then. They lose that eye-shine when they die. How many whelps did you count?"

"I couldn't count, Slim. The place was full of smoke and my eyes were running and the little wolves were milling around, all mixed up in a pile back of their mother. Might've been eight or ten or even more."

"We'll find out when you bring 'em outside. No hurry about that, either. Little as they are, the whelps won't leave the bitch's body. You set and rest a spell. Breathe some good air, let the red go out of your eyes." Then frowning, Slim asked, "You figure you can tote everything out in just one more trip?"

"I'd better be able to. I've only got one more trip into that cave left in my system, Slim. When I've made it, that's all."

Slim grinned. "Judging by how good you did on the first one, I got a feeling you'll make it do."

Anxious as he was to put the cave into his past forever, Lannigan did not make the mistake of going back in until his strength had returned, his eyes cleared, and the last vestiges of smoke had been exhaled from his lungs. Slim made a new torch, smaller than the first. Lannigan carried a gunnysack, and trailed the safety rope behind him, as before. He knew the tunnel this time; knew how to maneuver through the bottleneck, where he could walk upright, when he had to crawl. Most important of all, he knew there was no live bitch-wolf waiting in the den. He tossed the squirming whelps into the sack, then quickly tied the sack and the forelegs of the dead female onto his lifeline. He tugged on the rope twice, and Slim, waiting for the signal, began hauling on the rope from outside.

Sack and wolf-carcass slid along the smooth stone floor, Lannigan behind them, pushing when his help was needed. It took a few minutes to get the double load through the bottleneck; he had to lift the sack of whelps and the dead wolf through the narrow place with one hand, holding the torch in the other. Then the widening walls made progress easier. Lannigan emerged from the tunnel with his eyes smarting only a little bit, his throat feeling rough and raspy, but on the whole in much better shape than he'd been in after the first trip.

"How many whelps?" Slim asked.

"Nine. I counted them while I was putting them in the bag." Lannigan's reply was abstracted. He was getting his first real look at the wolf-bitch.

Her body lay in a stretched-out sprawl. The wolf was bigger than he'd remembered from the quick glimpse he'd had of it in the den. From the nose to the base of the tail, its body was nearly as long as Lannigan was tall, and had the animal been standing, its shoulders would have been higher than his waist. He studied the wolf's head. It was doglike in form, but different from any dog he'd ever seen, with a high-domed cranium above glazed yellow eyes, and a broad muzzle that ended in a black nose. Its black lips were open in a death-snarl to show fangs two inches long in both top and bottom jaws and behind them lines of jagged sharp yellow molars. The wolf's coat was smoky white, with a darker oval patch running along its sides; it had a pronounced ruff, now matted and bloodstained.

Slim, untying the gunnysack that held the whelps, saw Lannigan's absorption and said, "She'll weigh a good hundred and fifteen pounds, if that's what you're wondering, and I don't figure you to weigh more'n that."

Lannigan grinned wryly. "Last time I stood on a scale was at the livery stable in Chispos. I just topped one hundred twelve."

Dragging the gunnysack, the whelps inside sounding off in high, shrill whimpers, Slim walked up to the dead wolf and ruffled its furred flanks with a boot-toe. "Pelt's scruffy. Always is on a bitch that's just whelped. Skin won't be worth much."

He looked around, saw a sharp-edged length of stone that had surfaced at the foot of the bluff near the cave-mouth and dragged the gunnysack to it. He reached into the sack and brought out one of the whelps, holding it by the loose skin at the nape of the neck. The little animal kicked its stubby feet and whimpered. It was no more than eight inches long, and held its tail curled protectively between its legs. Its pale veiled-blue eyes showed as small slits in its blunt face.

"What're you going to do with it?" Lannigan asked, though he knew what Slim's answer would be.

"What I'm going to do with all of 'em, is put 'em away." He held the whelp by its hind legs and snapped its neck across the rock-ledge in a quick arc. He tossed the body aside and dragged a second whelp from the bag, dispatching it the same way.

Lannigan turned aside when he saw the second whelp die. Slim was reaching for the third when he saw the small man's move. He said, with no emotion in his voice, "You can't be squeamish and be a wolfer, Lannigan. These little bastards look cute and helpless now, but they'll grow up to be as big as their mama and kill twenty head of cattle a night."

"Who said I was going to be a wolfer?" Lannigan asked over his shoulder.

"I did. You damned feisty fool, you think I'm going to let you walk away? Anybody that'll walk into a den the way you did is fit to partner with." Slim smiled when Lannigan turned, surprise on his face. "If you've a mind to, that is. But I'll tell you somethin'. You'll make a hell of a lot more money partnering up with me than you ever will playing nursemaid to a bunch of steers."

Lannigan looked from the dead wolf to the bodies of the whelps, then his eyes traveled to Slim's expectant face. For a long moment he hesitated, then said, "Well. I guess you've got a partner, Slim."

For the first time since they'd met, the two men shook hands.

"There's a bottle of whiskey in the wagon," Slim told his new partner. "But I guess we better save it till we get back to camp."

Neither of them felt it was necessary to discuss terms and percentages, or to talk about writing down a formal agreement.

"Have we got something else to do here?" Lannigan asked.

"Nothing only a little clean-up. You tie that wolf hulk to the tailgate and we'll drag it along. If we get the hulk outa the way, there'll be another bitch using the den by the time we come back in two, three years to clear the Lazy S-X range again. I'll finish off the other whelps while you're doing that."

Lannigan observed, "You seem pretty sure we'll be back."

"I'd bet money on it. Hell, partner, the past few years I haven't had to break in no fresh territory hardly at all. I just go back and work over the ranges I've cleared before."

"Are there really that many wolves, Slim?" Lannigan was dragging the carcass of the bitch-wolf to the wagon.

"They breed like fleas. You'll learn about that, along with the other things you got to know, like making a set and mixing up scent and building deadfalls and such as that. Look here, now. We got nine whelps. If that bitch had stayed alive, she'd be dropping nine or ten more inside of three months. Work it out yourself. A young bitch'll be good for thirty whelps a year, easy."

"I guess they do breed like fleas," Lannigan agreed. He asked with a frown, "How come there's so many wolves up here and I never hardly seen one down on the Gulf Coast, where I been working? A lot of coyotes down there, but no wolves to speak of."

"That's old range down along the Gulf. They been working thirty years to clear it. The wolves got smart and moved, the coyotes stayed. Unless you're sheep ranching, it's wasting time to clear out coyotes."

"We had orders to kill 'em on the King spread. And they had two hunters after 'em all the time."

"Sure. King's a breeding ranch. Coyotes'll take down a calf, like they will sheep, but once a steer gets yearling growth, it's pretty much safe unless it's weak and sickly. Wolves kill the calves and the grown steers, too."

They were working as they talked, Slim putting the dead whelps in the gunnysack, Lannigan picking up the rope and fuke and canteen after tying the wolf carcass to the tailgate of the wagon. Slim swung the bag into the wagon bed and jerked a thumb at the carcass.

"Skin's not worth much, but I'll skin her out, anyhow. She's worth a bounty from the ranch, so's the whelps. We'll stay in camp tonight, go into the main house tomorrow, and square up. And we'll figure out what your share's going to whack up to."

"I've got no share coming, Slim. Nothing beside what I made going into the den." Lannigan climbed up beside Slim on the wagon seat. They started off, the wolf carcass dragging behind them.

"We'll wrangle about shares later on," Slim told him. "Come up with whatever we think's right. But we won't be short, neither one of us, with the county money and the pelts I got stored in the shed at the Lazy S-X.

"Have we got a new job to go to, now this one's finished?"

"Sure. Only we better head down to Fredericksburg first and get rid of them skins. We'll need a bunch of new traps, too, with us both making sets. And some of them traps I got now needs to be fixed up. There's a blacksmith down there that does good work."

"And then what?"

"We didn't partner up to loaf, did we? Soon as we're finished at Fredericksburg, we'll head for the Cross Tees." Slim hauled back on the reins as they arrived at the campsite. He told Lannigan, "I don't guess you know how to skin out a wolf hulk, but here's where you start to learn."

Lannigan had wondered why the wolfer's wagon bed was divided into several closed boxlike compartments instead of being littered with gear tossed in indiscriminately; now he found out. Slim opened one of the compartments and took out a thong-wrapped bundle of sticks; from another, a trio of wide-mouth glass jars filled with unidentifiable—at least to Lannigan—bits of fleshlike substance; and from a third compartment, a sheathed knife and well-worn whetstone.

"Getting ready takes more time than the skinning does," he told Lannigan as he began whetting the knife blade on the oily stone. He worked at the blade's edge for several minutes, dragging the edge lightly over his thumbnail from time to time until at last he nodded with satisfaction. He said, "It pays to keep one knife just to skin with, and whet it every time you start a fresh hulk."

Slim pulled the wolf carcass around until it was on its back, and slipped the knife into the crease between its hind legs. He made one stroke from back to neck, circled the neck, and then made cuts along the inside of each leg, connecting with the long belly-slash. He spread the animal's hind legs and sliced deeply into the anal area.

"There's a couple of glands back here that goes into the scent-mix, and so does her bladder and gall-sac," he explained.

His knife moving in swift, sure strokes, Slim removed the organs and put each one into one of the jars he'd taken from the wagon. When he took the lids off the jars, the air was filled with a strong scent of urine and musk.

"Them parts will keep a long time in these jars," he said. "I got some sublimate dissolved in glycerine in 'em."

"Smells like hell," Lannigan remarked, his nose wrinkled. "A stink like that'd drive me away from a trap."

"Works different on a wolf, though," Slim chuckled. Apparently, the odor did not bother him. "After I mix up a little bit from each one of these jars, I'll have me a smell that'll pull a wolf right up to a set. Works better'n meat does."

"And that's all you use for bait? I thought traps had to be baited with meat or some kind of food."

"Oh, I'll double-bait a set sometimes, use a chunk of fresh meat or a fish that's begun to get high. But mostly the scent does the trick. Keeps the coyotes away from the sets, too."

Closing the jars, he went back to the carcass and severed the tail at its base. Grasping the cut neck-skin, Slim turned the wolf on its side and planted a foot on its head. He pulled the skin back toward the tail, peeling it from the carcass. As the skin parted from the body it dragged with it long strips of nearly transparent integuments that stretched until they broke with a loud popping sound. Occasionally one refused to break and he severed it with his knife.

Within two or three minutes, the pelt had been peeled from the dead wolf as a glove might be peeled from a hand. There was surprisingly little blood, just a trickle from the anal area, where the scent-glands and bladder had been cut out. Slim spread the skin on the ground, hair side down, and picked up the sticks that were held together by a thong. Along one side of each slat, notches had been cut and at each end holes drilled into which pegs could be fitted to make a rectangular frame.

"I ain't too fond of this kind of stretcher," Slim told Lannigan as he fitted the slats together. I like ovals best, but they ain't so easy to carry as these knock-downs."

Lannigan watched with interest as Slim dragged the skin into the center of the frame and worked quickly with his knife, piercing the pelt at intervals around its perimeter. Then he wove the thong into the holes he'd made, looping the leather strip into the notches along the frame's edges.

"You see?" he asked Lannigan, holding up the hide on the stretcher. "You can do this in no time at all, once you've got the knack of it. Only thing you got to watch is to pull the laces just tight enough so they'll hold the skin flat, but not so tight it pulls out when the pelt dries and starts to shrink."

"How long does that take?"

"Oh, three, four weeks in a dry climate like this 'un. Skin won't be full hard by then, but it'll be stiff enough to handle." He took up his knife again, and with the frame propped against the wagon, scraped its inner surface with long, stroking swipes. "They don't stink so bad if you get the loose stuff off. Then, after it's scraped, you smear on that stuff in the box, yonder."

Lannigan picked up the wooden box and opened it. He smelled it, pushed a finger into the crystalline substance it contained. Slim looked up and saw what he was doing.

"Long as you got your hands in it, you smear the skin," he said. "Only, go wash your hands good after you finish."

"What is this?" Lannigan frowned.

"Arsenic and salt. Keeps maggots away; dries the skin faster."

Somewhat gingerly, Lannigan rubbed the arsenic mixture over the raw inner surface of the skin. While he was doing this, Slim scored the furred head from jaw to jaw beneath the eyes and pulled away the scalp. He told Lannigan, "Seeing as we're going to break camp right after we eat, we'll just let the hulk lay. Coyotes and buzzards'll clean it up, the bugs'll do the rest."

Lannigan looked at the wolf's carcass, pale and pink-spotted. Removing the scalp had exposed the yellowed teeth almost completely, and he wondered how he'd have reacted if the animal had charged him while he was trying to struggle through the cave to the den. It was a thought he pushed quickly from his mind.

Slim glanced at the sun and said, "If you ain't any hungrier than me, let's put off eating till we get to the Lazy S-X. They got a real bathtub there, too, out by the cookshack, and I can soak off this wolf-stink before I eat." Lannigan's face gave away his surprise, and Slim began to roar with laughter, bending and slapping his thighs as he guffawed. When the first burst had subsided, he said, "Gawdamighty, partner, you didn't think I like to smell this way, did you? Oh,

I seen your nose wrinkle when you first come in the other night, and I got to give you credit for not saying nothing."

"I just thought—" Lannigan began.

"I know what you thought. Well, that's something else you've learned, now, ain't it? When you're wolfing, you can't smell like a man at all. Wolves is terrible shy of human scent. But you'll get used to stinking, after we been making sets a month or so on our next job."

Bumping over rough trails that grew smoother and more clearly defined as they drew closer to the well-established settlements along the Pedernales and Colorado Rivers on the three-day trip to Fredericksburg gave the new partners a chance to get acquainted. The journey also gave China Slim the opportunity to begin educating Lannigan on the niceties of the wolfing trade. Most of the time, they talked shop. Lannigan learned, at least in theory, how to recognize a wolf-run and where along its perimeter to place his traps; how to make a set with bait as well as scent; how to rig a log deadfall; how to make a pit-trap; and all the other ways used by trappers to outwit their quarry.

They arrived at Fredericksburg, a neatly arranged cluster of dressed stone houses, shortly after noon of the third day. For the last dozen miles of the trip, Slim had been tantalizing his new partner with mouth-watering stories of saloons and beer gardens that served sturdy beers, finely lagered in the German style, and of the lavish free lunch tables the saloons maintained, loaded with bratwurst, weisswurst, blutwurst, zwibelwurst, leberwurst, rehebelwurst, bockwurst, knackwurst, and a dozen other kinds of sausages in addition to the more common corned

beef, ham, cheeses, boiled eggs, and pickles. The re-
cital excited Slim so much that he insisted they stop
at the first saloon they came to, to settle the dust in
their throats with a stein or so of beer and to treat
their empty stomachs to a few bites from the free
lunch counter.

Three steins and several dozen bites later, they got
back aboard the wagon with heavier stomachs and
lighter heads, and went on into town to Georg Helmut's fur-trading shop. Helmut spoke through a full
white beard in a thick German accent that defeated
Lannigan, but seemed to give Slim no trouble. The
wolf pelts from the Lazy S-X were quickly disposed
of, part of them for cash, the rest for new traps that
they loaded on the wagon.

They started for the smithy, to leave the old traps
in need of repair, and on leaving the blacksmith shop
were reminded by the saloon across the street that the
heat of the forge had dried their gullets, a condition
that required immediate remedying.

As they sat with foaming steins in front of them,
Slim said lazily, "Now we only got one more thing to
do, partner. That's to get us some new clothes, and
there's plenty of time for that before we pick up the
traps from across the way tomorrow morning." He
leaned across the table. "I bet you get horny as I do,
out on the job. I got a gal in a fancyhouse a little
ways out of town that I go see when I'm here. There's
some other nice ones there, too. How about we go on
out there right now and get fixed up?"

"Well—" Lannigan began, but said nothing more.
He was reluctant to confess to Slim that he'd always
been shy with women. Morals played no part in his
reaction, whether the woman was in the oldest profes-
sion or outside it. Lannigan's inhibitions were rooted
in his fear that every woman he met might find his

small stature unappealing, perhaps even something about which to joke.

Slim took his partner's temporizing for assent. He drained his stein and stood up. "This is a good time of day to go call on the girls. They get busy later on, and when I'm with Gertie I don't like to be hurried. Drink up, and we'll take off. It's been too long since I had a chance to dip my wick."

At the brothel, Gertie greeted Slim with enthusiasm, and somehow seemed to grasp Lannigan's problem after she'd glanced at him. "I know just the girl for you," she told him. "Nice and sweet, unless you—" She hesitated momentarily and then said quickly, "Well, if it makes any difference to you, Carlita's a Mex."

"No, no, I don't mind that," Lannigan protested.

Carlita was even smaller than Lannigan, short enough so that he towered over her by several inches. He felt immensely male when the girl looked up at him. Even when she made a joke about their small size, he did not feel offended, but laughed along with her.

"Don't let him fool you, now," Slim admonished Carlita with a tongue slightly thickened by the beery afternoon and evening. "He might not be no giant, but Lannigan's plenty of man. Went into a damn dark cave all by hisself and killed a wolf bigger'n he is."

"*Ay, mí!*" Carlita's eyes widened. "That is a brave thing to do, no? And when you do this great deed, Laneeghan?"

"Oh, a little while back," Lannigan replied, his face growing pink. "And it wasn't all that much."

"But of couse it is! To face a great, fierce lobo alone is *una cosa valoroso!* Tell me about it, Laneeghan." Carlita put the stress in her mispronunciation of Lannigan's name on the middle syllable, in the style of her native language, so that it came out as LanEEghan.

"No," he corrected. "My name's Lannigan."

"LanEEghan," she repeated. "LanEEghan." She grimaced. "Ay, it is a name too hard to say. It is better I give you a new one. I will call you Lobo, after the big wolf you kill!"

"Now, by God, that's a name fits him to a tee!" Slim roared. He draped an arm around Gertie, threw the other across Lannigan's shoulders, and grasped Carlita by the arm. "Come on over to the bar! I'm buying the drinks to christen my new partner! From now on, he don't answer to no other name than Lobo Lannigan!"

CHAPTER 5

While they were trapping out the Cross Tees range, and then on the job that followed at the O Slash O, Lannigan proved his right to the name Carlita had bestowed on him when he went into dens after bitch-wolves and their whelps.

Neither of these dens was as tortuous to enter as the first had been. On the Cross Tees, Lannigan had only to squeeze his head and shoulders into a narrow vertical slit and fire the fuke at the green eyes of the wolf, a dozen feet away. Getting into the den on the O Slash O was another matter. The wolf and whelps were at the back of a cavern that opened under the lip of a deep, sheer ravine. The cave's entrance was at the end of a narrow ledge along which a slender wolf could walk, with its four feet, but which was not wide enough for a man to traverse.

Lannigan could inch along the ledge sideways, pressing against the ravine wall, but when he tried to bend to enter the cave, his precarious balance was destroyed. He and Slim solved the problem with shovels; they dug into the cavern from the surface, then Slim lowered Lannigan down headfirst and held him by the ankles while he shot the bitch-wolf.

After finishing at the O Slash O, the partners treated themselves to a second trip to Fredericksburg. The trip wasn't really necessary, they agreed, even though they had a huge quantity of pelts to deliver to Georg Helmut. After some discussion around the supper fire they also agreed that delivering the skins meant cash in hand, and that cash meant nothing unless it was spent; that they had no job ahead; and that it was a damned sight more pleasant, with summer coming to its peak, to sit in a shady beer garden through a long afternoon and anticipate the pleasures of the oncoming evening.

A week of overindulgence in pleasuring proved to be enough. Bleary-eyed, gassy from beer, the last snack of assorted wursts lying heavily in their stomachs, the partners started north again. They took their time in covering the hundred miles northwest, to the high plateaus between the middle and north forks of the Concho River. It was an area where cattle and sheep ranches overlapped; China Slim had worked for most of the spreads at one time or another, and assured Lannigan that they'd be needed at the first place they stopped.

His prediction was not far off; it was actually the second ranch they inquired at that needed the wolves cleared from its range. The Diamond Dot was a long way from anywhere, in country so infertile that a sheep needed fifty acres of grazing land a year and a steer needed two hundred acres; a country where ranches were scarce and far apart and towns nonexistent. Slim had been right, though. Wolves that were being trapped and hunted in the richer range of central Texas were moving to the state's less thickly settled areas, and spreads like the Diamond Dot were suffering.

"We'll have another job ready before we finish this one," Slim said as they jounced on the wagon seat on their way to the edge of the Diamond Dot range, to set up camp. "One, maybe two more, around here, then maybe we oughta go north. I been wanting to run some snow-sets up above the Smoky Hill River in Kansas."

"Any special reason for going that far north?" Lannigan asked.

"None, except I get tired of dust and drought. And I got me a sorta hankering to take some prime pelts, the kind that's got thick glossy fur and brings prices high enough so's you can afford to work without no ranch bounty. I'd've tried it afore now, only a winter trap line's no place for a man by hisself."

"Just say the word when you're ready to start."

"Long as you're agreeable. We might just work our way north after we get through here. There's lots of new spreads up above the Red, along the Canadian. Chances are we'd be welcome on one of them till the time comes to push further along."

"North or south or here, it's about the same to me." Lannigan remembered having said something similar to Prod Seeton when he'd been fired off the S Bar T, and wondered idly where Hardcase Harris had wound up.

Slim said, "We'll hash it out before we start moving again. I never been above the Red, I'd sorta like to look it over, see what it's like up there."

"Be interesting, I guess," Lannigan agreed. "I never traveled that far north myself."

During the months since he'd joined forces with China Slim, Lannigan had let the older man initiate actions and make final decisions. Slim had been aware of the deference being shown him and had been careful never to take advantage of it. He'd been equally careful when showing Lobo the tricks of a trapper's trade and educating him in the ways of wolves never to make him feel uninformed or ignorant. By ignoring the younger man's diminutive stature and treating him as a physical equal, Slim had made Lannigan less self-conscious and touchy about his size than the small man could ever have come to be while sharing a bunkhouse berth with a group of joking, teasing cowhands. Lannigan was not conscious of the change his attitude had undergone, or of the degree of improvement in his self-assurance. He only knew that he felt a lot more comfortable as a wolfer than he had as a cowpoke.

They found a place to camp in broken country, fifteen miles from the Diamond Dot headquarters, near a sweetwater creek that surfaced for a few dozen yards before disappearing again into the underground channel through which it ran. The creek was a small one, a thread of water, and so shallow that they had to scoop out a depression in its bed in which to lower their water bucket when filling it. The only space level enough for their campsite was a hundred yards from the creek, on a little flat dominated by the hackberry tree that had guided them to the water. A few paces beyond the flat, a sprawl of dead mesquite provided firewood.

While Lannigan set up camp, Slim went to scout for wolf-runs. He came back with the news that he'd discovered three within easy working distance, two of them small, the third an exceptionally big one with several shorter runs branching from it. Three months earlier, Lannigan had not believed there were such things as wolf-runs. He'd thought his new partner was playing on him the kind of joke that old hands like to perpetrate on greenhorns, and only after Slim had taken him out and escorted him around a run did Lobo realize that they actually existed and that knowing how to read them was a key to successful wolfing.

Even after Lannigan's several months of work, Slim was still quicker at finding runs and reading them, but once Lobo had convinced himself that wolves were indeed creatures of habit and followed a relatively set pattern in their movements, he applied himself to learning all that the older wolfer could teach him about these wolf runways. He could recognize a run now when he crossed one, even a new run not deeply marked by the claws of the animals that used it. He could follow the run in its looping course, even on horseback, and could spot the places where wolves had left their sign, thanks to Slim's persistence as a teacher.

Lannigan's first lesson had been given on the Cross Tees. He'd listened with almost open skepticism to Slim's explanation that it was the habit of wolves to move to and from their hunting areas in loops or circles; the circles might have an irregular perimeter as short as eight or ten miles, but usually were twenty to thirty miles around and might be sixty or more miles in length. A big run might have several short runs branching off its perimeter in different directions, but always the pattern of the loop persisted.

After they'd ridden, and then hiked, around that first run on the Cross Tees, Lannigan had begun to understand. Slim had pointed out the shallow, almost imperceptible dust-dimples left by the wolves' paws on the hard soil, and had followed them to the nearest marking station, where a wolf passing would invariably stop to leave its own sign by urinating on some noticeable feature of the landscape bordering on the run.

"These places is a wolf's signposts," Slim explained. "They might be anyplace, like a bush or tree or a big old boulder or a rock outcrop, maybe even an old buffalo or steer skeleton. That wolf wants to leave his scent, show the other wolves he's around." Seeing the question on Lannigan's face, he anticipated it by adding, "Nobody really knows the why of it. I guess a dog-wolf leaves signs to draw a bitch to him, and a bitch might be looking for a dog to breed with." He'd pointed to long lines of claw marks beside and around the mesquite-stump that was the marker they were examining. "They'll most always scratch some by a sign post. Sometimes, they'll drop dung, too, but when they do that they scratch dirt over it."

"And we set the traps close to the markers?"

"Now you got the idea, only close ain't good enough. You got to study out which way a wolf's going to move when he goes up to leave his sign, and make your set where he's most apt to step."

"Don't coyotes leave sign, too? Seems to me you'd catch as many coyotes as wolves, there's so many more of them."

"Like I told you afore, coyotes won't go near where a wolf's left scent. Mostly, they stay clear of the runs, too."

During the beginning of their job on the Cross Tees, Slim had taken Lobo with him, making sets and clearing traps, but after the third week had sent him out alone. "If you can't do it with what you've learned now, you never can," he'd said. "Long as I'm along, you're going to look to me for help, but if you're by yourself you'll have to figure out the right way, and then you'll never forget it. Just work slow and don't do anything you haven't thought out and you'll be all right."

Though many of his first sets were unproductive, Lannigan's skill improved quickly. By the time they were ready to move to the O Slash O job, his sets were accounting for almost as many wolves as were Slim's, though he still hadn't acquired his partner's skill and deftness in setting traps.

"Give you another month or two, you'll be about as

fast as me," Slim encouraged him. "Just don't push yourself too hard. And remember, when your sets don't work after you've been on a run a while, move 'em to another one. Then, after you rest the old run a spell, you can go back to it and do real good again. But you could go out on your own right now, was you a mind to."

"Fat chance," Lannigan had grinned. "I like things just the way they are."

On the first day of their Diamond Dot job, Slim and Lannigan rode the runs together, deciding which runs each of them would work. It was commonsense practice, a precaution to make sure each would know where to look for the other in case of an emergency. Their real work began the next day, after they'd spent the evening checking the jaws, springs, and trigger of each trap, then boiling them in a big copper washboiler that was part of the wagon's equipment, to remove any traces of man-odor left by their hands. The jars of scent were almost empty, so Slim mixed a fresh batch. He stirred together glycerine and mercuric salts, added a dollop of wolf urine, and into this liquid base stirred minced bits of wolf bladder and shreds of the blue-gray anal glands they took from each wolf they trapped.

Lannigan and Slim went to sleep to the accompaniment of distant wolf howls. They woke before daybreak and left camp on foot, each leading a mule loaded with traps and their tools. At the run he was to work, Lannigan waved good-bye to Slim and turned off. He reached the beginning of the run as the sun's first rays were reddening the sky and began to look for the marking station where he'd make his first set. He'd noted the location in his mind the day before, when they scouted the runs. It was a stunted mesquite-bush a few paces off the run itself, and when he saw it ahead in the still-dim light he stopped the mule and tethered it.

Lannigan wore one of the trap-setting outfits he and Slim had prepared before leaving the Diamond Dot headquarters to set up camp. His jeans, shirt, and jacket had been boiled and sun-dried three times and his shoes and gloves scraped to raw leather, then the entire outfit had been buried in the big pile of drying manure by the corral. The small knapsack in which he carried a freshly boiled trap and his other gear had been buried with his clothing. After transferring the gear from the mule's spanniers to his knapsack, he walked to the mesquite-bush where he'd make the set and squatted on the ground a few paces away from it.

For a quarter of an hour, Lannigan studied the terrain, deciding on the precise spot where the trap should be placed. The location he finally chose was about eighteen inches away from the bush, where the ground was scored with claw marks and dotted with dry, dust-covered feces. Pulling the trap from the knapsack with gloved hands, he checked it carefully, though he and Slim had tested all the traps before putting them to boil in the big copper wash-kettle. The trap, still unset, looked from the side like a letter P, with the closed jaws forming the loop. The tail, or side, of the P held the trigger mechanism and springs.

In the arc made by the jaws, the trigger-pan sat at right angles to the closed jaws, above the trap's strap-iron base. The saucer-sized pan was attached to the trigger, an L-shaped piece of narrow strap-iron; the pan was on the short end of the L, and the long end ran down between the flanges forming the tail or straight side of the P. Inside these flanges, the springs formed two tight coils around square rods welded to the jaws at one end. The other end of each rod was rounded and passed through a hole in the base, in which it turned freely. A metal crosspiece on the long end of the trigger-lever fitted into shallow grooves scored on one side of each rod. The springs were fixed to the end of the frame and to the rods just back of the trigger, and were always held under tension.

Working with gloved hands no longer bothered Lannigan. He put the trap and his knapsack beside the bush and took out the rest of his equipment. His setting-cloth was a three-foot canvas square that had been deodorized with his clothes; he spread it and stepped onto it, carrying a big trowel of the kind used by bricklayers. Kneeling on the cloth, he dug a teardrop-shape hole wide enough to accommodate the trap's jaws when they were opened and just long enough to take the spring-end of the frame. The hole was shallow, just deep enough to sink the trap below ground-level after it had been flattened by setting.

Each trowelful of dirt he removed, Lannigan emptied on the setting-cloth. He scraped a little extra earth from the center of the hole's narrow end to accommodate the trap's trigger-lever. Picking up the trap, he snapped a check-chain through a hole drilled in the long end of its frame. Then he took his hatchet and drove a four-foot length of iron wagon rod into the pointed end of the hole. He locked the loose end of the chain to the rod by dropping two links of the chain, formed into a V, over it and wedging the last link on top of them. Only then did he set the trap by holding its base against his chest and pulling the jaws open until the crosspieces on the trigger dropped with twin clicks into the grooves of the rods through which the springs ran.

Now the trap looked like a misshapen paddle, with the frame that extended from the base forming its handle. It was less than four inches thick. Gingerly, Lannigan bedded the frame in the smooth dirt at the bottom of his excavation. He pressed it into the soil until the opened jaws were perhaps a half-inch below the level of the hole's edges. He laid the six-foot chain in even courses between the stake and the point at which the jaws began.

On the trigger-pan that now lay exposed in the circle of the opened jaws Lannigan placed a piece of stiff leather the width of the pan and long enough to extend over the trigger-lever; the cover would keep dirt from trickling into the mechanism. Scooping up handsful of loose earth from the setting-cloth, Lannigan trickled it onto the leather pad. He added a bit of dirt at a time, slowly, to avoid springing the trap. When he'd covered the pad almost to the level of the surrounding ground, he began dribbling dirt over the jaws and frame until the entire hole was filled, the trap covered by a concealing layer of loose soil less than a half inch deep.

To finish off the set, he took his brush, a wolf's tail with the bone left in it, and smoothed the dirt above the trap and the soil all around it until the loose earth blended with the untouched surface around the set. He swept with a light touch, for the trigger-pan now carried the weight of the soil that rested on its protecting pad, and a mere ounce or so of pressure would spring the jaws. A small heap of dirt remained on the setting-cloth when he'd finished, and after stepping off the cloth Lannigan picked it up by its corners and carried it a few paces away from the set before scattering it with a vigorous shake.

One final touch was needed. Taking the bottle of scent from his knapsack, Lannigan shook it hard, moved to the marking-station, and opened the jar. An acrid, penetrating smell of concentrated wolf assaulted his nose. Holding the jar at arm's length, he bent over the mesquite-bush and dribbled some of the liquid over the branches. He closed the jar quickly and stepped back. The odor was already spreading through the otherwise clean air, and would persist for several days, until the small summer breezes diminished its potency.

For several minutes Lannigan stood completely still, surveying the area around the set to make sure he'd overlooked nothing, had left no object carrying man-scent that would warn a passing wolf away from the bush, and that the earth covering the trap blended perfectly with that around it. Satisfied, he picked up his knapsack and went back to the mule, ready to move on to the next set. He'd ride the trap line daily, resetting traps and making fresh sets that would be necessary after he'd killed any wolves caught in a trap's jaws.

Setting a new run was a time-eating job, and darkness was full before Lannigan got back to camp, guided for the last few miles by the flickering firelight and the brighter yellow glow of the lantern that Slim had hung on the uptilted wagon tongue. Slim was sitting beside the fire, coffee cup in hand. He turned and waved, then settled back to wait. Lobo watered and fed the mule and tethered it, and shed his trap line clothes before going down to the fire.

"Sets take longer'n you figured?" Slim asked.

"A while. When we scouted, we missed a few marking stations, some of 'em looked better'n the ones we spotted. I could've made three or four more sets if I'd carried enough traps with me."

"We can fill in tomorrow, when we check up. Come on, set down. There's fried rabbit and flour-gravy in the skillet. Cornpones in the other pan. Coffee pot's full, so's the water bucket, and I dragged up enough wood for the breakfast fire."

"You've kept busy," Lannigan commented.

"Not hardly. I had a little run, easy sets, too. First day you make sets is always toughest, though. We'll sleep in tomorrow. Not any real rush about riding the lines early."

Instead of rolling out when the pale tinge of gray broke the night sky, the partners stayed in their soogans until the sun was well up. They breakfasted by daylight instead of pale dawn before starting to check the trap lines. On the probability that at least a few of the traps would hold wolves, they took the wagon. Lannigan slipped off the seat when they reached the run where he'd made his sets. He slung two freshly boiled traps over his shoulder and took his knapsack and other equipment from the wagon.

"Take your time," he told Slim. "I'll set these two while I walk the run, then cut over across to yours; help you load up. We can pick up any hulks from this run on the way back to camp."

There were no wolves in Lannigan's first two traps and the sets had not been disturbed. The third trap was empty, but had been sprung. Lannigan spread the setting-cloth and removed the loose dirt that had covered the trap. When he got down to the leather pad that covered the trigger-pan and shook the dirt from it onto the setting-cloth, a nubbin of flesh fell off the pad. He picked it up; it was a toe and claw. The wolf that lost the toe had sensed the trap when it stepped on the loose dirt and had pulled its leg up quickly, but hadn't moved fast enough to get completely clear. Lobo straightened up from his kneeling position and looked at the ground around the trap. There were spots of blood he hadn't noticed in the tracks left by the wolf when it escaped. With a shrug, he tucked the toe-nubbin in the knapsack; it had to be disposed of somewhere distant from the run.

After resetting the trap, Lannigan started for the next set. As he approached it he heard the growls and clanking of the drag-chain that told him the trap held a wolf. A few more paces and he could see the animal, a Texas red wolf, smaller than the big gray lobos, worrying at the chain, which it had pulled to its full length away from the wagon-rod stake. The wolf's left foreleg was held by the trap's steel jaws. Lannigan and the wolf saw each other at almost the same instant. The wolf stopped worrying the chain and froze to immobility, yellow eyes glaring at the man, ruff erected, fangs gleaming ivory in its gaping mouth.

Lannigan drew his pistol. This was the part of trapping that came hardest to him. He always hesitated to shoot. Time after time he'd reminded himself at these moments that as wanton cattle-killers wolves deserved no mercy, that killing the beasts was part of the job he'd taken on. He knew quite well that if he was helpless the wolf wouldn't hesitate to attack him. Indeed, many of those held in his traps had lunged at him on three legs, dragging trap and chain, snarling with fury. It was as though the wolves knew he was responsible for their plight and were trying to reach and maul him in retaliation for the end to which the trap had brought them.

Still, it always took Lannigan several moments to bring himself to aim and pull the trigger. This time was no exception. He stood holding the revolver, telling himself it was time to fire, then delaying in doing so. For a full minute he stared at the wolf before bringing up the gun and putting a bullet in its brain. The wolf dropped, twitched for a moment, and lay

still. Lannigan walked up to the carcass, still holding
his pistol, and prodded it with his boot-toe to assure
himself the animal was dead. Sitting beside their af-
ter-supper campfires, Slim had told him both facts
and legends of wolves and their ways. His stories had
included several versions of incidents when sup-
posedly dead wolves had come back to life and attacked trappers.

This wolf would not, Lannigan decided. He holstered the revolver, spread the trap's jaws wide
enough to release the wolf's leg, then dragged the
hulk aside and began the routine of renewing the set.
He left the carcass, when he moved on to the next
set; he and Slim would swing by and pick it up in the
wagon on their way back to camp.

All the other traps around the run were empty,
though one more had been sprung. Lannigan reset
this one, made the two new sets he'd planned, and
when he reached the end of his loop started walking
cross-country to Slim's run, a little more than a mile
away. He saw the wagon standing, a sign that his
partner had not yet finished running the line, and to
save needless walking, cut across the middle of the
run at an angle he was reasonably sure would bring
him close to the area where Slim's last traps were located. His calculations had been right; he saw Slim at
a distance and hailed him. Slim stopped and waited
for Lannigan to catch up.

"There's just three more of my sets to look at," he
said as Lobo came up. "There's three hulks for us to
pick up, back around the run. How'd your sets do?"

"One. About midway of the line. And two misses.
One of them was close, wolf left a toe behind."

"Two of mine was sprung, but they was all clean.
We better get on the trail of that cripple right away,

Lobo. If we don't track it down, we'll have to tell the Diamond Dot we left 'em a renegade."

A wolf that has escaped a trap never forgets the experience. It becomes almost supernaturally cautious, and generally more wanton in its killing than others of its kind. Among the stories that Slim had told Lannigan were tales of renegade wolves that by themselves had destroyed as many as sixty head of cattle or a hundred sheep in a single night of killing.

"We'll have to be lucky, then," Lannigan said. "If all them yarns you've told me're true, about how smart renegades are."

They were walking around the run as they talked, and before Slim could reply they heard the angry yelping snarls of a trapped wolf arising just ahead of them.

"Sounds like we'll have another hulk to haul back," Slim remarked. "You'll have to hump to keep up, Lobo. This'n makes it four outa my sets to just one outa yours."

"I'll catch up. Don't worry."

By now they'd come in sight of the set and could see the wolf in the trap. It was held by its right foreleg and had its head down, worrying at the leg where the jaws of the trap were closed on it. The drag-chain was pulled out to its full length. The wolf either heard or scented them just before they stopped, twenty feet from the set. It stopped gnawing at its imprisoned leg and glared at them, slitted yellow eyes seeming to glow even in the bright afternoon sunlight. It was another Texas red wolf. Its tongue was lolling from one side of its mouth, from which long strings of saliva drooled, and its jaws were open to show menacing fangs.

"Hell, it's just a little one," Slim said. He'd drawn his Navy Colt, but now he holstered the gun and took a short-handled hatchet from his knapsack. "No use wasting good powder and lead on this button. It's little enough so's I can club it."

Hefting the hatchet, Slim walked toward the wolf. The animal tried to hobble to meet him in spite of the six-pound trap, but the drag-chain was already pulled taut and the wolf's struggles did nothing but raise wisps of dust as the chain rose, then fell back on the dry soil. Man and wolf were within two yards of one another. Slim stepped to one side, choosing the angle at which he'd close in on the wolf. Lannigan was opening his mouth to caution his partner; there was something about the animal's behavior that disturbed him. Before he could speak, everything happened.

A pace now separated Slim from the wolf; he was moving very slowly and the animal was tugging at the trap, trying to leap. Slim took a half step. The wolf hunkered down and launched itself again. Its trapped leg tore off with a spurt of blood. Freed from the trap, the wolf sprang. Slim tried to bring his hatchet around to catch the animal in midair, but his looping blow missed. The wolf's jaws closed on Slim's hand.

Lannigan drew his gun when he saw the wolf's leg tear off, but he could not shoot; Slim was between him and the wolf. Slim's hatchet was rising and falling as he tried to club the wolf off his left hand. Before Lannigan got to his partner's side, Slim had knocked the wolf away. The animal lay at his feet, kicking convulsively. Lannigan grabbed Slim's arm and pulled him back. Slim's hand was streaming blood.

"How bad did it get you?" Lannigan asked. He reached for his partner's wrist, to hold the wounded hand and examine it.

Slim jerked his arm away. "It don't hurt much." He

pulled the glove off the injured hand, wincing as the rough leather scraped over raw flesh. Lannigan bent to look just as Slim yelled, "Quick, Lobo! That damn wolf ain't dead!"

Lannigan drew as he pushed Slim aside. He turned, gun in hand. The wolf was on its feet, hobbling toward them as fast as it could on three legs and a stump. He fired. The slug tore into the wolf's head, but did not stop the animal. His second shot went squarely into the wolf's gaping mouth and stopped it in its tracks. It shuddered and dropped to the ground, shook convulsively once, then lay still.

"I never saw a wolf act like that before," he said, turning back to Slim.

"I have." China Slim's voice was low and sober. "I seen 'em come on at you after they was shot dead. Not just wolves, either. Dogs, coons, skunks. That wolf had hydrophoby. Lobo, you're looking at a dead man standing here."

CHAPTER 6

Lannigan's brain started working again. He asked, "Are you sure?"

"Look at the jaws on that hulk." Slim pointed, and both of them stared at the dead wolf. On the blood that had gushed from its throat when Lannigan's killing slug tore in, blobs of white foam were dotted, and flecks of thick white froth smeared its jaws and muzzle. Slim went on, "I seen wolves with hydrophoby before. Dogs, too, and skunks. That's how their mouths foams."

"There's got to be something we can do." Now Lannigan's voice was as somber as Slim's. He knew that the bite of an animal suffering from hydrophobia always meant death to the person bitten, and that no cure was known for the disease. He looked at his partner's hand, still dripping blood, though Slim was trying to stem the flow by holding his wrist tightly with his right hand. "The bite doesn't look all that bad."

"Don't matter whether it's a big bite, or just a scratch. I've seen it, Lobo. Seen a fellow bit by a skunk, didn't hardly break his skin. He was a goner in three days."

"If we start now, and hurry to a doctor—" Lannigan began.

Slim cut him short. "Where's the doctor going to

be? Four, five days hard riding. Anyhow, doctors got no medicine for hydrophoby."

"Damn something that's got no cure!" Lannigan said angrily. He knew Slim was right, but refused to accept it.

"There's one thing we might try." Hope crept into Slim's voice. "Seems to me I heard about somebody getting over a mad-dog bite after they cauterized the place where the dog's teeth sunk in."

"Let's do it, then!" Lannigan looked at the torn hand and added, "But I never cauterized anybody before."

"Hell, there's a first time when you do anything," Slim retorted. "Let's hit for the wagon. Sooner we get at it the better. There's a big old Wilson buffalo-skinner knife in the necessary box. It's good steel, oughta heat up enough to do the job right."

At the wagon, the thick back-curved blade of the Wilson knife thrust into a small fire built with buffalo chips and the few scraps of wood Lannigan could scrounge up, they waited for the steel to heat. Lannigan used the time to sponge off Slim's hand with a scrap of shirttail wetted with water from their canteen. The wolf had clamped down at the heel of the palm, and on both sides its jagged teeth had laid bone bare. Though Slim kept pressure on the veins in his wrist, fresh blood welled out constantly.

"It don't look so good, does it?" Slim asked calmly, and, when Lannigan shook his head, added, "Don't feel so good, either."

"Think you can stand the hot knife blade?" Lannigan looked at the fire, where the skinning-knife was beginning to turn from cherry-red to bright orange. Its handle was beginning to char.

"Don't bother about what I can't stand. You push that steel in wherever my hand's tore up." Slim's eyes followed his partner's to the knife. "Looks like the blade's plenty hot. Steel won't stick to flesh after it's orangey that way. I'll hold steady as I can."

"You sure the blade's hot enough?"

"I'm sure the quicker you do it, the better off I'm going to be. Pick it up, Lobo. Let's get it over with."

Lannigan found the haft of the knife too hot to handle until he'd wrapped his bandanna neckerchief around it. He looked at Slim, who was holding his wounded hand out in readiness, elbows braced in his ribs. Lannigan pressed the flat of the glowing blade to the wound. There was a hissing when the hot steel touched moist flesh and blood. Sweat suddenly drenched Slim's face, and his lips compressed with pain, but he held his hand steady, turning it under the glowing blade as Lannigan pressed the fading steel over the wound. The sweet-sick smell of burning human flesh was gagging both of them before he took the knife away. Its blade was now a dull blue. Slim was swaying, his eyes closed, tears welling between tight-pressed lids.

"You all right?" Lannigan asked. He dropped the knife, helped Slim to the wagon, and steadied him while he eased down into the shadow cast by the wagonbed.

"It don't—hurt much worse—than the bite did," Slim replied through clenched teeth. "Git out the whiskey bottle, Lobo." A long, deep gulp followed by a series of shorter sips helped Slim a little. After he'd begun to feel the whiskey's effect, he said, "I'm all right now. You can leave me to set here and rest while you go back and finish up."

"Finish what? I'm not going to leave you."

"Like hell you ain't. You got to go back and burn that wolf hulk. Suppose another wolf or a pack of coyotes comes by and starts to worry it? There'd be hydrophoby all over the place."

"But, Slim—"

"Don't give me no buts, Lobo. We can't leave that hulk lay. You know how quick a hulk brings coyotes and racoons and skunks and birds. Just go do it. And don't touch anything with your hands. Burn the hulk, my gloves, sear the trap good."

"I don't like leaving you here by yourself."

"Ain't a thing you could do for me, here or any-place. And there sure ain't going to be nothing worse happen to me than's already happened. Now, go on. I'll be all right."

Reluctantly, but recognizing the need to do so, Lannigan followed Slim's instructions. He gathered fuel: twigs, dry grass, dead brush, buffalo and cow chips, anything that would burn, and when the fire was blazing high, pushed the wolf's carcass on the pyre with a mesquite branch. He noticed the animal's leg-stump while moving it, saw that the trap had shattered the bone and that the wolf had gnawed away the flesh and skin around the break. It must, he realized, have been just at the point of liberating it-self when he and Slim arrived. He kept feeding the fire until even the wolf's bones were calcined and he could grind them to powder with his boot-heel. As he worked, he tried to keep his mind off the future, but was not very successful in doing so.

Several times that night, after a supper for which neither of them had any appetite, Lannigan roused and looked over at Slim's hotroll. As far as he could tell, his partner was sleeping, aided by several mas-sive slugs of whiskey before turning in. The next day was one of inactive waiting. Slim claimed he felt fine except for the throbbing of his hand, which was puffed with huge blisters from the heat of the cauterizing steel. Together they drained the blisters, pricking them at the edges to let the liquid flow out. Lannigan suggested a bandage, but Slim refused.

"It ain't too much for me to stand," he said doggedly. "I been hurt a lot worse, and if I get past this, I guess I'll be hurt again some time up ahead."

Lannigan did not ride trap lines the following day, ignoring Slim's suggestion that he check the sets. He stayed close to camp, going only far enough away to drag up a supply of dead, well-dried mesquite limbs for the fire, to take the animals to water and stake them out in a new grazing area, and to bring fresh water for drinking and cooking. They ate the stock rations always carried in the wagon to tide over periods of bad hunting: jerky shaved thin and boiled with potatoes and onions; bacon and cornpones, bacon and fried potatoes. The food was monotonous, but neither of them felt hungry. It was while they were sitting beside the fire in the gentle dusk that Slim was taken by the first convulsion. The spasm grew gradually, beginning with a tightening of the neck muscles that ma⁻¹e him twist his head in an effort to ease the strains.

Lannigan watched for a minute before asking, "You're hurting, ain't you?"

"Some." Slim's voice was thin and strained. "I got this kinda cramp in my neck."

Lannigan got up to help, but Slim waved him back. "Don't touch me, Lobo. I don't want you to get it, too."

"Damn it, I'm not going to catch anything just by touching you!" Lannigan took the other man's head in his hands and tried to stop its twisting, but the muscles in Slim's neck seemed to have taken on a strength that defeated any effort to hold or move them. While he was trying to restrain the rolling and tossing of his partner's head, Slim's arms and legs began to twitch. There was nothing Lannigan could do except to lower him to a prone position and kneel by him, trying to help the afflicted man hold the spasm in check. The convulsions stopped suddenly, and Slim lay quiet, somehow diminished in size, gulping for breath in great rasping gasps.

Between efforts to breathe, he said hoarsely, unbelief battling fear in his voice, "I guess that's the way it starts."

"Don't be a damned fool!" Lannigan snapped, holding the fear out of his own tones. "It might not happen again."

"It will," Slim prophesied. "You watch. It'll keep getting worse and worse till I can't stand it no more, or till I jump on you like that crazy wolf jumped on me."

"But there's a chance it won't! You might not get worse. It might go the other way, and you'll get well."

"No. Lobo, I'm going to die. The death-cold's in my bones." He was silent for a long minute, then said, "I want you to do something for me. You and me both know I'm as good as dead now. Make it faster than it's going to be otherwise, Lobo. Shoot me, will you?"

"I can't do that, Slim! Don't ask me to!"

"Why not? You'd shoot a crippled horse or a steer or mule to get its misery over fast. It'd be a kind thing to do for me."

"You know I couldn't pull a trigger on you, Slim."

"Maybe you think so now, but wait'll you see me slobbering and twisting and hurting all over. That's how it'll be when the damned hydrophoby takes hold good. You think about it, Lobo. If I got to die, I wanta go clean and quick. You got to help me!"

"I can't, Slim. Not as long as you've got a chance to get well."

"Thing about it is, I ain't going to get well. There's not any kind of medicine that'll cure me."

"Hang on a while. I'll do what I can to help you."

"There's not but one way you can help, Lobo. What I got ain't going to let go. But I'll tough it out a while. When you see I'm right, maybe you'll change your mind."

Slim's prophecy that the rabies would not let him go was proved accurate before daybreak. Lannigan did not try to sleep, but sat bundled in a blanket beside Slim's soogans. In the middle of the night the convulsions returned. The seizure was worse and more prolonged than the first one, and left Slim like a balloon that has collapsed after losing its air. Nothing that Lannigan could do helped him.

When he'd regained strength to talk, Slim whispered, "You see, Lobo? It's just like I told you. Next time, it'll be worse."

"It just seemed worse because it's dark. Sun'll be up after while, you'll feel better then."

"Please, Lobo. You got to see I'm right. Help me die easy."

"As long as you're alive, Slim, there's hope."

With his old asperity, Slim retorted weakly, "Anybody who'd figure there's still hope ain't right bright. And I ask your pardon for saying that, partner, but it's the damned truth."

"No offense taken, Slim. But you feel all right now, don't you? How do you know you won't start getting better after a while?"

Slim sighed. "All right, Lobo. Let's see what daybreak brings."

Daylight came without Slim's having suffered another attack. He seemed in better spirits as the sun spread its brilliance over the arid countryside, and when Lannigan asked how he felt, said, "Well, I don't hurt, except my hand. I do feel sorta puny, acourse." He tried to sit up in his bedroll, but fell back. He sighed, "I don't know. We better just see what happens the rest of the day."

"You want some breakfast? Or maybe just some coffee?"

"I guess I don't feel much like eating. You go ahead." As Lannigan was turning away, Slim added, "No, wait a minute, Lobo. They say when you got hydrophoby you get to where you can't drink anything. I guess a drink of fresh cold water'd go down right good. It might be the last one I'll get to enjoy."

"Stop talking that way, now!" Lannigan's harsh scolding did not cover his concern, though. He said, "I'll just go down to the creek and fill a bucket fresh."

He'd put the bucket into the hole they'd dug in the creekbed and was waiting for the trickle of water to fill it when he heard the shot. Leaving the bucket, he ran back to camp. Slim was sprawled on top of his bedroll, the butt of his big Navy Colt still gripped tightly in his uninjured hand, the revolver's muzzle inches away from his head. The other side of Slim's head, where the bullet had torn its way out, wasn't pretty to look at.

Although he'd known when he heard the shot what would be awaiting him, Lannigan could not come to accept the reality of it. He stood staring at Slim's body for several minutes. He was about to move away when he noticed the folded slip of paper sticking out of Slim's shirt pocket. He fished it out and unfolded it, recognizing it as a sheet from the tablet Slim had kept in the wagon to write down a record of the wolves trapped.

"Lobo, we was both right," he read. "I feel them

cramps coming on again. A man's got no right to ask somebody else to do a job he can't handle hisself. You been a good partner. Too bad we couldn't of gone on. Take the traps and gear. And what money I got that the trader in Fredericksburg is holding. Good luck, Slim."

If China Slim had been nervous when he wrote the note, his handwriting did not show it. The letters flowed in clean, even lines without shakiness, and the signature was firm and clear. Lannigan swallowed hard. He tucked the note in his pocket, then took the shovel out of the wagon. He walked around the level area where they were camped, not quite sure what he was looking for, but recognizing the right place when he saw a natural rock outcrop that looked like a head-stone standing on a quick narrow rise that overlooked the waterhole.

It was wolf and coyote country, so he lined the grave with rocks when he'd finished digging, and piled the heaviest boulders he could move on top of Slim's body before he shoveled the dirt back in. Not being a praying man, Lobo didn't quite know what to do after the grave had been filled. He stood unde-cided for a minute, looking up at the sky, seeking words, but couldn't find any words that he thought were good enough for Slim. He gave up trying after a while and walked away. The shovel over his shoulder seemed to weigh a ton.

There was a lot of day left. He wasn't hungry, and to have started a fire would have been a commitment to stay longer. He bundled all the camp gear into the wagon and hitched up, tied his pony to the tailgate as always. It was quiet working without Slim, and the place already had a ghostly feeling.

He ran the trap lines. There were eight wolves caught, between his sets and Slim's, and several more

traps had been sprung. Lannigan had no hesitancy
about shooting the trapped wolves now. He felt that
every time he fired he was somehow collecting a toll
for Slim's death. He didn't bother to skin the wolves
or even to take their scalps to collect the bounty due
on them.

When all the traps were piled into the wagon, he
drove the fifteen miles to the Diamond Dot main
house and, using the fewest number of words possible, told the foreman what had happened. He gave
the man the location of Slim's grave, in case a line
rider might run across it before it had weathered into
the landscape and disturb it, trying to learn who'd
been buried there.

Then he got back into the wagon seat and headed
north, for no other reason than that north was the way
Slim had planned for them to go.

From the Diamond Dot range on the North Concho
Branch to the JA Ranch on the Prairie Dog Town
Fork of the Red River was not quite two hundred
miles as a homing bird might fly, but Lobo Lannigan
did not travel as a bird would have. He rambled,
veering sometimes east and sometimes west, following
the easiest way across the upsloping plains. There
were no roads, seldom even a trace left by wagons
that had gone that way earlier.

Sometimes the wagon jounced a hundred miles to
cover fifty in a straight northward line, until he came
across the old Comanche Trail and started to follow
it. Lannigan didn't know or care that the trail was a
century older than he was. It had been beaten hard
by the hooves of Comanche war parties' mustangs on
their way to raid *haciendas* in Mexico, and defined
still more sharply by the mules and horses they drove
back as loot.

He followed the trail until it petered out in the southern mouth of Palo Duro Canyon. A few miles further north, two weeks now from the Concho, he was hailed by a line-rider off the JA, who offered him the hospitality of supper and a bunk for the night in a line shack. It was a fortunate evening for Lannigan. Sam, the JA hand—Lannigan never did learn the man's last name—was a fountain that spouted information instead of water.

"So you're a wolfer," Sam said thoughtfully. They were sitting outside the shack after supper. "Well, save yourself riding to the JA. Colonel Goodnight keeps a wolfer on the place regular."

"Wolves are that bad hereabouts?" Lannigan asked.

"Bad enough. Buffalo used to winter in the canyon, so did the Comanches with their horse herd. Wolves still come looking."

"How about the other ranches close by?"

"Them with range that joins the JA splits the wolfers' pay. Was I you, I'd strike straight north, up to the Canadian. I'd bet a fancy Appaloosa pony to a spavined mule that Ed Clark on the YL would be right glad to welcome you."

When Lannigan left the next morning, his head was crammed with landmarks and directions Sam had given him: creek crossings, rock formations visible from afar on the prairie, which side to take when circling the biggest buffalo wallows, the burned-out remains of a big Murphy wagon, the crumbling walls of a long-deserted sheepherder's adobe. In some places there was even the vestige of a trail to follow, the ruts left by Murphy wagons loaded with buffalo hides bound for Dodge City, or of Army supply trains servicing the forts and cantonments that had dotted the prairie during the days of the Civil War and the Comanche campaign. The ruts had a habit of appearing briefly and vanishing after a few miles, but Lannigan had no doubt that if he just kept his mules heading in the right general direction he'd arrive sooner or later at Tascosa, and the YL spread just beyond the old town.

After the wagon topped the caprock when coming out of the canyon, the character of the land changed instantly. The caprock was the dividing line between the plains and prairie, which now at summer's peak stretched brown-yellow on all sides. At first glance the country was flat and featureless from horizon to horizon, but after he'd traveled a score of miles Lobo realized that the featureless flatness was an illusion. There were rolling rises and downslopes beyond them that slanted so subtly they could not be seen, but only felt by the amount of effort the team was putting out. There were gullies, some of them mile-wide slashes that cut the land sharply, yawning in abrupt dropoffs, which were invisible from a hundred yards away.

Nearly everywhere Lannigan looked, bleached buffalo skeletons humped white above the shortgrass. Most of the skeletons were clumped together, a half dozen to a hundred lying within a radius of two or three hundred yards. These marked the places where hide-hunters had found a small group of animals that had drifted from the main herd and had taken advantage of the stragglers by dropping all of them with spaced-out shots from their big Sharp .50s.

Rarely, a line of brush or trees fuzzed the horizon, marking the course of a creek or the rising of a spring. The prairie was essentially water-sparse and treeless, and the presence of one indicated that of the other. When Lannigan reached the creek that meandered northward to the Tascosa crossing of the Canadian, he'd have identified it even without Sam's description.

Wheel ruts in the soft ground on both sides of the creek led him to the crossing. At the ford downstream from the creek mouth, the river was split by a narrow island, more sandspit than solid ground, on which maturing cottonwoods rose amid the stumps of what had been older trees. Slick lemon-green trunks of even younger cottonwoods, not much more than saplings, lined the grassy north bank of the river. Between their thin boles and low broad-leafed branches, the rich, deep brown of adobe plaster gleamed mellow in the afternoon sun and outlined the walls of a score of houses. Lannigan geed the team across the strip of yellow-orange sand at the river's edge and splashed through the shallows to the town.

Tascosa was not, Lannigan thought, as much of a town as Sam had made it out to be. The main street came to within a double-lariat length of the river. Houses started there, buildings straggled on both sides of the dusty thoroughfare beyond them. The first big building bore a sign declaring it to be a livery stable, and up the street other signs identified other businesses.

Lannigan was more interested in the building across from the stable, which had a welcome message scrawled across its front, "SALOON—Cold Beer." Three or four horses stood at the hitch-rail outside it. Lannigan pulled in and knotted the team's reins on the rail. He looked along the street; it was deserted. With a shrug, he pushed through the swinging doors of the saloon.

There were three men standing at the bar, their heads close together. Something about the middle one seemed vaguely familiar to Lannigan, but he ignored memory's nagging tugs and walked up to the bar.

"That sign outside really mean what it says?" he

asked the white-aproned barkeeper. "Your beer really cold?"

"It's cold as you'll find anywheres around here." The man put a stein under the tap and started a foaming stream flowing. Lannigan glanced sideways along the bar. The middle man of the trio was leaning forward, and Lannigan recognized Hardcase Harris just as Harris recognized him.

Harris said, "Well, look what blowed in on a bad wind. Couldn't you find a job down south that was little enough for you to handle?"

"I've done all right." Lannigan turned away, showing Harris his shoulder. He tossed money on the bar and picked up his beer.

One of Harris's companions observed, "Your little friend don't act too happy to see you, Hardcase."

Harris threw up his hands in mock alarm. "Now, you ought not've said that, Slane. The runt gets right mad if anybody notices he ain't no bigger'n a button. And then he starts tossing knuckles."

"You don't say!" The man called Slane was playing along. "You think the three of us is enough to handle him?"

Lannigan said, "Tell your friend to shut his face, Harris. I'm not looking for trouble, but I won't walk away from it. You know that."

Harris seemed disappointed that Lannigan hadn't responded any more angrily. He set his jaw and began pushing to stir up Lannigan's short temper. He said, "I was hoping we'd meet up again somewheres, runt." He brought up a hand and fingered his scarred ear. "I still owe you for this, remember."

Before answering, Lannigan drained his stein. It gave him time to study Harris's companions. None of the men wore gunbelts. He told Harris, "I come in here for a beer, not a fight. I had the beer, so I'm leaving. If you're smart, you'll stay."

Without waiting for a reply, he walked to the door, moving as fast as he could without giving the appearance of making a running retreat. As soon as he was outside he sprinted for the wagon and pulled Slim's old fuke out of the box where it traveled. He turned, leveling the shotgun, just in time to cover Harris and his friends as they dashed out of the saloon. They stopped with skidding heels when they saw the fuke.

"I see you know what this'll do," Lannigan said conversationally. None of them replied, so he added, "It's got both barrels loaded with number ought buck, and the shot starts spreading two inches out of the muzzle. Now, you can go back into the saloon, or you can walk away. I don't give a damn which, as long as you don't get closer to me."

"Ah, now, wait a minute!" Harris protested. "We wasn't going to hurt you."

"That's right," Slane affirmed. "We was just funnin' you."

"You had your fun," Lannigan replied. He stared at Harris and asked, "Now then, Harris. What's my name?"

In a voice choked with anger, Harris said, "It's Lannigan."

"Good. You remember to call me by it if we run into each other again."

Slowly, looking back occasionally, the trio walked away. Lannigan waited until they turned off the street before he tucked the fuke into his elbow and went back into the saloon.

"Think I'll have another beer," he told the barkeep. "Had to drink that first one so fast I didn't have time to enjoy it." He put the shotgun on the bar beside him. "I'll just keep this handy, if you don't mind, in case them three come back. Don't worry about it going off. It's not loaded."

"You faced them three down with an empty fuke, mister?"

"Well, I didn't have time to load it, and none of them had on a gun, so I figured they wouldn't know the difference. I sure as hell wasn't going to fist fight all three of 'em. Me and Harris tangled before when we worked for the same spread down on the Brazos, the S Bar T."

"How long ago was that?" The barkeep stopped midway to the backbar where the beer steins were stacked.

"Early in the year. February. I didn't look to run into him again, but I guess people and towns up here aren't so thick that if you stay around a while, you'll meet all of 'em. Mind if I ask why you're so curious?"

"Slane and Whitehead, the two he was with, are supposed to've taken over what's left of Billy the Kid's old gang."

"And who might Billy the Kid be?"

"You mean you never heard of Billy Bonney? Famous outlaw. Pat Garrett shot him not much more than a year ago, over in New Mexico. Billy used to stop off regular here in Tascosa."

"Sorry, I never heard of him. Never figured Harris for an outlaw, either, but then I never did know him all that good." He thought for a moment before asking, "If those three are outlaws, how come they didn't have gunbelts on?"

"Things aren't as free and easy as they used to be, in Tascosa. Tom Pape, our new city marshal, won't let anybody wear a gun in town." The barkeep had been filling a stein, he passed it across to Lannigan. "On the house."

"Thanks." Lannigan's arm brushed the fuke as he

picked up the stein. "You think your marshal might object to this? It ain't exactly a pistol, and I ain't exactly wearing it."

"You'd have to ask Tom, I guess."

"Tell you what. I'll pull out as soon as I finish my beer. Then your boss won't have to fret about the place getting shot up if Harris and his friends come back looking for me."

"Mister, I'm the boss. Name's Pat Garrity."

"Pleased. Mine's Lannigan, Lobo Lannigan."

"Stopping, or just passing through?"

"Little bit of both, I guess." Lannigan sipped his beer. "So you got Harris tagged for an outlaw. Interesting."

"Now, I didn't say he was," Garrity replied quickly. "All I know is, he came into town five or six months ago, and it wasn't a week before he'd hooked up with Slane and Whitehead. And nobody's really sure they're running Billy's old outfit; it's just talk."

"Well, it don't matter to me. We never was what you'd call friendly." He drained the stein and put it on the bar. "I'll be obliged if you'll set me on the trail for the YL. Which way do I head out?"

"Go right through town, north, and follow the track that cuts a little bit west after you leave Hogtown. Can't miss that. The girls will have their red lanterns lit up by now."

"Thanks. Can I make it before dark?"

"Easy. It's not too far."

Lannigan pushed through the batwings and peered along the street before leaving their cover. There were no more people around than before. Just the same, he loaded the fuke before he geed up the team, and kept it lying handily beside him on the wagon seat as he followed the trail that would lead him to the YL.

CHAPTER 7

"A real, live by-God wolfer!" exclaimed Ed Clark, the YL ranch manager, when Lannigan introduced himself. "I'm right glad to see you, Lannigan. There's times I think we've got as many wolves as steers on this spread. Damned varmints are driving me crazy."

Clark's words did a lot to dissipate the nervousness that had been building in Lannigan's mind during the ten-mile ride from Tascosa. It was the first time he'd been faced with setting up a job; always before he'd stayed in the background while China Slim negotiated with the owner or foreman of a ranch.

"Come on inside," Clark invited, peering down at Lobo through oval gold-rimmed spectacles. The ranch manager was taller than Lannigan by a foot. He wore a heavy untrimmed mustache that protruded an inch or more on either side of his thin, tanned cheeks, and his clothing was that of a working cowhand. He led the way toward the headquarters building, walking in the double-jointed fashion of men who spend more time in the saddle than afoot and seem to find their balance unsettled when they have earth under their bootsoles.

Lannigan looked around as he followed the ranch manager to a bowed-back adobe structure that stood at right angles to a smaller but similar building. In front of the second house a trio of cowhands were standing, watching their boss and the stranger. There was a third adobe building, open-fronted, a hundred yards distant, which Lannigan took to be a stable.

All three buildings had the same haphazard, unkempt look that Lannigan had noted about the houses in Tascosa, and he thought that he was probably seeing the headquarters structures at their best in the soft sunless twilight. He wondered idly why they'd been built of adobe, then realized that given the generally treeless condition of the Panhandle's prairie, a building that used anything beyond a minimum of lumber would be an ostentatious luxury.

Clark's office was small, just big enough to accommodate a rolltop desk, two chairs, and the inevitable squat iron safe. The ranch manager indicated a chair as he took off his hat, showing a nearly bald white pate that contrasted with his windburned, suntanned cheeks. He said, "Tell me something, Lannigan. Are we getting more than our share of wolves up here? Three or four years ago, they weren't nearly as bad as they are now."

"They're drifting up this way, I'd say. The spreads down south have been clearing wolves off their range for a long time, now."

Clark shook his head. "We run a string of a hundred brood mares on the YL, to keep our cavvies up. Every one of them carried a foal going into last winter. You know how many colts we had when it come time to bring the mares out of the nursery pasture?"

"Half," Lannigan guessed.

Clark snorted. "We had exactly eleven. I chased my butt over half the Panhandle swapping steers for colts, just trying to put together the remuda we need for roundup."

"I'd say you must've lost considerable cattle, too, then."

"Enough to hurt. We never did find all the dead ones, but I'd estimate we lost close to a thousand head, mostly calves and yearlings." The manager seemed glad to have someone new, someone not on the YL payroll, on whom he could unburden his problem. He went on: "It wasn't that we didn't try to hold the wolves down. I had the hands out on wolf drives three or four times."

"Wolves make tricky targets. You won't make much headway going after them with guns."

"You don't have to tell me that. Nineteen men, the best drive we put on we shot seventeen wolves. Seems like the bastards know just how far a rifle carries and keep their distance."

"Well, if you really wanta clear your range, I'm here and ready to start trapping," Lannigan suggested.

"What kind of bounty you expect to get?"

"South of the Red, they're paying five dollars a head, half-price for whelps. And I keep the pelts, give you the scalps to pay me on. I don't look to you for grub or anything else."

Clark passed a hand over his bare scalp. "Five dollars sounds high. All I get for a fat steer at railhead in Dodge is six, maybe six-fifty."

"More like twelve or fifteen dollars for the steers you consign to a commission agent to sell in the stockyards at Kansas City or Chicago." Lannigan had listened to China Slim deflate the arguments of ranchers who claimed that the bounty on a wolf was about the price of a steer. He went on: "It's not high, Clark. Not when a wolf's likely to drag down anywhere from ten to fifteen or even twenty head in one night, or maybe a dozen colts."

Reluctantly, Clark nodded agreement. "I know.

Thing is, I'm tight for cash right now. The YL's owned by a bank in Boston, and they've been damned close-fisted the last year or two. It'll be better in a few months, though. I got a letter from the owners last week saying they've sold the spread to some outfit in England. New owners will take over pretty soon."

Lannigan made no reply to this, considering it none of his affair. He hadn't given much thought to who actually owned the spread, but wasn't too surprised by Clark's revelation. Everybody connected with Texas cattle-ranching, from the lowliest jinglebob boy to the owners or managers of brands further south, knew that all but a small handful of the big new ranches sprawling over the unfenced, unclaimed land in the Panhandle were owned by a bank somewhere back East, or by a syndicate based in England or Scotland.

Cattle ranching on the limitless prairie, where range boundaries were measured in scores of miles, seemed to have a fascination for investors in the tiny, tight British Isles, where fifty acres was a big farm. Financial England, from the smallest merchant banker on the fringe of the City of London to the titled nabobs who handled the affairs of the Old Lady of Threadneedle Street were forming stock companies almost daily to buy Texas cattle land. British pounds, each pound worth five United States dollars, were pouring in an endless stream into the Panhandle. To the English mind, such huge undertakings, based on vast acreages of land and beef-cattle by the thousands, could not fail to return immense profits.

Almost from the time the buffalo-hunting Cator brothers, themselves sons of a British Navy captain, saw the buffalo herds declining in '73 and began running cattle on their old hunting grounds, Eastern and

English money started to flow West. The Cator ranches were in what was then Comanche treaty country, thirty miles north of the Canadian along Palo Duro Creek. They toughed it out with their small herds until '74, when MacKenzie's cavalry broke the backbone of Comanche power in the battle of Palo Duro Canyon, sixty miles south of the Canadian. The troopers destroyed the Comanche horse herd and confined the defeated tribesmen on reservations in Indian Territory.

Gunsmoke from the big battle had barely cleared the canyon when Goodnight moved a herd in from the south and set up the JA. At about the same time, Littlefield drifted a big trail herd over from New Mexico and established his LIT north of the Canadian. Littlefield was the first of the new ranchers to sell his spread to the British, and the pattern he set was followed by most of those who came in between '75 and '80. Before the 1880 decade was two years old, there were twenty big spreads on the newly opened range that covered nearly two thousand square miles of unclaimed virgin prairie. Four out of five of the big new outfits owed their existence to Eastern or English financing. Most of the small brands were nester outfits, owned in many cases by hands working for the big spreads, trying to maverick their way into herds.

Lannigan decided it didn't make much difference who owned the YL, as long as he'd made a deal with the man in charge. He asked Clark, "You going to stay on, work for the Englishmen?"

"As far as I know. There's always a chance they'll want to put their own man in, of course."

"Even if they did, a deal you'd made would stand. From what you said, if you don't start clearing the YL range of wolves, that bank in Boston's not going to have much of a herd to sell."

"That's a sure thing," Clark agreed. He thought for a moment. "All right, Lannigan. I'll pay your five dollars a scalp, as long as you understand you might not get all your money until the new owners take charge of things."

"I'm not in any hurry. You just tell the Englishmen that if they don't want to keep me on, they can call the deal quits. I guess it's all right if I bunk here tonight, start in tomorrow?"

"You can start in tonight for all I care," Clark smiled. Then he sobered quickly and asked, frowning, "You don't use poison, I hope?"

"Not a speck," Lobo replied emphatically. "Slim—he was my partner until he died a little while back—Slim used to say poison on a cattle or sheep range is as bad as wolves. I never did use it, but he told me how poisoned wolves slobber before they die and when cattle graze over the slobbered-on grass, they die, too."

"He was right," Clark agreed. "Some of the brands around here have started poisoning, but I sure don't like it. Well, we've got a deal, Lannigan. I'll get my *segundo* to ride with you tomorrow and show you our range limits, where we've got line shacks, places where the wolves have been thickest, things like that. The rest is up to you. Just give me a clean range, that's all I want."

When they'd talked, Lannigan had discounted part of Clark's wolf worry as being the inclination of a manager to exaggerate his problems. He discovered he'd been wrong, after riding over the YL range with the *segundo*, Dave Morton. Everywhere the evidence of wolf attacks was visible. Steer carcasses were scattered over most of the grazing grounds, some of them old, but far too many of them fresh. Among the herds, steers that had survived attacks of the predators showed big patches of new skin on their flanks and hindquarters, growing to cover huge chunks of flesh that had been bitten out by the marauders.

There were bobtailed steers and yearlings, their tails snapped off by the wolves' strong jaws. Many such steers would be lost, for they could not switch away the horn flies, buffalo flies, and botflies that lighted on the animals' rumps and backs to lay maggot-producing eggs under their hides. The horse nursery pasture used earlier in the year was strewn with the rotting carcasses of colts and mares the wolves had killed. There were so many that the scavenging coyotes and birds had not touched some of them, and on these carcasses gaping wounds in bellies and hindquarters showed where the killers had eaten a bite or two and then abandoned the dead animal to pull down another.

"We guarded this damn nursery till all of us was too tired to stay in the saddle," Dave Morton told Lobo. "The wolves sneaked by us at night, when we couldn't see to shoot 'em, and they'd drag down ten or a dozen colts before we could ride in and chase 'em off. We just give up, after a while."

"Other spreads hereabouts in this bad shape?"

"It's bad all over, but most of the brands have begun using strychnine now. Ed won't have it on the YL, I guess he told you that."

"I don't like it, either," Lannigan said. "A steer's just as dead from eating poisoned grass as it is if a wolf drags it down. My business is getting rid of wolves, not cattle and birds and all the other little meat-eating animals that a poisoned carcass wipes out."

"You've got a lot to do here, Lobo. Sooner you get at it, the better off the YL's going to be."

Lannigan lost no time in scouting the wolf-runs, which were plentiful, and in making his sets. There was never a morning when he found all the traps empty, and he counted as lost a day that did not take at least four wolves. On one record day, the traps held nine. He soon saw the job was too big for single sets; riding a line of thirty traps was more than a man could handle alone in one day. If left unattended too long, the traps yielded only pieces of paws and stumps of legs where the wolves had gnawed themselves free, and Lannigan worried about creating so many renegades.

With tools borrowed from the YL forge and young cottonwoods that he cut along Big Blue Creek, Lannigan began building tilt traps along the runs. Making such a trap was a three or four day job, depending on how hard the digging was. The trap's base was a circular pit fifteen feet deep, with its sides undercut to make the hole ten feet in diameter at the surface and twenty feet at the bottom. A cone of dirt was left standing in the center of each pit, and at the cone's top Lannigan implanted the trunk of a young tree, burying it six feet deep and leaving an equal length sticking up from the top of the cone. Through a hole bored in the trunk at ground level he inserted a wagon rod to serve as an axle, and on top of the rod he mounted a platform of tree branches woven into a circular pattern that filled the gap between the support and the edge of the pit.

To finish the trap, he nailed a crosspiece near the top of the tree trunk at right angles to the wagon-rod pivot. Rawhide thongs attached to the ends of the crosspiece dangled strips of hide liberally doused with scent; the strips were a foot above the platform.

A wolf investigating the scent was forced to step on the edge of the pivoted platform, which tilted under the animal's weight and dropped it into the pit. Relieved of the wolf's weight, the carefully balanced platform returned to its horizontal position. Because the platform covered the pit and because its sides had been undercut, the wolves could not scramble up and escape from the pit, or jump out of it.

Makeshift as their assembly was, Lannigan's tilt traps worked. He was somewhat surprised that they did, for he'd built them from descriptions given him by Slim, and had never seen one himself. Each of the three tilt traps he built began to take four to six wolves daily, so Lannigan could reduce his sets to a dozen traps on the more active runs and have a job he could handle, working alone.

Building the traps during the hours he had left after running his sets kept Lannigan busy for nearly two months. He'd made his headquarters at a line shack located near the biggest wolf-runs and now needed to go to the YL's main house to replenish his supplies. He rode the traps early, returned to the line shack to load the scalps and skins he'd accumulated, and set out across the prairie. He wondered if Ed Clark was going to have money enough to pay for the more than 350 scalps that were in the wagon with the skins.

He saw the flagpole when he was still three miles from the ranch headquarters, and wondered about it until he got close enough to identify it. His amazement grew as he got closer and saw the sunshine dancing off a dazzling foursquare two-story building that glistened with fresh red paint and white trim. The contrast between the new structure and the swaybacked old adobe houses he remembered was so great that Lannigan wondered if he'd mixed up his direction somehow. It was not until he pulled up the mules in front of the gleaming new building and saw behind it the old adobes he remembered that Lannigan was certain he'd reached the right destination.

Dave Morton came out of the new building and walked over to the wagon. He pushed his hat back on his head and said, "Well, there she stands, Lobo. What'd'you think about it?"

"Just what the hell took place here, Dave?"

"Oh, the new owners've taken charge. Decided the old place wasn't good enough, so they bought up all the lumber and fittings that they could find up at Dodge and hired a crew to come in and put that thing up. Gotta admit, it's better'n the old houses."

"Mighty fancy, all right."

"It is that. You wanta look inside? Can't tell much about it, the carpenters are just startin' to fence it into rooms."

"No, thanks. I'll wait till it's finished. I just come to get some grub and drop off these pelts. Got the scalps to match 'em; thought I might as well get a tally started."

Morton looked at the wolfskins piled high in the wagon. He whistled. "Looks like business has been pretty good, Lobo. Those new traps you said you were goin' to make must've done the job."

"They work." Lannigan nodded. "Well, I better find Ed and get started off. I wanta ask him can I store my pelts in the old stable until the job's finished and I can haul 'em to the traders."

"Ed's not here any longer. The new owners let him out."

"Hell, you say. Well, he figured they might. Too bad, but I guess it happens. Maybe I better talk to the new boss, then."

"Bosses. We got two now. Fellow named Hemphill,

he's from England. Other one's George Sessions, he's from Philadelphia. Hemphill's going back home for a while, but Sessions is running things."

"He ever run a ranch before?"

"If he has, he don't say much about it. Or show it much, by the way he behaves."

"Then I guess he's the one I better talk to."

"Afraid you can't, right now. He's taking Hemphill to Dodge to put him on the train going east. Won't be back for three or four days."

"You're still the *segundo*, though?" Lannigan asked Morton.

"Nobody's fired me yet, so I guess I am."

"Then I'll just tally the scalps with you. And if you don't mind me using a little space in the stables, I'll unload my pelts."

"Sure. How many scalps you got?"

"Just over 350. I didn't count too close, knew I'd have to make a tally here anyhow."

Morton whistled. "Damned if you're not going to get rich, Lobo. All your wolfing jobs pay off this good?"

"Not likely. You just got a lot more wolves on the YL than you need."

"All right. I'll climb on and you pull over to the stable. There's a corner someplace in there where you can keep the hides."

"Pelts," Lannigan said automatically, remembering how Slim had corrected him. "Steers got hides. Wolves got skins, we call 'em pelts."

They'd finished tallying the scalps, arriving at a total of 364, and were almost through unloading the skins, working in a corner of the stable where the light was obscured by the wagon and team that stood between them and the door, when a woman's voice called, "Dave? Is that you back there?"

"It's me, Miss Judith. What's the trouble?"

"No trouble, but the carpenter foreman wants you. Something about where they should put the stairs up to the attic."

Lannigan was straining his eyes to see the speaker, but her back was toward the stable door, her face in shadow.

Morton said, "Now, Miss Judith, I don't know nothing about that building. It's for your uncle to decide where the stairway goes."

"They said it can't wait until he gets back. They can't do anything on the second floor until they know where the stairs go." She was aware that Lannigan was staring at her and was returning his openly curious gaze.

Morton caught the exchange of looks and said, " 'Scuse me. Miss Judith, this here's Lobo Lannigan. He's the wolfer that's clearing our range. Lobo, make you acquainted with Miss Judith. Her uncle's the new YL boss I was telling you about."

"Right pleased, ma'am." Lannigan remembered in time to remove his hat.

"I'm glad to meet you, Mr. Lannigan." She looked at the pelt he was holding, and those already stacked against the wall. "Goodness! What a lovely fur. I suppose it's from a wolf?"

"Yes, ma'am."

Morton remarked, more to himself than to them, "I guess if the wood-butchers are in a bind, I better go see about it."

"They really do need you to tell them what to do," Judith said. "I'll be along in a minute or two, I want to look at Mr. Lannigan's furs."

"Sure." Morton turned back to Lannigan. "Come on over to the cookshack when you're finished and we'll fill out your grub list. Stay on to supper, if you've a mind to."

"Might, at that. Thanks, Dave."

Morton started for the door. Judith asked, "Do you mind if I touch the fur, Mr. Lannigan?"

"Handle it however you want to, miss." Lannigan was suddenly embarrassed, wanting to look at her, too bashful to do so. He held out the skin, jumping nervously when their hands brushed. He was glad he'd taken the time to wash and shave before leaving the line shack. Judith stroked the pelt, first with the lay of its fur, then backward, so that the brown-flecked reddish hairs rippled under her fingers in waves.

"Why is the skin so stiff?" she asked. "All the furs I've seen are soft and flexible."

"This ain't rightly fur yet, Miss Judith. After it's cured and tanned, it'll be soft, like you say." He pulled a gray wolf pelt from the few skins that remained in the wagon. "That one's off of a Texas red wolf. This here's from a Texas wolf, too, but it's a timber wolf, the kind they call a lobo."

"But your name is lobo," she exclaimed. "Isn't it?"

"Oh, that's just a sorta nickname." Lannigan did not want to discuss the name and its origin. He said hastily, "I guess you'll excuse me if I go on and finish unloading?"

"Of course. I'll watch, and when you're through we can walk up to the house together." Judith was stroking the gray wolf pelt. She said softly, "It's beautiful. Both of them are." Looking at the big stacks of skins, she went on, "How can you bear to kill such lovely animals, Mr. Lannigan?"

"One reason's because it's what I get paid to do. But wolves ain't really beautiful, if you see 'em pull-

ing down steers or horses. They can be ugly and
mean and sometimes right scary."

"They're just doing what Nature intended them to,
hunting for food."

"You'll excuse me, Miss Judith, but that ain't quite
the way it is. Might've been years back when the
wolves hunted elk and buffalo and suchlike, but a
steer won't fight back like a wild animal will. They
ain't a real fair match-up for a wolf."

"Uncle George says Texas steers aren't much more
than wild animals. Do they fight when a wolf is after
them?"

"Just like anything would if it was trying to keep
from being killed. And I'll grant you a Texas steer
ain't like a muley-cow in somebody's farmyard. But,
damn—oh, excuse me, Miss Judith. I just let that slip
by accident."

"I've heard the word before, Mr. Lannigan. It
doesn't shock me, even if I'm supposed to pretend it
does." Seeing that Lannigan's embarrassment had broken his train of thought, she went on. "It looks to me
as though you've finished unloading. Why don't we go
up to the house? We can talk more about wolves
later."

Outside, in the growing dusk, Lannigan got his first
really good look at Judith Sessions. She stood a half
head taller than he did, but her slenderness somehow
reduced her stature. Her arms and hands were slim,
too, and her face was thin, perhaps too thin for
beauty. There was a delicacy about her, an aura of
fragility, that seemed to command the world to treat
her gently.

As they walked to the old adobe headquarters
house, Lannigan studied her covertly. In spite of its
angularity, her face was symmetrical, her features
regular, though perhaps her mouth was scaled a trifle

too generously. Her eyes were deep-set, a lustrous hazel, alive and inquiring under thin, straight brows. Her hair, though almost hidden by the broad-brimmed hat she wore, was a russet-brown. Lannigan could not guess her age; it might have matched his own, or been a year or two greater or less.

Judith chatted easily about her impressions of Texas, filling gaps that Lobo's frequent silences would have made awkward. His life, spent in the womanless world of bunkhouses and line shacks, his only feminine contacts saloon girls, made conversation with a woman difficult. He would have liked to talk with Judith, to learn more about her, to find out why she was at the ranch, but did not quite know how to begin.

At supper, which they ate in the old headquarters building, Dave Morton's presence made it easier for Lannigan to talk. Much of the conversation revolved around the YL, and from it he got the answer to the question that had interested him the most.

"I hope I'll be able to stay here long enough to see the new buildings finished," Judith remarked at one point, when they were talking about the new headquarters house. "Even if they aren't going to include a school."

"Who'd want a school on a cow ranch?" Lannigan frowned.

"Someone who didn't know there weren't any married couples with children on one," she replied, smiling. "In this case, my uncle. People in the East don't realize that ranches out here aren't like family farms. Uncle George planned for me to teach school here."

"So you'll have to go back east now?"

"A lot sooner than I'd thought. And there are so

many things I still want to see and find out about, things I've only heard about."

"You want to see if what you've heard back there jibes with the way it really is," Lannigan suggested.

"Yes. And I want to see a roundup, and a herd of cattle start out on a trail drive." Judith looked challengingly at Lannigan and added, "And now that I've seen your wolfskins, I want to know why you men think you've got to slaughter all those beautiful animals."

It was Morton who took up the challenge. "If you saw what they do to cattle and horses, you might not think they're all that beautiful, Miss Judith."

"They're just following their instincts," she retorted. "They kill for the food they need to keep themselves alive."

"No, that ain't exactly right, ma'am," Lannigan said. "A lot of times wolves kill just for the hell of it." He put his hand over his mouth, his face reddening. "If you'll excuse my language, please."

Judith shrugged an acceptance of the apology as she demanded, "How can you say a thing like that?"

"Because it's the truth," he replied hotly, his embarrassment stripped away by his irritation. "Wolves is my business. If you want to know what they're really like, I'll sure show you."

A half smile came to her lips. "That sounds like you're offering me a dare."

"Well, I din't aim to, Miss Judith. But if you want to take it that way—"

"I do," she interrupted. "I'll take your dare. Now, when will you show me what wolves are really like?"

Lannigan thought for a moment. "Day after tomorrow? But I got to warn you, it'll keep you up all night."

"That doesn't bother me."

"And you'll be on a horse most of the time."

"I'm willing to do that. And able to. I've been riding since I was five years old, so don't worry about me and horses."

"All right, then. I'll ride by just about sundown." Lannigan stood up. "Now, I got a ways to get. I better get moving."

"Stay the night, Lobo," Dave Morton urged. "Plenty of room in the bunkhouse."

"No thanks, Dave. I got to ride trap line tomorrow."

"And kill more wolves?" Judith asked with mock sweetness.

Stung, Lannigan shot back, "You're da—" he caught himself in time. "You're right, Miss Judith. Maybe you'll find out why it don't bother me to kill 'em. I hope your nerve's up to it."

"You'll find my nerves equal to the occasion, I'm sure, Mr. Lannigan. I'll be ready, just before sundown."

Riding back to the line shack, the wagon bounding and rattling under its light load, the prairie almost as light as day in the full moon, Lannigan hoped the half-formed plan that had jumped into his mind when he challenged Judith Sessions would work out. He went over it, point by point, and decided it had better than a fifty-fifty chance.

"And that's as much edge as a man's got a right to ask for," he said aloud, addressing the mules or the moon or the night or perhaps just the open prairie. He had the habit, common to men who work alone, of talking to himself. "Damn fool, ought've not let her get under my skin." Then he added, "But there's something about her, all right. Even if—ah, hell!"

He rode the rest of the way to the line shack in silence.

CHAPTER 8

Lannigan swung off his mustang at the hitch-rail of the old YL headquarters house just as the sun disappeared under the rim of the flat horizon-line. There was a horse standing saddled at the rail. Before he could reach the door, it opened and Judith came out, followed by Dave Morton. Lannigan took off his hat.

"I told you I'd be ready," she said with a smile.

"Oh, I didn't misdoubt you would, Miss Judith." Lannigan looked questioningly at the *segundo*. "You going to join the party, Dave?"

"Afraid I can't. I still got half a day's paperwork to catch up. If the boss was back, I'd go along, but I want to have everything right up to snuff when he pulls in."

Lannigan said, "We might as well be moving, then, Miss Judith."

She went to her horse. Lannigan belatedly hurried to help her mount, but by the time he got to her side she was already in the saddle. Looking down at him, she said, "I hope it doesn't shock you that I'm not riding sidesaddle."

"Hadn't thought about it one way or the other," he replied, mounting his own pony.

With a wave to Morton, they started off. Judith seemed to feel a need to explain her failure to conform to female riding customs. "I had this old skirt remodeled so I could ride astride. I wouldn't dare do such a thing at home, but I didn't think anybody would mind, out here in Texas."

"Don't imagine they will," Lannigan agreed. "Come to think of it, I don't recall seeing many ladies on cowponies before."

They rode in silence for a while, Lannigan watching Judith from the corners of his eyes, assuring himself that she could handle her horse. When he saw that she rode easily and confidently, he increased their pace to a lope.

"We got a ways to go," he explained. "Better part of ten miles. By the time we get there the moon'll be up, and I don't want to spook any wolves that might be prowling. Just might do that if we go clattering up to the place, so we'll clatter now and slow down when we get closer."

"You sound very sure there'll be wolves where we're going."

"I can't guarantee you, but it's more'n likely there will."

Conversation was difficult, nearly impossible, at the faster pace their horses were holding. They rode abreast, Lannigan avoiding any sudden changes of direction, but swinging in a gentle arc to the section of range that he'd spent most of the day preparing. As they drew closer to it, he hoped his work hadn't been wasted.

There were three runs on which he'd as yet made no sets, and he'd scouted all three for recent wolf-sign. All of them bore fresh tracks, but on one of the runs most of the tracks were those of a small pack. It was a family pack, Lannigan was nearly certain; from the size and pattern of the paw tracks he judged the pack to be made up of a dog and bitch and three almost grown cubs. There were old tracks and new, but none of them had been left within the past few days. The run looped around several areas of broken ground where a pair of riders could lurk unnoticed.

After deciding the run was the best choice of the three, Lannigan rode zigzag across the range, toward the working pastures, until he came across a small bunch of YL cattle. He cut out a scrawny but mature steer and a sickly-looking yearling and drove them to the run, staying with them until late afternoon, turning them back when they started to drift away. He knew they'd drift after he left, but the grass was reasonably good in the vicinity, and he counted on their staying fairly close at hand.

Late in the day, allowing himself just enough time to get to the YL headquarters by the appointed hour, he'd dribbled a series of scent tracks from the perimeter of the wolf-run inward toward its center. Working from horseback, he spaced the trails like spokes of a wheel, a dozen yards apart. He took care to deposit the smallest possible quantities of scent, just enough to pull a wolf from the perimeter of the run to its inner area.

By the time he and Judith got to the run, the full moon was climbing the sky. In the clear night air, details of the landscape were almost as easily seen as they would be by daylight. A short distance from their destination they encountered the steer and yearling. Both animals were lying down, and lurched to their feet when the riders approached. Judith gasped when she saw them move. She reined in, acting by instinct, and Lannigan pulled up, too.

"Nothing to worry about," he assured her. "Just a couple of critters I moved over here to give the wolves some meat to work on."

"I'm sorry," she said. "They startled me, it's been so quiet."

"They're our bait. Ride back of me a ways, now, while I chouse 'em where they ought to be."

Moving slowly, Lannigan drove the animals ahead of them until they reached the center of the run. He left them standing, the yearling blatting uncertainly, and guided Judith to the broken ground where he'd decided they would wait.

"All we got to do now is set," he told her. "And we don't want to talk a lot, because wolves can hear sounds a long ways off."

"Can't they smell us, too?" There was a shiver of apprehension in her voice.

"Sure they can. Only I put out some scent to cover ours up and draw the wolves this way. Once they're close enough to scent them steers, they won't be thinking about much else." In hopeful afterthought, he added, "If they show up at all."

They waited in the saddle for almost an hour, then dismounted and tethered their horses in the gully Lannigan had selected for their lookout post. The moon moved higher, casting thinner shadows as it rose, revealing more detail of their surroundings to the watching pair. The steers, after milling uncertainly for a while, had settled down close to the center of the run. The silence was uncanny, unsettling to one who was not used to it. Judith paced nervously, three or four short steps in each direction from their mounts.

"It'd be better if you was quieter, Miss Judith," Lannigan suggested in a half whisper. "Or, if you're tired of waiting, we can go back."

"No, I'm all right. It's just that everything's—well, spooky."

Almost before she'd finished speaking, the eerie howl of a distant wolf vibrated faintly and broke the night quiet.

"Is that—it was a wolf, wasn't it?"

"Sure wasn't no coyote. But it's maybe four, five miles away. Calling for company. Might be—" Lannigan stopped abruptly, he did not know quite how to phrase what he'd started to explain.

Judith saved him from embarrassment. "You mean, it's a mating call?"

"Something like that, the way it sounded. That wolf wasn't hunting. When they're trailing something, they mostly keep quiet until they catch up, then they start yapping."

As though on cue, a series of barking snarls broke out close at hand. Lannigan levered a shell into the chamber of his Winchester. He'd taken the rifle out of its saddle scabbard when they dismounted.

"Get on your pony," he whispered. "Look at the steers."

In the saddle, their heads were above the rim of the gulley. Both steers were on their feet now, circling in little more than their own length, trying to decide which way to run. The yearling took off, moving away from the place where Judith and Lannigan were concealed. Before the animal had covered a score of yards a streak of gray, ghostly in the moonlight, dashed in front of it to cut off its flight. The yearling stopped short and reversed its course. The older steer began running in the opposite direction. From nowhere three more wolves appeared and trotted into a rough arc in front of the steer. It stopped and began turning aimlessly.

Now a fifth wolf joined the others. It ran up to the steer and circled with it, avoiding the bigger animal's clumsy efforts to hook it, darting away from the swinging horns to snap at the steer's back hooves. The three other wolves began closing in. The steer could not move in any direction; wherever it turned its head it saw a snarling wolf with shining teeth bared in gaping jaws. The yearling, some distance from the attacking wolves, started running again, but the wolf that had halted its first effort to escape turned it back with a series of quick rushes punctuated by growling snarls.

Judith covered her ears with her hands as the angry staccato yelps increased in volume, but she could not draw her eyes away from the attack. Lannigan leaned across the little space between them and pulled away her hand. He said, "Watch, now. Watch the wolf that's back of the big steer."

For a moment, the steer under attack by the pack continued to circle and try to hook its tormentors. It grew either dizzy or tired, for it stopped briefly. Like a missile released from a catapult, the wolf that had been worrying the steer's heels leaped up and closed its jaws on the animal's tail. The steer bleated and swung around in narrow circles, trying to throw the wolf off. It had made only a half-dozen quick turns when a cracking pop rang out above the yelping pack and the wolf dropped off, holding the severed tail in its jaws. It trotted to one side and began to worry the tail, tossing it into the air, swinging it from side to side with quick shakes of its head.

Not as much to Lannigan as to herself, Judith gasped. "Oh, the poor thing! That wolf bit its tail off!"

"Sure did," Lannigan agreed. "Look close, now. They're about to finish off the steer."

Even as he was speaking, two of the three wolves in front of the steer ran to either side of it and began to snap at its hind legs, much as the single wolf had done earlier. The steer kicked, but the agility of its attackers defeated its efforts, it could not land a hoof on either wolf.

One of the wolves leaped for the tiring steer's hind

leg. Its jaws closed on the hamstring and severed it;
the steer began limping on three legs. The second
wolf moved in on the other leg, which the steer could
use now only as a pivot. The attacker's fangs found
the vulnerable tendon in the uninjured leg and
snapped down.

Its second hamstring now bitten through, the steer's
hindquarters sank to the ground. Supporting itself by
its forelegs, the steer could not move, but continued
to try to hook the wolves as they circled it, closer and
closer, until one of the wolves caught the steer's
muzzle. The steer kept on blatting, but now the blatts
were muffled, smothered.

At the same time, the two wolves that had
succeeded in hamstringing the steer moved up to its
flanks and began tearing at the disabled animal. They
worked with sidewise slashes, burying their fangs in
the thinly fleshed flanks, tearing out chunks of meat,
which they chewed once or twice before swallowing.
Weakened by the loss of its blood, which was streaming from its opened sides, the steer sank slowly to the
ground, still blatting feebly. The wolf that had been
holding the steer's nose joined those in the rear and
dug into the steer's hindquarters. The fourth wolf,
which had been worrying the tail, came up to tear off
a bite or two.

Judith sighed, a drawn-out shivering exhalation.
"Well, at least the little steer will get away now."

"No, Miss Judith. Three of them wolves is young-
sters, the big ones are giving them lessons. Watch,
now."

A deep-throated bark from the wolf that had been
guarding the yearling called its companions from the
fallen steer. They left the victim, its muscles still
twitching, its ribs still rising and falling in faltering
inhalations, and went to attack the yearling.

This time the two biggest wolves stood off to one side and let the three smaller ones carry out the killing. Their moves were almost a step-by-step repetition of the attack on the big steer, though carried on at a faster, more excited tempo. In less than five minutes the yearling was prostrate, the wolves ripping into its belly.

"They'll eat the kidneys and liver and some of the guts," Lannigan told Judith. "If it was a mama cow carrying a calf, they'd gobble down the calf and maybe take a bite or two off of the mama." He raised the rifle.

"You're going to shoot them, I hope," Judith said angrily.

"If I'm fast enough, I might drop two," he replied. He triggered the Winchester, and one of the wolves dropped. The others began to run; from a standing start they reached full speed before Lannigan could chamber another shell. He fired at one of the ghostly fleeing forms and it began to limp, then its hind legs gave way. The wolf continued to pull itself ahead, using only its forelegs, until he hit it with another slug. The remainder of the pack had vanished.

"At least you got two of them," Judith said. There was grim satisfaction in her usually soft voice. "It's too bad you didn't kill the others." She dismounted and walked over to one of the wolf carcasses. Lannigan followed her.

He asked, "You still think it's all right to let wolves do what's natural to them?"

"Please don't remind me. I owe you an apology, Mr. Lannigan."

"No you don't, ma'am. You just didn't know what a wolf's nature is like. But if you want to do something I'd be right grateful for, you could quit calling me

'Mr. Lannigan,' and just cut it down to plain 'Lobo.' If you don't mind, that is."

"I will if you'll stop calling me 'miss' and 'ma'am.' It reminds me too much of my school classrooms."

"Suits me fine, if that's what you want." Lannigan was silent for a moment. "You still think wolves is too pretty to kill?"

"No. What they did was savage. Oh, they're beautiful, but I can understand why ranchers kill them. Tell me something, Lobo. If you hadn't shot when you did, would they have eaten more?"

"Not very likely. Maybe a few bites. But if there'd've been any more steers around, they'd've gone right on killing."

"And the way that one bit off the steer's tail? Do they do that very often?"

"A lot of the time. Me, I think that's one of the ways they play."

"Their jaws must be tremendously strong, to go through bone."

"Right powerful. China Slim, he was my partner till he died a while back, showed me something when he was learning me to wolf. He poked a tree limb thick as my arm at a wolf we'd caught in a trap, and that da—that wolf snapped it in two with one bite."

Judith shuddered. "I'd hate to have one snap at me."

"You don't have to worry too much. Generally, they won't jump people, unless they're starved or you're hurt. But it still don't pay to take chances."

"I don't intend to."

Lannigan was looking at the dead wolves. He said, "Sorta hate to leave them hulks, but I don't feel much like skinning 'em out now, and by the time I could get back the coyotes and kit foxes'll have 'em ripped to pieces. Would you mind if I scalped 'em, Miss—I mean, Judith? Only takes a minute, and even if I lose the pelts, I'll still get my bounty."

"Do whatever you need to do, Lobo. Then, we'd better get back to the ranch. It just occurred to me that you must have work to do tomorrow—or today, I guess, by now." She shivered. "But at least I've had a night I won't forget."

A week passed before Lannigan saw Judith again, though few hours passed when he did not think of her. Long periods of solitude are spent by different men in different modes of thought. Some turn their minds backward and waste time recalling past mistakes or in reliving triumphs once achieved. Some project ambitious, improbable, and unrealizable futures. Others, such as Lannigan, forgo both introspection and retrospection. They concentrate on the present and the deed of the day, the people with whom they are in immediate contact.

Lobo Lannigan did not think of himself as falling in love with Judith Sessions. She was a woman from a world different from that he knew, and he did not equate his growing interest in her as anything except curiosity about her world. She irritated him as much as she attracted him, with her failure to understand what he thought of as reality. He did not quite understand how she'd become a challenge to him or why. He still carried in his mind the belief that had inhibited him since early youth, that his size repelled women. Yet, as he went about his familiar routines, there were many times when, to his surprise, he'd find himself thinking of something he should tell Judith about the world as he knew it.

Lannigan had not had any visitors since settling in at the line shack; he was not prepared when Judith, Dave Morton, and a pair of YL hands rode up a week after he'd taken Judith to watch the wolf-kill. It was early morning and he was getting ready to ride his trap line. Judith and Morton dismounted, the two cowpokes stayed in their saddles. Lannigan exchanged greetings with his visitors, but spoke first to Morton.

"Thought the only outfit you ride now was a desk and chair."

"I'm off that rig, now the boss is back." Morton grinned. "About time I was. I got a lot of drifted stock that needs to be pushed to winter range before the weather turns."

"You think it's about to? It's only into September."

"It'll hold for a while. Real winter don't set in here until December, most years. But when I told the boss I was riding this way, he wanted me to stop by and ask you to come talk to him."

"And I invited myself to come along," Judith volunteered. "I thought I'd come out with Dave and then go back with you."

"Well, I was going to clear my sets, but I guess they'll wait till later on. Make yourself at home, Mi—Judith, while I saddle up."

"We'll push along, then," Morton said. "See you later, Lobo."

Judith had been looking over the line shack since she'd dismounted. It was more soddie than house—a slope excavated to form a floor and three walls, a front wall of boards, roofed over with shakes from the salt cedars that grew profusely in the Canadian River brakes. She asked Lannigan, "Do you mind if I look inside?"

He pulled the door open. "Make yourself comfortable as you can while I saddle my pony. There's coffee in the pot on the stove, if you want some."

She went in and stopped just inside the door to let

her eyes adjust to the dim interior; there were no windows. The shack was both bare and crowded. It was barely eight feet square, its back and side walls and floor hard-pounded dirt. The ceiling was low, its cottonwood limb rafters unfinished, and seemed to press down on her. A double-tier bunk filled the back wall, the top bed rising nearly to the ceiling. Blankets were crumpled on the bottom bunk, clothes piled on the upper. At right angles to the bunk, stretching along one side wall, was a bench, a small raw-wood table in front of it, and two chairs pulled up to the table.

At the other side wall there was a low, oblong monkey stove that served for both cooking and heating; a coffeepot rested on it. Wooden packing cases had been nailed to the planks of the front wall for cabinets. She noted that Lannigan was a neat housekeeper; there were no dirty pans, or plates in evidence. Wherever there was an unused square of floor space, dried wolf-pelts were stacked; their animal aroma hung in the air. The shack had the temporary feel of any structure left unused for long periods and then occupied only briefly by transient lodgers.

Lannigan came in. He saw the astonished disapproval in Judith's eyes and asked, "It ain't much, is it? Not like what you're used to."

"It's terrible, Lobo! Uncle George ought to be ashamed, expecting you to live in a place like this."

"Now, don't go blaming him or anybody else. This shack was built before he ever heard of the YL. Anyways, line shacks wasn't meant to be lived in, they're just places to shelter in a little while when the weather's bad."

"You're living in this one."

"It'd be stretching the truth to say so. I cook on the

stove, take my grub outside to eat. Half the time, I sleep outside, too."

"I still think it's terrible."

"It'd look that way to a lady like you, that's used to built-up towns and regular houses. It don't bother me." He looked around. "It don't bother a cowhand, either, when he's caught out in a blizzard."

She shook her head. "It's hard to get used to Texas, Lobo. People are satisfied with so much less than we expect, back home."

"Most everybody can get used to doing with a lot less than they do, most of the time."

Judith surveyed the shack again. "You're right, I suppose. I'm not sure I'd want to, though." She waited for Lannigan to agree or argue, and when he said nothing, added, "You said you've got a lot of work to do today. Shouldn't we start for the ranch?"

They talked very little while riding to the YL. It was as though Judith's remarks about the line shack emphasized the gap between them. Lannigan was irritated at her criticism of his quarters, of the way people adjusted to life on what was still a frontier. He felt no enthusiasm for conversation.

Even before they dismounted at the hitch-rail, Lannigan heard the dogs yapping. He turned, frowning, and asked Judith, "Is that dogs I hear?"

"Oh, I didn't think to tell you. Uncle George brought back a pack of hounds. Some friend of his in the East breeds them. Uncle had written him about the wolves and coyotes, so his friend shipped him a pack of dogs to hunt them with. They came in just before Uncle George started back from Dodge City."

"What kind of dogs are they?"

"Goodness, Lobo, I don't know. Greyhounds? I think that's what Uncle calls them."

"Hmpf. Well, dogs is something I don't know

about. Seen a few sheepdogs around, but they was just dog, no kind of breed."

"Come look at these. Uncle George is really proud of them."

Judith led Lannigan around the corner of the gleaming new headquarters house. A lariat had been guyed between two wagon rods driven into the ground and strung on it by the hand loops of their leashes were eight long-legged, long-muzzled gray dogs with deep chests and thin, sunken bellies. A short distance away, a man in his early forties was standing watching the hounds. He was stocky, almost fat, with a florid face and heavy mustache. From his dress, a store-new creamy Stetson, pleated jacket, whipcord pants, and leather leggings, Lannigan guessed he was George Sessions. Judith confirmed the guess.

"Uncle George, I'd like you to meet Lobo Lannigan. He's the—"

"I know who he is," Sessions replied. "Morton's told me." He did not advance to greet them, but stood with hands in his jacket pockets, examining Lannigan inch by inch. "Hm. You don't look big enough to handle a banty chicken, let alone a wolf."

Lannigan held back the words that came to his mind first. He replied mildly, "There's enough pelts out in the stable to show I can, Mr. Sessions."

"Yes. I've heard about your hides, too. We'll talk about that later." He waved toward the greyhounds. "What do you think about them?"

"Thin-coated. Be hard to winter them in this country. Look like they could use a square meal, too, but that's not my business."

"Greyhounds aren't supposed to be fat, Lannigan. It's pretty clear you don't know anything about hounds."

"I never said I did. Wolves is my line of work."

"Those hounds are going to finish your work a lot quicker than your traps ever will. They won't sit around waiting for the wolves to come to them. They'll go after the wolves where they live."

"I bet they will, at that. I wouldn't bet so strong that any of 'em would come back."

Disbelief was in Sessions's face as he stared at Lannigan, and in his voice when he asked, "Are you saying they can't handle wolves?"

"No, sir. I'm just saying I never heard of a dog yet that could. You ask around, find out why none of the ranches in wolf country keeps dogs."

Judith broke in. "Sheep dogs? Don't they fight wolves and drive them away from the flocks?"

"Sheep dogs back off and yelp till the herder comes," Lannigan told her. "Mostly, they stay clear of trouble and back away from a wolf till they get help."

"Nonsense!" Sessions said decisively. "You've admitted that you don't know anything about dogs, Lannigan, so just leave these to me. All I want you to do is show me where to turn them loose, where the wolves are."

For a moment Lannigan didn't reply. Then he said thoughtfully, "They look like nice dogs. I'd hate to see 'em all killed."

"They're not going to be killed!" Sessions exploded. "I'll agree that if it was one of them going against one wolf, the wolf just might win. But these dogs run in a pack, they'll outnumber the wolves."

"Wolves run in packs, too, Mr. Sessions. So do coyotes. I don't give these dogs much of a chance even against coyotes, and a coyote's a little bit smaller than your hounds here."

"I'll prove you're wrong," Sessions retorted. "Now, I want to work them as soon as possible; tomorrow'd be fine. All you've got to do is lead me to the best place to turn the hounds loose."

Lannigan started to protest that he wasn't on the YL payroll, and that he had his own work to do, but he knew he'd have no rest until the ranch manager had his way. He nodded. "All right, Mr. Sessions. Tell you what. I'll finish up what I got to do today. Then tonight I'll ride back here and take you and your dogs out tomorrow. We oughta start about an hour after midnight. That suit you?"

"To a tee!" Sessions exclaimed. "And you'd better be ready to eat crow, Lannigan. These hounds are really going to show you something!"

"I wouldn't be a bit surprised if they did," Lannigan replied quietly. "No, sir, not surprised one little bit."

CHAPTER 9

A late-rising crescent moon hanging high obscured rather than illuminated the prairie when Lannigan arrived at the YL to lead the wolf-running party. Sessions was waiting with Dave Morton, their horses saddled. A spring wagon, team hitched, stood nearby, and two YL hands, Spud Jensen and Pecos Daniels, were loading the greyhounds. The dogs were still secured to the lariat by their leash-loops.

Lannigan asked Sessions. "Is Miss Judith coming along?"

"Why should she? This is man's business."

"I just thought—"

"I know what you thought, Lannigan. I've heard all about that damned fool midnight exhibition you inveigled her into, how she's been visiting you out at the line shack. I'll be obliged if you'll keep out of her way from now on."

Lannigan choked back a hot reply. He'd see Judith, he thought, when they got back, and get her side of things. He said, "If you're ready to go, then, we might as well start."

He led them west at a long slant from the area where his traps were. The after-midnight air was nippy, as most nights had been for a week; the drawn-out prairie autumn had arrived to warn that real winter was due in another month or two. They pulled their collars up around their ears as a thin, chilling breeze hit them once they'd left the shelter of the ranch buildings.

Sessions and Morton flanked Lannigan, ahead of the wagon. All of them were sleepy, and they did not talk. The hounds were the only ones that showed much animation. They knew something was beginning that involved them and showed it by their constant high-pitched whines. The noises made by the dogs and the occasional groaning and rattling of the wagon were the only sounds that broke the night as they rode the gentle upslope of the prairie, which was beginning its almost imperceptible tilt that would top off in the mesa lands of New Mexico Territory, less than fifty miles distant. Lannigan had chosen the direction not only to avoid his traps, but because the western range was flatter and less broken than the rest of the YL. He'd scouted it; knew there were wolves moving over it most of the time, transients on the way to the runs where he had his sets. They rode for almost three hours in a straight line before he signaled a halt. The creaking of the wagon stopped, the noise of the dogs increased. Behind them, the sky showed its first signs of predawn paling.

"Is this the place?" Sessions asked.

Lannigan was still nursing his anger after their verbal brush at the ranch. He said curtly, "It's as good a place as any."

"You're sure there are wolves around here?" Sessions insisted. He was squinting into the darkness-shrouded landscape.

"They're here. But I wouldn't set the dogs loose till it's light enough so we can see to follow 'em."

"If Lobo says there's wolves, there's wolves," Dave Morton assured his boss. "He knows where they are a lot better'n we do."

"All right," Sessions said. He called to the men on the wagon, "Might as well get the dogs down on the ground, give them a chance to loosen up their legs before we turn them loose."

Jensen got into the wagon bed while Daniels walked back to the tailgate and dropped it. Sessions dismounted and went over to help Daniels get the dogs to the ground. They had the entire pack out of the wagon when somehow—afterward, nobody could explain exactly what happened—the greyhound at the end of the string pulled its leash free of the lariat. Both Sessions and Daniels let go the lariat and began chasing the freed hound. The remaining greyhounds started after their packmate, and the lariat straightened out as they moved, their leash-loops slipping off the rope one by one.

Lannigan and Morton, still on their horses a short distance from the wagon, did not realize the entire string of hounds was free until Sessions shouted at them to head the dogs off. Both men kicked up their horses, but trying to contain the hounds was like trying to collect wind in a sieve. Within seconds the entire pack had disappeared in the darkness, and a half hour of circling, trying to find them, convinced the riders they'd be wasting time looking for them before daybreak. They rode slowly back to the wagon, where they found Sessions tongue-lashing Daniels and Jensen for their clumsiness.

"Now, you can't blame Spud and Pecos, Mr. Sessions," Morton pointed out. "It was an accident. They didn't let loose your dogs a-purpose. You was right there working with 'em, and you didn't aim to let the hounds go free."

"Damn it, Morton, shut up!" Sessions snapped. "I know well enough what happened, you don't have to tell me!"

Lannigan said, "There wasn't—" He did not finish. A cacophony of dog barks and wolf yelps sounded on the quiet night. The noise seemed to be all around them.

"Let's go find them!" Sessions called, running toward his horse.

Lannigan shook his head. "No use. Not until it's light enough. You can't follow sound on the prairie, Mr. Sessions. You head in one direction, pretty soon you'll find out the noise is coming from someplace else."

"But I want to get close enough to see what's happening!"

"Sure you do," Lannigan replied. "But finding that bunch of hounds has just got to wait until daylight. Soon as I can see, we'll track 'em down." He listened. The noise of the animals was growing steadily fainter. "No use in us flubbing around out there now. They'll leave tracks, we'll catch up with 'em."

They waited, stamping around the wagon to keep warm. Eventually a gray streak of dawn appeared and spread slowly, imperceptibly, across the sky. The brightness grew. Pink glowed on the eastern horizon, and now the ground could be seen clearly. Lannigan said, "I can read trail now. Let's ride."

Daniels and Jensen stayed with the wagon, to start after the trio on horseback had gotten well ahead. Lannigan fanned his companions out, Sessions to the right, Morton to the left; he rode in the center spot a short distance in advance. Morton saw the first greyhound before they'd gone more than a mile. They converged on the dog's carcass, Sessions swearing loudly at the sight of the hound's slashed flanks and ripped throat. Lannigan made no comment. He did not dismount, but circled in a widening spiral around the dead dog until he picked up the tracks of the other greyhounds and the wolves, and called the others to follow him.

"Well?" Sessions asked as they started, moving at a walk, Lannigan keeping his eyes on the ground. "Well? What about the rest of them?"

"They'll be up ahead. Or what's left of 'em." They rode on in silence. Lannigan noticed the changed pattern of the tracks, and did not like what he saw, but he had to tell Sessions sooner or later. He decided there'd be no point in delaying what he had to say. "I'll tell you what begun to happen when your hounds got right along in here, Mr. Sessions. The wolves maneuvered your hounds and got 'em strung out."

"What do you mean, strung out? Those greyhounds were trained to run in a pack!"

"They broke their training, then. You can read it in the tracks. Right where we are now, there's one wolf running ahead of the dogs, the other wolves run on the sides to keep the hounds from bunching up. When one of the hounds starts to straggle, the wolves in back gang up and kill it."

"Damn it!" Sessions grated. "My hounds don't have a chance that way! One of them against an entire wolf pack! How many wolves are there against them, Lannigan?"

Lannigan rode in silence for a long moment. Then, without raising his eyes from the scratches that marked the trail across the dry prairie soil, he said, "It's not much of a pack. There's only three wolves. Hard to tell, but I'd say it's a dog and a bitch and one of their half-grown young'uns."

"Three? Oh, now, you can't be right about that. Eight greyhounds are more than a match for three wolves. You heard how much noise those wolves were making, it sounded like there were fifty of them. No, you'll have to prove what you're saying before I'll believe it."

When they reached the body of the next dog, Dave Morton joined Lannigan in interpreting the tracks for the ranch manager. The marks of claws and paws were plain enough even to such a relatively inexpert tracker as the *segundo*. The thin pads of the greyhounds and their blunted claws could be distinguished easily from the broader pads and sharp claws of the three wolves. The tracks showed how the wolves had worked, one attacking from the front, the other from the rear, while the prints of the third wolf were mixed in with the remainder of the greyhound pack.

As they followed the trail, the bodies of the dogs lay in an almost straight line. They were closer together, a sign the dogs were tiring. In each case, the pattern of the wolves' attack was the same. Toward the end, the fights must have lasted only a few seconds.

They did not try to follow the trail of the wolves beyond the place where the body of the last dog lay. Sessions angrily ordered Jensen and Daniels to dump the bodies of the other dead greyhounds they'd picked up. He said not a word on the long ride back to the ranch, and brushed past Judith angrily when she ran out of the house to greet them and get the news of their morning. Bewildered, she turned to Lannigan.

"What's the matter, Lobo?" He pointed to the empty wagon, which Daniels and Jensen were just wheeling past the house. Her eyes grew wide and she clenched her lower lip between her teeth. "Not all of them, surely? Not all eight?"

Lannigan nodded. "Happens to men that won't listen."

"What will Uncle George do now, do you think?"

"I don't much care what he does, Judith." He knew he should stop and talk with her, tell her what Sessions had said to him, but the morning's angers and frustrations were seething in his mind. "I got my own work to do, and I better get at it. I wasted two days on this foolishness, and that's all I aim to put in. If your uncle wants to talk to me, he knows where I'll be at."

Several days passed before one of the YL line riders stopped by to tell Lannigan that the ranch boss wanted to see him. Lobo did not hurry to respond. He ran his trap line, removed three wolves from the sets, and emptied the tilt traps of the eight wolves they held. Back at the line shack, changing from his wolfing outfit to everyday clothes, he decided to make his trip to the YL do double duty, and loaded the wagon with the pelts he'd accumulated since his last haul there.

Sessions gave him a cold greeting and plunged brusquely into the reason he'd summoned Lannigan. "You're dragging this job out too long. At the rate you're going, we'll have calves and colts on the range before you get the wolves cleared off."

"Between my sets and tilt traps, I'm taking ten or twelve a day. There was eleven in my traps this morning."

"It's still going too slowly, Lannigan. I've decided we'll finish the job with poison."

"And mess up your range for two or three years with poisoned grass that'll kill your stock, your horses?"

"Other spreads use strychnine. They don't seem to lose too much stock that way."

Lannigan shook his head. "Wolves, they ask for kill-

ing. I don't like to mess up a range, or kill harmless
critters like kit foxes and coons and birds and jackrab-
bits. Or even coyotes, come to that. All they bother is
sick calves that'll likely die anyhow. Besides, I told
Ed Clark before I took this job on that I wasn't going
to put out strychnine."

"I take that to mean you'll quit, then?" Sessions
asked.

"I guess so."

"That suits me. Clear out of the line shack as soon
as you can. I don't want you squatting out there all
winter."

"I'll be gone before sunup tomorrow." Lannigan
held himself back from retorting angrily to Sessions's
slur. "We'd better settle our account right now. I got
a batch of fresh scalps out in the wagon that ain't
been tallied yet. We'll add them to what I tallied
with Dave Morton a while back, and you can pay me
off."

"That's another thing we've got to work out. Five
dollars a scalp is too much to pay for what you're
doing."

"Now, hold on, Mr. Sessions. A deal's a deal, and I
got one with the YL. You can't go back on it now."

"If you wanted to bet on that, Lannigan, you'd lose.
You didn't make a deal with me or with the people
that own the YL now. If I feel like doing it, I can cut
you off without a penny, but I want to be fair and pay
you what the job's really worth."

Lannigan said nothing. He was battling down the
anger boiling up inside of him, trying to keep it from
showing on his face. He felt that he'd just stepped
into something over his head; in his experience, men
didn't welsh on deals, whether their own or those
they'd inherited. He knew there were laws that'd help
him, but going to law was looked on as a sneak's way

of settling a dispute. Besides that, the law in Texas wasn't something a poor man used to fight a big spread. It was something the big ranchers used to fight each other with. He decided it'd be wise for him to make the best deal he could and move on as fast as possible.

"What sort of price do you call fair?" he asked Sessions.

"How many wolves do you claim you've trapped?" Sessions countered.

"I tallied three hundred sixty-one scalps with Dave. I got another two hundred fifty-four out in the wagon. That'd make six hundred fifteen all told."

"At five dollars, that's just too damned much money. I may be new here in Texas, but I know what a job such as you're doing is worth."

"Ed Clark knew what it was worth when we made the deal, and he wasn't green hereabouts."

"You're not dealing with Clark now. You're settling with me. I think a fair price is a dollar a scalp. To make you feel better, I'll give you a dollar fifty, and that'll probably be more money than you've held in your hand any time up to now."

Again Lannigan let the insult go by. He said, "That's not a fair price, and you know it, Mr. Sessions. I can't come out ahead if I get that little for my time." He thought about the skins, for which he'd get three to four dollars apiece. "But I'll cut my figure down to two-fifty a scalp, and that's being more than fair to you."

Sessions was determined that he'd set the price. "Two dollars. And that's as high as I intend to go, so if you're smart, you'll take it."

Lannigan took his time answering, staring grimly at Sessions while he deliberated. Finally, he nodded. "All right. Two dollars."

"I'll have to give you a draft, I don't keep that much extra cash on hand." Sessions took a pad of bank drafts from his desk drawer, scrawled figures on it, and signed it, then pushed the slip of paper across the desk. "You can take this to the Howard & McMasters store in Tascose. They'll cash it for you."

Lannigan looked at the draft. "You're shortening me. I ought to get twelve hundred and thirty dollars for six hundred fifteen scalps. This is for twelve hundred even."

"I understand you've been getting your food and supplies from our kitchen storeroom," Sessions said. "I doubt thirty dollars will cover what you've had, but I'll settle for that."

"I was aiming to pay for what grub I drawed. If you think I'm short, tell me how much, and I'll give it to you."

Having won, Sessions could afford the gesture. "Never mind. I'll consider the thirty dollars as full payment."

"You're real big-hearted, ain't you, Mr. Sessions?" Lannigan stood up and started out. At the door, he said, "I'll be leaving as soon as I clear out the pelts that I've got stored in the stable."

"Wait a minute. We didn't say anything about them. If they're off wolves you trapped on YL range, they're YL property, not yours."

Lannigan felt his patience snapping. "Now, you look here! My deal with Clark included me keeping the pelts!"

"Your deal with Clark doesn't apply, remember?" the ranch boss retorted. "The only deal you've got is the one you just made."

This must be how a wolf feels, Lannigan thought, when it tries to jump out of a tilt trap. He glared at Sessions. "I'll tell you something. I got a load of pelts in my wagon outside. They ain't yours, and they won't be. I aim to ride out with 'em, and I'm ready to lock horns with you or anybody else that tries to stop me!"

Sessions did not answer. He looked beyond Lannigan's eyes, at the door. Lobo waited until it was clear the ranch boss wasn't going to argue or threaten, then slammed the door and strode thumpingly through the hallway, out of the building.

Judith was on the veranda. He started to brush past her, but she grabbed his arm. "Lobo! What's the matter? Have you and Uncle George been arguing? What's going on?"

"It's already gone on. Your blatherskite uncle cheated me. I'm getting off this damned spread." He pulled his arm free, hurried down the steps, jerked the tether-rope from the hitch-rail, and was slapping the reins over the mules' backs before he'd settled into the wagon seat. He turned once to look back before he got away from the headquarters area. Judith was still standing where he'd left her gazing after him, her mouth open in shocked surprise.

There was not enough daylight left for Lannigan to pick up his traps. He slept at the line shack and spent the next morning clearing the trap line. The day dawned gray, the wind began to pick up while he worked, and a line of blue clouds in the north promised colder weather. The night had brought five more wolves to the tilt traps and three to the sets. He skinned them and let the hulks lie where they were.

By the time he'd finished pulling up the sets and loading the traps, it was early afternoon, and the blue clouds were moving fast, pushed by an increasingly cold north wind. When Lannigan got to the line shack to pack out, a note from Judith lay on the table. It read: "Lobo, when you aren't mad any more, come back to see me. Please." He snorted. He wanted nothing more to do with Easterners. The note went into the monkey stove along with the little clutter that was left after he'd straightened up the shack and finished loading the wagon.

Tascosa had not changed much since his last visit, as far as Lannigan could tell in the early dusk. The norther was howling now, clearing the street of anything but scudding dust-babies that looked like blown snow in the rectangles of yellow lantern-glow that spilled from the narrow windows of the stores and saloon. Lannigan stopped at the Howard & McMasters store to cash his draft.

"Mr. Sessions told me you'd change this for money," he told the square-faced man behind the counter, handing him the draft.

"YL drafts are good as gold." The storekeeper looked at the slip of paper, raised his eyebrows and asked, "I suppose your name is Lannigan?"

"That's right. Just come off a wolfing job at the YL."

"Pleased to meet you, Mr. Lannigan. I'm Jim McMasters." The merchant's attitude was noticeably warmer after seeing the figures on the draft. He turned to an imposing safe that towered head-high back of the counter and began turning the combination dial.

A thought occurred to Lannigan. "You trade pelts here? I got a pretty good lot of wolfskins outside in my wagon. If I could dicker a trade with you, it'd save me hauling 'em around."

"Afraid I can't accommodate you on that, Mr. Lannigan." McMasters heaved a canvas sack from the safe to the counter. "If you're heading east, try at Mobeetie. The sutler at Fort Elliott does some business

in pelts and furs. The next closest place I know of is
at Westport, up in Kansas. But that's a regular wolfers' rendezvous, so I suppose you know about it."

Lannigan hadn't heard of Westport before, but he
didn't say so. He tucked the name into his memory
and asked, "How far's Mobeetie?"

"A good three days, in a wagon. Trail's easy to follow, though. A lot of wagons are moving between
there and Tascosa these days." He put his hand into
the sack. "Now, then. How'll you have your money,
Mr. Lannigan? Gold, or greenbacks?"

Even if Lannigan had been in a sweat to get to
Mobeetie, the icy blast of the norther that was now
raging full-blown would have frozen his desire to
travel any further that night. He swung the mules
across the street and left them in Mickey McCor-
mick's Livery Stable, then plodded with his head
down the short distance to the Exchange Hotel. There
he paid twenty-five cents for a hot tub bath, fifty
cents for a steak and eggs supper, and another fifty
cents for a room. He slept that night with his bulging
purse under his pillow and by habit rolled out at
dawn. Pulling up the collar of his heaviest jacket
against the biting wind, he started for Mobeetie.

From the beginning to the end of the three-day trip
across the Panhandle the norther stayed with Lannigan. It cut his face with gusting blasts as the mules
joggled over the prairie, wave after wave of wind
quartering his path. It chilled his hands even through
gloves, started his nose dripping, and dried and
hardened his lips until they cracked whenever he
opened his mouth. The wind sneaked with invisible
icy trickles into his soogans the first night out of Tascosa, no matter how snugly he pulled the blankets
over his head. He dropped off the caprock late on
the second day, into the cuts and draws that striated

the land as it sloped down to the North Fork of the Red River, and that night he slept more warmly; the gullies provided windbreaks.

Late on the third day, Lannigan came within sight of his destination. Mobeetie, and Fort Elliott to the north of the town, loomed across the prairie, growing larger and appearing further apart the closer he got to them. He headed for the fort. No need, he thought, to waste time going into town first. Mobeetie, supper, and a bed could wait until he'd finished the business he planned at the sutler's store.

"Wolf pelts, eh?" the sutler said, cocking his head to inspect Lannigan from hat crown to boot soles. He was a greasy man, with small squinty eyes. In defiance of Army regulations that denied the civilian sutlers the right to wear any article of military clothing, he had on a forage cap with a brass troop insignia on it. "You been trapping around here?"

"West. The YL range, up from Tascosa."

"I know where it is. You do all right?"

"Fair. Got about two hundred fifty pelts out in my wagon."

"Well, sir—I didn't get your name?" The sutler's voice gave no clue that he was interested in buying.

"Lannigan. Most folks just call me Lobo."

"My name's Tobias. Well, Lannigan. If this is your first stop, you need a drink to cut the cold. Icier than a witch's tit outside, ain't it? Whiskey keg's over in that corner there. First one's on me. After that it's a dime a dip. It's easier for a man to dicker when his brain ain't half froze."

Lannigan found the idea appealing. He went over to the keg, took a tin cup from the half dozen that stood on the table beside the keg, and ladled out whiskey with a dipper that hung from a peg. It wasn't very good whiskey, he discovered when he sipped it, but it was good enough to cut the chill he'd ridden with for three days. He went back to the counter. The sutler passed a hand over his oil-shiny face that was three days past a shave and bobbed him a grin.

"Them skins of yours, now. They come off wolves you trapped, or did you poison?"

"I don't use poison. Just traps."

"That's good. Skins off of poisoned wolves ain't worth much after the wolves been let lay and ripped at by coyotes and foxes. I guess I better take a look at what you got." Tobias followed Lannigan out to the wagon and ruffled quickly through a pile or two of the pelts. Back in the store, he said, "They're pretty fair. Not rightly what you'd call prime, but better'n most I see around here. What you figure they're worth?"

"Where I've been trading, down at Fredericksburg, skins like that bring four or five dollars."

"Umm. I guess there might be some of 'em worth that much, can't say without grading. I got to ship 'em out, you know; costs me a little bit to handle 'em. I'd say yours is mostly summer fur, thin. I'd go higher for prime winter skins, maybe up to six dollars, but the best I can do for your lot is three."

Lannigan had drained his cup, in slow sips. He started for the keg, but Tobias called him back. "I got a bottle of high-grade stuff for whoever I'm trading with," he whispered. "Hold out your cup. No charge, since we're going to do business."

"Not unless you come up on your bid, we're not," Lannigan told the man. He took a swallow from the replenished cup and couldn't tell that it was any better than that from the keg, though it did taste different. He went on: "Unless I can get four, I'd be of a mind to go south, sell 'em where I always do."

"That's a long trip, for wintertime. Man might freeze something off on the trail going down there. Well, I'm a reasonable man, Lannigan. You say four and I say three. Want to split the difference?"

"Three-fifty?"

"For the lot. How many did you say you got?"

"My count's two fifty-four. Some Texas reds but mostly lobos."

"Three-fifty'd give you a nice pocketful of cash." Tobias tilted his head back and gazed briefly at the smoked-up ceiling: "Eight hundred and eighty-nine dollars, I make it." He dropped his eyes to gaze questioningly into Lannigan's. When the small man didn't reply, Tobias said wheedlingly, "Tell you what. If I round it out to nine hundred even, cash on the line, have we got a deal?"

Lannigan took another mouthful of whiskey to give him stalling time. After he'd swallowed, he said, "I guess we have. I don't like the idea of hauling 'em south where I'd get a better price."

"You only have to haul as far as my storeroom, right around in back." Tobias raised his voice. "Cibolo! Got a job for you!"

A door at the end of the store opened and a man lumbered in, a big man, bigger than any Lannigan had ever seen. He had to turn sidewise to get his shoulders through the door and his head was almost as big as the whiskey keg. From the color of his skin he appeared part Indian.

"Cibolo, show the man where the storeroom is," Tobias ordered. The big fellow started for the door. Before Lannigan could follow, the sutler dropped his voice and told him, "Real biddable, Cibolo is. I can't twist my tongue around his real name. I call him Cibolo because it means buffalo over in New Mexico Territory, where he comes from. Now, let him do all the work. He's buffalo-strong, too. Why, he'd make three or four of—" Tobias let the remark hang unfinished when he saw Lannigan's eyes narrowing. He said hastily, "Come back when you've unloaded and we'll square up."

Cibolo's muscles made unloading fast work. Lannigan was back in the sutler's within a half hour. Tobias refilled the cup he'd left on the counter, put the bottle away, and dug into a pocket of his heavy coat. He pulled out a bulky leather pouch and dumped its contents on the counter, a mixture of gold and silver coins and currency. Lannigan sipped at the whiskey while the sutler spread the money with a sweep of one pudgy hand and flicked out double eagles from the scrambled money. He stacked them, nine stacks of five of the twenty-dollar gold pieces, and shoved them across the counter to Lannigan. "There you are," he said. "Nine hundred even."

"Thanks." Lannigan scraped the coins into his hand and dropped them in his jeans pocket. They weighed very pleasantly against his leg when they joined the purse he'd filled in Tascosa. "Pleasure to do business with you, Tobias." He yawned extensively and went on, his voice drowsy. "Getting tired, I guess. Better head on to Mobeetie and find a place where I can put up for the night."

"Sleep good," Tobias called as Lannigan left the store. "Come back when you got more skins to trade."

For the first few moments after he'd left the fort and set the team on the well-beaten track to Mobeetie, frosty gusts of the dying norther swirling around his face drove Lannigan's sleepiness away. Gradually, the drowsiness returned. The wind no longer seemed as cold. His eyes closed for a moment, and he snapped them open with a start to find himself leaning forward in the wagon seat.

"Must be the whiskey," he muttered, settling himself upright and bracing his knees on the dash. "Ain't used to it, guess I don't drink enough of it."

When sleep came the next time he was powerless to fight it off. A wave of somnolence swept through his body, relaxing his arms and legs. He slid slowly off the seat into the bed of the wagon. Something roused him briefly, but his mind registered only the disturbance, not its source.

When Lannigan woke next, he was in a jail cell.

CHAPTER 10

A throbbing headache and dry mouth were Lannigan's first sensations when he woke up. His eyes focused slowly, first on the bars of the cell, then on the cot on which he lay. He understood then that he was in jail, but had no idea how he'd gotten there or why. He got to his feet. still a bit groggy, wobbled to the door, and grabbed its bars. The door swung outward and almost threw him down. The jail was small, two cells on either side of a central corridor. A solid door was set in the wall at the end of the corridor. Lannigan went through the door into a room occupied by a young chunky man standing in front of a heat-radiating potbellied stove. The man turned when he heard Lannigan enter. A deputy sheriff's badge was pinned on his vest.

"Finally roused up, I see," he said. His voice sounded friendly enough, Lannigan thought.

Lannigan asked him, "Where in hell am I? What'd I do to get put in jail for?"

"Don't get riled, mister. You wasn't locked up, was you? If you don't know, you're in Mobeetie, and I put you in here last night because when I found you, you looked drunk. We don't lock people up for that here. If we did, we'd have half the town in them cells."

"Why, then?" Lannigan demanded. "The last thing

I remember, I was in my wagon, on the way here from Fort Elliott."

"Oh, you got here. Somebody come running in, said there was this wagon with no teamster going up the street. I found you curled up between the seat and dashboard. Sound asleep. Smelled like whiskey. Tried to rouse you, but couldn't. Brought you in here so's you'd be safe from harm and wouldn't freeze. Any time you got a notion to go, you're free to."

"I wasn't drunk," Lannigan said flatly. "I had a drink or two of whiskey in the sutler's store out at the fort, that's all."

"You sure you didn't forget how much you really had?" The deputy grinned in friendly understanding. "It'll happen that way."

"It didn't happen that way to me. I had one drink while I was selling my pelts and another one to seal the deal. Then after my wagon was unloaded, he topped off what was left in my cup. . . ." Lannigan remembered his money. He pawed his pockets, found them empty. "It's gone. Did you take it off me and put it where it'd be safe?"

"I take it you mean your money's gone?" The deputy shook his head. "Mister, you wasn't carrying a dime. Nor any kind of papers that'd tell me where you come from and who you are."

"Name's Lannigan. Lobo Lannigan."

"Mine's Bert Coogan. They call me resident deputy, which is just one way of saying my boss over at Wheeler blames me for everythin' that goes wrong in the east part of the country."

Lannigan acknowledged the introduction with a jerk of his head. "Are you real sure there wasn't any money on me last night?"

"I'm sure. I looked myself. Went through all your

pockets trying to find something that'd tell me who you was, what you do."

"I'm a wolfer. I just wound up a job over on the YL. Mister, I had twelve hundred bucks in gold and greenbacks in a purse in my pocket, and another nine hundred in double eagles that I got from selling my pelts to the sutler at the fort."

Coogan whistled. "That's a hell of a lot of cash for a man to be packing around. You sure you didn't buck some of our games here in town while you was drunk?"

"I went to sleep before I ever got to town." Lannigan frowned, trying to remember. He knew he'd gone to sleep suddenly, and recalled vaguely that he'd somehow been disturbed or moved after he went under. He told the deputy, "All of a sudden, I got sleepy, between town and the fort. That's all I'm sure about, but it seems like I remember somebody feeling of me, maybe moving me. I just don't recollect anything about it, though."

"Maybe this'll help you." Coogan reached a cup from a shelf behind the stove, poured coffee, and passed it to Lannigan. "There's some fried spuds and bacon left in the skillet. You're welcome to 'em if you're hungry."

Lannigan realized he was. "Thanks. Guess I might feel better if I ate something." The coffee was easing his headache and the groggy feeling was leaving him.

Coogan slid the food from the skillet onto an enamelware plate and handed it to Lannigan. The first few bites gagged him, but once he'd swallowed them, the food tasted good. With his mouth half full, he asked, "Where'd my money go, Coogan? And my horse and mules and wagon? That wagon's got all I own in it."

"They're out back. I put your stock in the stable; left the wagon in the yard behind the office here. I didn't go over the wagon last night, it was too damn dark and cold."

"You think somebody followed me from the fort and robbed me?"

"It's happened before. Mobeetie's about the toughest town in the Panhandle, Lannigan."

"There's only one thing could've happened," Lannigan said grimly. "That sutler and the big hulk of a breed that works for him was the only ones knew I had any money on me."

"Tobias? And the breed he calls Cibolo, about twenty hands high and wide as a stable door?" When Lannigan nodded, the deputy went on: "Like I said, it's happened before. I'd say it's a pretty safe bet Tobias slipped you something more than whiskey."

"To make me go to sleep," Lannigan nodded. "Then the breed followed me and did the robbery?" Coogan nodded agreement, and Lobo went on: "No wonder that greasy bastard was so easy to deal with! He knew all along he was going to get my skins free!"

"That's about the way of it. We've had suspicions about Tobias, but we never have been able to prove anything on him."

"What kind of suspicions?"

"Well, he come over here from New Mexico Territory about two years after the fort was built; that'd be about seventy-nine or eighty. There was some stories about him, that he'd comancheroed while he was in the territory, and that he bought stuff that Billy the Kid and his gang stole when they was rampaging."

"If you think he's a crook, why don't you tell the Army?"

"We have, Lannigan. Lots of times. Thing is, Tobias has got a half brother or cousin or some such kin who's a Congressman back in Washington. And the Army's got to get along with Congress."

"You're telling me in a roundabout way to kiss my money good-bye, ain't you? At least, that's how I read it."

"About that. I'm sorry, Lannigan. I just don't want you to expect too much from me."

"That's sure one hell of a note!"

"I agree with you," Coogan replied soberly. "But look at it from the law's side. You really know who robbed you? Or if you was even robbed the way you think it happened?"

"I know I had more'n two thousand dollars when I left that sutler's, and it was gone when I woke up this morning."

"I believe you. But try telling that to a judge and jury. You know what they'd think? That you got orrey-eyed and blowed your wad at the tables in the saloons here. Unless we got a witness or some kind of evidence, there ain't a thing we can do."

"Well, if you can't do anything, I sure as hell can!" Lannigan stood up, started for the door and stopped short. "Did whoever robbed me get my guns? I had a .30 Colt and a Winchester under the seat, and there was a Remington and a fuke and a Navy Colt in the wagon."

"The ones under the seat was still there. Whoever shook you down must've missed 'em in the dark. I'd guess the others are all right, too. The back end of the wagon didn't look like it'd been gone over. You'll find the Colt and Winchester in that cabinet there."

Lannigan opened the cabinet to which Coogan pointed and found his weapons. He strapped on the pistol. Coogan said, "That's something else that'd make a jury doubt you was robbed. Guns are just like money hereabouts."

"Maybe so. And maybe they'll get my money back for me."

"You figuring on going out to Elliott and facing Tobias down?"

"I aim to talk to him. Might aim one of these if I don't like what he tells me."

Coogan stood up and sighed. "I'll go along, then. The colonel in charge of the fort's a Yankee hardnose. He don't recognize Texas law; says the fort's Federal territory. Was you to do something sudden, like gunning Tobias down, he'd have you up in front of a firing squad before you knew it was happening."

"I was robbed on Texas land. Don't that give you a look-in?"

Coogan sighed again. "We'll see. After we listen to what Tobias has to say."

Tobias said nothing helpful. He was sorry, of course, he told them, that Lannigan had been robbed, but everybody knew Mobeetie was full of thieves and the like. Cibolo? Oh, he was away, hauling Army goods up from Fort Griffin, be gone a couple of weeks, likely. And would Lannigan and Coogan take a drink of whiskey? His treat, of course.

"I had all your kinda whiskey a man can take," Lannigan said.

"Now, wait a minute, Lannigan." Tobias's voice was soft and as greasy as the neckband of his shirt. "You can't blame me because you took a drop too much and let somebody get to you after you left here."

"Nobody's accused you yet," Coogan told the sutler. "The man just wants to find out where his money went. Two thousand dollars is a damn big wad for anybody to lose."

"Two thousand?" Tobias frowned at Lannigan. "You only got nine hundred from me."

"I was paid off for a wolfing job; cashed the draft at Tascosa."

"Now, you see, I didn't know about that. Well, I'm

downright sorry." Tobias frowned thoughtfully.
"Maybe I can help you a mite, though. If you're
broke, you'll want to go to work again. Was I you, I'd
mosey up north, to Westport, over on the east side of
Kansas. That's a wolfer's heaven. No ranches to collect bounty from, but country between the Smoky
Hill and the Republican is fine winter trapping.
Whatever pelts you get between now and March will
bring top price."

"Keep your advice, Tobias," Lannigan said sourly.
He turned to Coogan. "You going to ask him any
questions?" When the deputy shook his head glumly,
Lannigan said, "Then, let's get back to town. Hanging
around here sure won't get my money back."

As they rode into the jailyard after a virtually silent
trip from the fort to Mobeetie, Coogan asked, "You
got any more ideas about going after Tobias?"

"No. To get back what's mine, I'd have to rob him,
and that ain't my style, Coogan."

"Good enough. I'll take your word. Now. What're
you going to do? Stay around here, or move on?"

"You asking, or inviting?"

"Asking."

"There's a fur trader down south, at Fredericksburg
that's holding some money me and my partner left
with him. Guess the best thing to do is go down there
and get it."

"Didn't know you had a partner. Where is he?"

"He died a little while back," Lannigan replied
curtly.

"Oh." Coogan hesitated before offering, "I'll put
you up in the jail a few nights, if it'll help."

"Thanks." Lannigan walked over to his wagon to
put his guns under the seat. "I'll see how I feel after a
while. Might ride out from town a ways and camp,
might take you up." As he shoved the rifle under the

wagon seat something glistening caught his eye. He fished it out of the corner and found himself holding a twenty-dollar gold piece. He held it up for the deputy's inspection. "Whoever robbed me must've dropped this one." Somehow, finding the money made him feel better, small as the amount was. He said, "Well, so long as I ain't flat-ass broke, I might look around town before I decide what to do."

Twenty dollars didn't let a man do much in Mobeetie, Lannigan discovered when he started looking for a place to sleep. The town's main industries seemed to be gambling and girls. Every saloon had both, and their free lunch counters were tucked away between the gambling tables. Anybody who wasn't playing found himself jostled away when he reached for a bite to eat. The town's two hotels were attached to saloons and balked at renting to anybody who couldn't or wouldn't rent a girl to go with it; those who wanted only a place to sleep were turned away. There were two boardinghouses that offered rooms without companionship, Lannigan found out, but they were full. Discouraged, he returned to jail.

"Guess I'll take you up on that invite to sleep in your jail again tonight," he told Coogan. "If it won't put you out. I can't pay the prices they get in this town of yours."

"Mobeetie's sure no place for a man with a case of shorts," the deputy agreed. "Pick out any cell you want. The only time I'm full up is army payday and Saturday nights."

For a long while Lannigan lay awake listening to the street noises that drifted into the cell. He wasted no time regretting the predicament he was in. Lannigan lived by the frontier code: if a man wasn't smart enough or tough enough to hold on to what he had, it was his own fault if he lost it; and if he got into a tight corner, he pulled himself out of it without whining for help.

There wasn't much of a chance he could see to pull himself out of his financial hole as long as he stayed in Mobeetie. Coogan had confirmed what he'd heard, that the ranchers in that vicinity all used poison on wolves. Going east wasn't a solution; Texas stopped thirty miles in that direction and turned into Indian Territory, where there were no ranches, only reservations. Backtracking had no appeal; he didn't know how much influence Sessions would have with other ranchers, but he had a hunch the YL boss would blacklist him, if such a thing was possible. New Mexico Territory didn't look too bright; all he'd heard about it was that things were wilder there than in the Panhandle.

Push come to shove, Lannigan told himself, he wasn't too damned in love with the Panhandle. It was being taken over by Easterners and Englishmen, who, according to his book, didn't live up to their word. There was north, but winter was settling in; and from what everybody said, the further you went, the hairier it got. Going south, he'd run into places that would remind him of China Slim. He thought for a while about Fredericksburg, but that only made him feel worse about Slim. He decided he didn't want to go there until his memories of his dead partner had faded. He still hadn't made up his mind what to do, when he fell asleep.

Coogan woke him the next morning with a cheerful call: "Roll out if you're hungry! Coffee's boiling and breakfast's on!"

Midway during breakfast, Lannigan realized that he'd made up his mind while he slept. He told Coogan, "I got no reason to lollygag around here. Guess I'll put out soon as I finish eating."

"Heading where?"

"North. There's that place up in Kansas where winter trapping's supposed to be so good. Up between the Smoky Hill and the Republican. I got no idea how far it is."

"Far enough to freeze your butt off. I been up there, when I soldiered. Winter settles in and don't let up, not like the way it is here, where it'll snow a day and warm and melt and then wait a week or so before it snows again. Up in Kansas it snows and stays. Gets deep enough to bury a man."

"I'll manage."

"Got long-handled drawers? Plenty of bedding?"

"Everything I need except bacon and cornmeal to see me through the trip. I'll stop on the way out of town and buy them." Lannigan pushed his empty plate away. "Setting here don't make miles. Soon as I get hitched up, I'm pulling out."

He was just getting ready to climb into the wagon seat when Coogan came into the stableyard, one shoulder sagging under the weight of a buffalo robe. He threw the robe into the wagon bed.

"You better take this, Lobo. Teamster put it up for bail last summer, then got hisself killed before he come to trial. All it'll do in jail is get eat up by moths. You'll need it where you're heading. It's a good robe. Comanche tanned."

"Now, look here—" Lannigan began.

"You look. I got no use for the damn thing. Do me a favor and take it. I wasn't much help to you in getting your money back, maybe this'll make it up a little."

Lannigan grinned. "All right, Bert. And I thank you for the help you give me. If I pass this way coming back, I'll stop in."

"You do that. If you don't get swallowed up in the snow."

There was little snow as Lannigan rode north, a few vagrant flakes now and then, drifting from a low gray sky. What the weather lacked in snow, though, it made up for in cold. During the eleven days it took him to locate Westport and travel there, he not only lost Thanksgiving Day, but almost lost Dodge City, where he'd planned to stop and ask directions. The railroad track finally led him to Dodge, and he dipped down into the big saucer of western Kansas that started at the Arkansas River and ended at the Republican, the sharp-edged north wind constantly attacking his face and finding openings in his clothing that he hadn't known were there. After the first few harsh days of shivering Lannigan rode with the buffalo robe draped around him until he looked like a mummy. With its protection, it took him only an hour or two to warm up after he'd climbed into his soogans at night. He was lucky, he told himself, that he didn't freeze completely stiff.

Westport was a skeleton of a town, its flesh of buildings eroded away. Only a half-dozen houses and one big store building showed signs of habitation, and as he pulled into the place Lannigan wondered if he'd been following a dead trail that had led him to nowhere. It never had been a big town, he thought, looking at the broken-back barns and snaggle-window houses that were about to collapse on themselves. The store encouraged him a little bit when he reined in at its door. It was a big building and showed signs of having been kept up. The rusting strap-iron cage sitting in front of it indicated that there'd been some kind of activity in his line going on in the past, if not the immediate present.

When he met the proprietor, Jules Renier, he found the activity had been in the past. Renier was a hawk-nosed Frenchman who might have descended from a member of Venderye's original group of trappers who had opened the fur trade far to the north a century earlier. He looked at Lannigan with unconcealed astonishment on hearing that the newcomer planned to trap wolves during the winter.

"But, you are the first wolfer to come here for years. In the seventies, we would have a dozen, in the sixties, we would have a hundred or more on the prairie to the west, but when the northern Territories opened up, they moved."

"How about the wolves? Did they move, too?" Lannigan asked.

"Farmers!" the old man spat. "Farmers and poison did for the wolves."

"I didn't notice a lot of farms on the way here," Lannigan observed. "At least, not after I got north of the Smoky Hill. Or maybe I missed seeing 'em, maybe the farms here are like the cattle ranches in Texas, twenty miles from the gate to the front door."

"No, no. The farmers have moved, too. Drought, dreams of better land further west. And the wolves are coming back. Yes, you will do well here, young man. It is a good sign that you have come." Renier was making no effort to hide his pleasure.

"I guess if I bring in pelts, you'll buy 'em?"

"Even if only to keep for myself, I would buy them, just to be trading again. But do not worry, I can sell all the prime winter skins you bring me, and we will both make a profit. Only tell me, have you trapped in the snow before?"

"No. This's my first shot at it. But I learned how to go about it from my partner, before he died."

"Do you have snowshoes?"

"Never owned a pair in my life. From the way the ground looks, I won't need any now, either."

"Ah, that's where you are wrong. But I can help you. Wait." Renier disappeared through a door behind the counter. There were noises of objects being moved, and in a few minutes he returned carrying two wide pieces of wood about four feet long, with upcurved ends. He held them up for Lannigan to inspect. "Norwegian snowshoes. They are the easiest kind to use. Only one needs remember to keep one's toes pointed straight and slide along without lifting one's feet."

"What's wrong with me just walking the way I always do?"

Renier looked Lannigan up and down, measuring his height with his eyes. He said, "The ground is bare now. In a week, two weeks, three at most, the snow will begin to fall. In a single night there will be drifts higher than you are tall. They will not go away. You are a small man, it is true, and weigh little, but without these on your feet you will flounder and sink and be buried, believe me."

"What about riding my sets on my pony? Lead a mule with my gear and to tote back the pelts?"

"Your animals will be useless. They cannot move, and without a good shelter they will freeze. You must leave them here with me. I will attend them until the season is over."

"What about me? Don't I need a good shelter, too?"

"Of course, but that is easy. There are many sod houses and dugouts that have been abandoned. You will repair one of them before the snows begin and it will be your headquarters. I will see that you make a good choice."

"Looks like you're sorta taking charge," Lannigan said dryly.

"If I am, it is only because I wish for you to have a good season, and live to enjoy its profits. There are other things you need. Food, of course. Tallow for baits. Tobacco for your pipe. Ammunition. Coal oil for your lantern, and candles. Don't worry, I have all these things, I will supply you."

"Hold up a minute, Renier. You better know it right now. I got robbed down in Texas. I figured you'd let me pay off in pelts."

"But of course, that is my usual arrangement. We will balance our account when the season is over. I will see that you have everything you need to keep your camp until spring."

"Wouldn't it be better if I just come in every two or three weeks? Pick up what I need when I need it?"

"My young friend, you will be twenty miles from here, much too far to travel on snowshoes during the bad days. I will send my grandson out to guide you to an abandoned farm with a sod house that is in good repair, and he will help you set up your camp. He will bring your animals and your wagon back."

"Sounds easy, the way you tell it."

"Nothing is easy on the prairie, young man. One plans to have what is needed to survive, but one must still work to do so."

Lannigan cocked his head at the storekeeper. "How come you're doing all this for me? You never laid eyes on me till I walked in an hour ago."

"But, I have told you. You are an omen, a sign, the first wolfer to return. Look, young Lannigan, I am a dealer in furs; so was my father and his father, far north in Canada. This store, it is a nothing, a convenience, useful only to help trappers who will bring me furs. Do you understand that?"

"I guess." Lannigan looked at the dim interior of

the store, the empty shelves and wall pegs, where supplies and traps had once been. He said, "Guess I'm lucky to be the first. Well, let's get an outfit together. Soon as I'm fixed up, I'll be heading out."

CHAPTER 11

Lannigan fought sleep. He rubbed his eyes hard, pulling off a glove, his hand chilling instantly once its skin was exposed, then peered through the winter-bared branches of the brush in which he'd taken shelter. The wolves were still there, and at a glance it seemed to him there were as many as before.

He'd counted eighteen of them when they'd first closed in on him more than an hour earlier, appearing without warning at the crest of a high drift while he was resetting a trap that had been sprung the night before. There'd been no distant growls or yelps to warn him. He'd looked up and seen the wolves poised in a half circle atop the drift. Most of them had their jaws open in what he'd heard people who knew no better describe as a "wolf's grin." This time he tallied seventeen, the one killed by the pack making the difference.

Lannigan hadn't been especially worried when the pack first showed up. They made no effort to advance, but kept their distance, studying him as he was studying them. When he'd finished his set and scattered the tallow chunks he was using in addition to the scent, he picked up his rifle and started slowly up the sloping drift toward the wolves. Instead of retreating, as Texas wolves did, they held their places. Lannigan levered a shell into the chamber of his rifle and aimed at the animal he'd identified as the pack leader. The wolves retreated when he brought up the gun. He followed his target in the sights and squeezed the trigger. The hammer thudded down, that was all.

Swearing to himself, Lannigan ejected the dud shell and tried again. The same flat clack of the hammer was the only response the gun made. He ejected the second dud shell and picked it up, looked at the primer. The mark of the firing-pin was crisp and clean, which told him what his trouble was. The shells in the magazine were from a box he'd bought from Renier. In fact, all the rifle cartridges he was carrying, all that he had at the soddie, were those he'd bought at the store in Westport.

"And God knows how long they've been on the shelf," Lannigan muttered to himself. "Primers corroded. Most likely drawn damp. Or might be Renier was shipped a bad lot from the factory." He levered the rifle again and again, aiming each shot just in case, until he'd emptied the magazine and a heap of dud bullets that had not fired lay off to his side on the snow-crust.

While he'd been trying to get the rifle into action, the wolf pack had stopped retreating. That the animals had run at the sight of his rifle told Lannigan they were gun-wise. Through some mysterious means of communication, wolves that had been shot at seemed able to transmit to others the knowledge that men could kill at a distance, and to define for others of their kind the limits of that distance. When no burst of noise, no whistling bullets, came from the rifle, the wolves began edging back toward Lannigan.

Now it was his turn to retreat. He shuffled back downslope past the set, moving clumsily in his Norwegian snowshoes, and shouldered his knapsack. Lannigan still was not greatly concerned. He had his pistol with five shells in the cylinder and perhaps another fifteen or twenty cartridges in his coat pocket. Since he'd started snow trapping, Lannigan had used the rifle more often than the pistol to kill trapped wolves. He'd found that stakes did not hold well in the snow, and had switched to the drags that he and Slim had used in loose, sandy soil. The big hooks were heavy enough to dig through the snow-crust when a wolf began dragging a trap, slowing the animal's progress and leaving a wide trail to follow. Using the drags meant he could not get close enough to a wolf for a quick killing shot with a pistol, and he'd relied on the rifle's longer range.

Lannigan knew almost to a step the distance that lay between his position and the soddie that was his headquarters. He had five miles to travel and two more hours of daylight. He was sure that the number of shots he could fire with his revolver would keep the wolves from closing until he got to the soddie. He started confidently, moving in the short, shuffling steps made necessary by the Norwegian snowshoes. Now and then he glanced back quickly. The wolves had started moving when he did, but they were not running after him. They were darker wolves than he'd encountered in Texas, their fur neither the creamy hue of the lobos nor the reddish tinge of the small Texas wolves. These animals were brownish-gray, with tan underfur; they were smaller than the lobos, but bigger than the Texas red wolves.

A loud angry wolf cry, neither howl nor bark, tore through the still, cold air. Lannigan turned and looked back. One of the wolves, drawn by the tallow chunks and the scent dribbled in the snow, had stepped into the just-set trap, and its jaws were closed on the animal's leg. The wolf hobbled away from the set, dragging the trap. The drag-chain tightened suddenly and the wolf went down.

It struggled to its feet, yelping. The pack had stopped when the trapped wolf first cried out, and now the other wolves began to edge in. Three or four of them circled into the area close to the set, discovered chunks of tallow the first wolf had missed, and gulped them down. The taste of food seemed to trigger their voracity. They started to circle their trapped fellow, forelegs stiff, the long fur on their necks and shoulders bristling, their hindlegs bent, ready to spring. For a few moments they circled the trapped wolf, and the air was filled with barking growls. One of them leaped. The others followed almost at once, and within a few more seconds the entire pack had closed in.

Lannigan watched with increasing astonishment. The wolves were doing something that he'd never seen before; it was accepted as gospel by men who knew wolf ways that the animals did not feed on their own kind. These were, and Lannigan suddenly understood that the pack must be starving, that it was hunger that had driven them to approach him so closely in the beginning. He looked at the tangle of bobbing, growling wolves, and his assumption that he was in no danger of being attacked by them evaporated as swiftly as did the vapor from the breaths he exhaled into the icy air. He turned and began hurrying toward the soddie as fast as he could push his Norwegian snowshoes across the snowpack.

At Beaver Creek the wolves caught up with him. Their yowling had been growing steadily louder behind Lannigan, though he'd lost sight of the pack after dropping down under the shoulder of the high wind-formed driftline atop the rim of the shallow valley that led down to the stream. He'd stopped at the

edge of the ice to take off his snowshoes. The creek
was only twenty feet wide, but he'd tried walking
across ice when learning to manage the snowshoes
and had a bad fall. The slick surface was hard
enough to cross without the added hazard of the
wooden slats.

Just as Lannigan stepped off the ice into the narrow
line of winter-stripped willows and alders that ran
along the creekside, the first wolves appeared on the
drifts above the streambed. He halted in the brush to
put on the snowshoes again, his gloved hands working
clumsily trying to reknot the thongs that held them
on his feet. The wolf pack was straggling in a long
line down the slope toward the ice by the time he'd
gotten the snowshoes firmly attached.

"Them sly bastards know I'm here," he muttered.
He picked up his rifle and started out of the brush.
Just as he broke from cover, a half dozen of the
wolves ran through the brush upstream and circled
back, paralleling the creekbed, cutting off his retreat.
They were too near him for Lannigan's comfort. Even
though he knew they were out of range, he drew his
pistol and fired at them. The wolves backed away
from the brush when the shot sounded, but didn't
change their positions. They still closed the route he'd
have to take to reach the soddie.

"Mexican standoff," he said under his breath. "They
ain't going to come after me, I ain't going out in the
clear where they can circle me and drag me down.
Best thing I can do is stay holed up and see do they
give up and go away."

He settled down into an alder crotch, where by
turning his head he could see in all directions. The
wolves paced for a while, then settled, too, some
along the far bank of the creek, others in the snow-
drifts beyond the brush. They were not close to him,

but Lannigan still felt uneasy. He fingered the pistol cartridges in his coat pocket and counted fourteen; with the five already in the cylinder of his revolver, that made nineteen. Too few, he thought, to be sure of quick kills of seventeen darting wolves should they attack.

Inactivity brought the cold seeping into his body, and with the chill came drowsiness. Behind low clouds he could see the glow that marked the sun's position; he had about an hour of daylight left to cover the three miles that now remained between him and the soddie. He caught himself dozing and fought sleep, rubbed his eyes, and quickly put his glove on again. He fingered the shells in his pocket, wondering if he'd have time and be accurate enough and fast enough in reloading to kill all the wolves. He wondered how he'd be able to handle any survivors with his knife and his bare hands.

Sleep left him suddenly as he remembered a story China Slim had told him around one of their evening supper fires. He drew his knife and peered closely at the blade, although he knew that his constant honing kept its edge sharper than most men's razors. He looked behind him at the iced surface of the creek. Taking his rifle, he inched down to the ice and tapped it with the butt. It took all his strength to start a crack, and he nodded with satisfaction. Working with the rifle butt, Lannigan broke out a chunk of ice a little over a foot in diameter and almost six inches thick. It was heavy, and by the time he'd gotten it up on the bank his hands were wet and freezing. He hurriedly put his gloves back on and after a short time felt the tingling burn of life returning to his fingers.

With his hands gloved, Lannigan could work, and he worked quickly. He dipped the hilt of his knife into the open water he'd created by removing the ice chunk, and pressed the dripping butt to the center of the cake of ice lying on the ground. The water running down the grip froze at once when it hit the chunk of ice, leaving the knife standing erect, its blade point-up, on the chunk's flat surface. Steeling himself, Lannigan pulled off a glove, and with his cupped hand scooped water from the creek and let it trickle down the handle of the knife. The water was warmer than the air; it smoked, but it froze as it ran down the knife-grip. After pouring only a few hand-scoops of water on the knife, it was embedded in a cone of ice firmly frozen to the chunk. Above the cone, the blade stood erect.

Thrusting his stiff hand inside his coat, Lannigan warmed it in his armpit until he could use it again. He slipped his glove back on and tested the firmness of the embedded knife. It did not move, and he grinned with satisfaction. He took a chunk of tallow from his knapsack and rubbed it along the blade of the knife. The tallow was frozen, but the friction of rubbing it caused flakes of the fat to stick to the colder steel of the knife blade. He worked until he had a thick coating of tallow on both sides of the blade, leaving the keen cutting edge almost bare.

Settling his knapsack on his shoulder, Lannigan picked up the chunk of ice and broke out of the grove's cover. The wolves were already restless, disturbed by the sharp sounds they'd heard when Lannigan was hammering on the ice; they looked up and started to stir. There were nine of them on Lannigan's side of the creek, now. He swung his head to keep their tawny forms in sight. Before he'd gotten more than a half-dozen yards from the brush, the wolves were forming a semicircle in front of him.

They were still out of certain pistol range, but Lannigan needed time. He bought it by wasting one of his scarce cartridges. The wolves scattered and ran. Lannigan ran, too, after he'd again picked up the chunk of ice. He carried it fifty feet from the line of brush and set it down with care, pushing through the snow-crust to bring the top of the ice level with the snow. He stamped around its edges to seat the ice solidly, the knife blade jutting upright.

While he was working the wolves drew back until they were only a score of yards from him, slinking up with their bellies flat on the snow-crust. Lannigan watched them closely. He could not afford to waste even one more cartridge, but he drew his pistol in the event one of them should get within the range at which a killing shot was certain. They held off, though, while he fumbled in his knapsack for lumps of tallow, which he strewed scantily around the knife, then tossed a few pieces in front of the watchful animals. Then he hurried back to the brush cover by the stream-bank.

For several minutes the wolves remained motionless. One of them caught the scent of tallow, inched forward until he was sure his nose had not been deceiving him, then trotted up to the knife and nosed a tallow chunk out of the snow, chomping it down with a crunch and a gulp. A second wolf joined him, and when the others saw the two eating, they trotted up to get a share. They followed the scattered pieces Lannigan had tossed out. One of them nosed the tallow-coated knife blade, then began to lick at it. The knife ripped into the wolf's tongue and blood spurted. The wolf did not appear to notice that its tongue had been cut, but went on licking at the tallowed blade until the snow around it was bright red in the fading light.

Now the remaining wolves got the blood-scent, even more attractive to them than tallow. Three of them leaped on the bleeding wolf. It tried to run but was already weakening. It covered only a short distance before it was pulled down in a tangle of jaws and legs amid a chorus of snarls. The wolves on the far bank heard the others feeding, and crossed the stream to investigate. One of them smelled the fresh blood-scent, warm and appetizing, and licked avidly at the knife. Its slashed tongue started to spurt redly, and the wolf was set on by two others. It fought, but went down when the rest of the pack joined the attack. There were now two wolf carcasses, and the pack divided itself, fighting to get to the cannibal feast.

Wolf tore at wolf. The smell of fresh blood, fresh meat, drove the wolves amok, submerged their instinct of pack loyalty in the far more dominant instinct to survive. Lannigan watched until the pack had reduced itself to a half-dozen living animals gorging on the carcasses of the dead. When he was sure that his movement would not be noticed, he pushed through the brush parallel to the creek until he reached a place where he was sure the wolves would not notice him when he broke cover. He left the brush and emerged onto the open prairie, starting in a beeline for the soddie. The wolves did not pursue him.

At daybreak the following morning, Lannigan filled his pockets with pistol ammunition for both his own revolver and Slim's Navy Colt. With a gun at each hip, he started running his trap line. He detoured to retrieve his knife. It was still there, sticking up in the snow, frozen blood turning it into a crimson stalagmite. For a hundred yards around the knife the snow was blotched with blood and on its crust lay bits of torn furred hide, gobbets of raw flesh, gnawed and broken bones. Lannigan counted eleven wolf skulls.

There was no sign of the surviving members of the pack.

Never during the remainder of the short winter was he endangered in similar fashion, and never did he see a single wolf pack as big as the one that had besieged him. During the long nights he was often awakened by wolves howling near the soddie, their deep ululating cries drawn down the chimney by the blowing wind, echoing tinnily in the stovepipe that passed up through the earthen roof. A few times, wolves scratched at the soddie door, or dug into the great heaps of buffalo chips that lay just outside it. Lannigan tried making a set close to his fuel pile, but the trap was never tripped.

Winter nights dragged slowly. Lannigan had learned that trapping in deep snow was a different matter from the bare-land style he'd used elsewhere. In the snow, traps could be set closer, in a straight line rather than around the perimeter of a run; neither man nor wolf could locate runs under the snow-cover. He experimented until he hit on a satisfactory pattern, four lines of ten traps each, the sets radiating from the soddie in the arc of a half circle. He could start in the morning, work one line going out from the soddie, cut across to the last trap of the next line, and follow that line back to camp by noon. In the afternoon, when he'd eaten and rested and gotten warm, he ran the other two lines in the same fashion, returning to his base in time to stretch pelts and do household chores before dark.

Full daylight lasted less than eight hours; sun-time, not clock-time, ruled his days. By clock-time, there was enough daylight to see by just before nine in the morning, and darkness began to creep over the white, cold land before five in the afternoon. Fuel for the small stove in the soddie had to be rationed carefully, so did the kerosene for the lantern. Both were needed to keep the sod house livable. With the door closed to keep out the bone-stabbing cold, the soddie was as dark inside by day as it was by night, since it had no windows. When the stove and lantern were extinguished, the chill inside soon became just a shade less intense than that outdoors. Never spacious, the soddie's interior grew more and more crowded as the stacks of wolf-pelts multiplied and demanded their share of the room.

When he was not working on his sets, Lannigan learned quickly that the bed was the best place for him to be. The bed was a crude bunk without springs or mattress that he and Renier's grandson had repaired when they were making the soddie habitable. By tucking half his buffalo robe under him for a mattress and folding the other half over his soogans, the bunk was transformed into a warmly comfortable bed, and the long hours he spent in it gave Lannigan time to think.

While the quick, busy days and endless nights flowed through the short prairie winter, he repeated to himself the words of the note Judith had left for him at the line shack, those three months ago that now loomed like a year. When the days began to stretch and the hours of darkness grew fewer, the memory of the message and of Judith herself occupied most of Lannigan's night thoughts. Her features grew more mistily beautiful, her response to his presence during the few hours they'd been together seemed warmer, and her attraction for him became greater, as reality was drowned in his hopeful memory.

As the memory of Judith brightened and glowed, Lannigan's anger with her uncle blossomed afresh. It was not quick, hot physical anger, the emotion with which he'd reacted to Hardcase Harris's personal denigrations, nor the unhappy resentment that followed his victimization by Tobias, but a rankling irritation at having been cheated out of the fruits of a job at which he'd labored long and honestly. Like any workman whipsawed by a power-holder, Lobo felt diminished in stature. He began thinking of ways by which he might get the remainder of his earned payment.

None of the schemes that passed through Lannigan's mind were completed. Some stayed in the background, half formed and all but discarded when the quick explosion of spring in a cascade of sunshine and warmth melted the snow. He hiked across the muddy, snow-patched ground to Renier's store, reclaimed his team and wagon, and hauled his pelts back. While the old trader sorted and graded the skins of more than two hundred wolves taken during his nine weeks on the frozen prairie, Lannigan lounged in the sun in front of the weather-beaten store, savoring the warm breeze.

"Good pelts," Renier called to him. "Come in. We will talk of how much I will offer you." Lannigan went inside. The old man was holding a pelt, his gnarled stiff hands stroking the glossy fur. "Only a few are below prime," he told Lobo. "For the lot, I offer you nine dollars each. It is a fair price, no?"

"It's a fair price, yes," Lannigan replied. "We got a deal."

After he'd paid for the supplies and provisions Renier had furnished at the season's start, Lannigan left the store with the comfortable bulge of more than sixteen hundred dollars in greenbacks nudging into his hip from his back pocket. He was walking to his wagon when the rusty iron cage that stood in front of the building caught his eyes. In an instant, a new plan to square accounts with Sessions rushed fully formed into his mind. This one, he was positive, would work. He went back into the store.

"Think I wanta buy that old cage you got out there," he told the storekeeper. "How much you figure it's worth?"

Renier looked at him questioningly, but replied promptly, "It is worth nothing. It is only in my way. A homesteader had it made to hold wolf-whelps that he planned to tame and train as hunting dogs. It was a dream, of course, and like all dreamers he left soon to follow a new vision that seemed better. If you have use for the cage, I will give it to you."

Lannigan had planned to start south at once, but he delayed long enough to scout the moist earth around his old trap lines, where the wolf hulks that he'd pulled off to one side after skinning them were thawing and beginning to smell noisome. There were fresh wolf-tracks in abundance, and he made a half-dozen new sets where the tracks were thickest. He also made himself a pole-noose, a slipknot at the end of a sturdy ten-foot branch.

During the next five nights the newly set traps took eight wolves. Lannigan salvaged four whose legs had not been maimed or broken, slipping the noose of his pole-snare over their heads and tightening the slipknot until the wolves lost consciousness. Then, working quickly, he freed them from the trap and put them in the cage on the wagon bed before they became active again.

For the first few days as he hauled the animals south, the caged wolves snarled and nipped at one another; if the cage had been bigger, they would have fought. Lobo fed them just enough to allay their hunger, but not enough to cause them to lose their gaunt look of winter starvation.

Hunting meat did not mean wasting time. At almost predictably regular intervals the wagon rolled past big squares of land where green tips of corn or wheat sprouted thickly; fields plowed and planted by homesteaders who'd given up. The land they'd planted had begun to reseed itself from the unharvested crops they'd left behind. In most such plots, deer and antelope grazed placidly, undisturbed by the wagon's approach. Lannigan had tested Renier's stock of ammunition until he found an undamaged box of rifle shells. He waited for the easy shots and took all the fresh meat he needed for himself and his wolfish cargo.

South of Dodge City, he turned onto the Tascosa-Dodge cattle trail, which led in a reasonably straight line to the Canadian. The trail was not quite a road. It was a wide swathe through the landscape that had been marked across the untouched prairie on both sides by the decade during which it had been pounded by the hard hooves of trailed steers. It showed the easiest course to take around the gulches and gullies and the infrequent rises that jutted abruptly from the rolling land, and led to the easiest crossings of the creeks that wove through it. From the top of any high spot along its course, little heaps of black charred cinders could be seen, stretching away into the distance like mileposts, the marks of places where chuck wagons had stood for a night on scores of cattle drives.

With each mile that fell behind him as he neared the YL, Lobo found his winter-night fantasies fading just a little bit, and the reality of the past autumn became clearer. Sometimes silently, but as often aloud, in the fashion of men who spend much time alone, he argued with himself, debating whether he'd read into Judith's note more than a courteous invitation.

He wondered with increasing worry whether she would welcome him as warmly as it had seemed she would during his winter vigils, or whether he'd be better advised to give up the idea of squaring scores with George Sessions, and swerve away from the YL. In the end, he held to his original plan, though when he pulled to a halt in front of the ranch headquarters his feet were chilled in spite of the afternoon's warm sunshine.

Sessions must have seen the wagon pull in, for he appeared on the veranda before Lannigan could alight. "What in hell are you doing here?" he demanded. "I thought we'd seen the last of you."

Lannigan had been rehearsing his reply for days, and delivered it unsmilingly, without deviating from the wording he'd worked out so carefully. "You recall what you told me when I left here, Mr. Sessions? About the wolves I'd trapped on the YL range being yours? Well, over the winter I got to thinking that some of them pelts I took away with me must've been yours, the way you reckon things. I don't want any man on two feet to claim I cheated him, so I brought you some wolves to seed your range in place of them I took. There's two dogs and two bitches in that cage, and I aim to take 'em out and turn 'em loose where they'll breed without nobody bothering 'em. I figure in about two years you'll have the YL's wolf stock all built up again." He stopped, caught Sessions's widening eyes with his own, and added, "I didn't figure out how many steers and colts these wolves is going to kill while their whelps is growing up, Mr. Sessions. These four's full-growed and hungry. I guess they'll start right away on your yearlings and colts. Oughta work out to twenty, twenty-five head a night for a while, anyhow."

"Lannigan, what the devil's gotten into you?" Sessions asked. "Talking about turning wolves loose on YL range! That's something only a crazy man would do!"

While Sessions was talking, Judith appeared behind him. She waved, but Lannigan did not see her, his attention was on the YL boss, and Sessions's wide body hid the slight figure of the woman.

Lannigan said, "Now, don't call me crazy, Mr. Sessions. It's just that all winter I been worried you might feel like I cheated you by taking YL wolfskins away when I left. So, I aim to pay up, like any honest man would do. By end of summer you'll have about twenty or thirty, and by spring there ought to be more'n enough to make up for the YL skins I took. All you got to do is trap 'em."

"Listen here, Lannigan, I don't want my range infested by wolves again!" Sessions's face was growing purple. "Now, you get the hell off YL property, or I'll—" He stopped, his mouth open.

"You'll do what? Call some hands to throw me off?" Lannigan shook his head sadly. "You reckon I don't know all your men's out on the far range, doing the spring gathers? Why, I bet the only one you could call is a cookhouse flunky." When Sessions still said nothing, he went on: "Now, I'll pull on out and turn the wolves loose. I just wanted you to know I was paying my debts."

"Wait a minute!" Sessions called hoarsely.

He started down the veranda steps, and Lannigan saw Judith for the first time. He almost backed away from completing his plan, but he'd gone too far now to retreat. He lifted his hat and said soberly, "Howdy,

Miss Judith. I got your note last fall, and you see I taken your invitation."

"I'm glad you did, Lobo," she replied.

Sessions, halfway to the wagon, turned in surprise when he heard her voice. "Judith, go inside. This is man's business, no concern of yours."

"No, Uncle George. I'm very concerned with what you call man's business. I'll stay while you and Lobo finish your talk."

Sessions hesitated, but he was more concerned with Lannigan than with his niece's defiance. He said, "Lannigan, I'll have the law on you if you turn those wolves loose anywhere near the YL."

Lannigan rubbed his chin. "I don't see you could do that, Mr. Sessions. Wouldn't be my fault if they got loose by accident, say the cage was to fall off the wagon."

"I know your game! You're trying to hold me up! That's blackmail, and I won't stand for it!"

"That ain't a nice thing to say, Mr. Sessions. I'm just paying what I owe you."

"You've said that twice, now. I suppose you're suggesting that I owe you something?"

"No, sir. We closed the deal, and I'm not complaining. I'm giving you these wolves so you don't feel shorted."

"Well, I don't feel you owe me anything, so get the damned things off the YL."

"No, Mr. Sessions." Lannigan shook his head soberly. "These are good wolves. Northern wolves. I want you to have 'em. They'll outkill Texas wolves two or three to one."

Sessions had known minutes earlier that he was beaten, but it hurt him to surrender, and he showed it. "Would you—I don't suppose those wolves are for sale?"

His voice dripping innocent surprise, Lannigan replied, "Now, you know, that just hadn't occurred to me. Of course, if you're in the market to buy, I might think about it."

"How much?" Sessions grated.

Lannigan took his time in answering, looking at Judith while he waited. He kept his face straight and his voice level. "Seeing you're anxious, I might let the lot go at five-hundred dollars apiece."

"Five hun——" Sessions choked. "That's robbery, and you know it." The ranch manager made an effort to control his temper, and succeeded to a degree. More calmly, he said, "It seems to me that we were about fifteen hundred dollars apart on our last deal. Suppose I paid you three hundred apiece for the wolves. Does that sound fair?"

"Not quite." Again Lannigan took his time. "Unless I was to get four hundred, I'd still be obliged to turn 'em loose. Looks like we don't deal, Mr. Sessions." He reached for the reins.

Judith said, "I think you'd better meet Lobo's price, Uncle George. He seems to have his mind made up."

Sessions glared at her, but quickly turned back to Lannigan. "All right. Four hundred, then."

"We got a deal. The cage goes with the critters, no extra charge."

"I assume you'll be satisfied with a draft instead of cash?"

"Like the man at the store in Tascosa told me, Mr. Sessions, a YL draft's as good as gold."

"All right. You pull the wagon around to the old stable. I don't want that damned cage sitting here in front." He looked around, remembered there was no one he could call on to help him, and said to Judith, "I suppose you'd better go with Lannigan, make sure he doesn't accidentally let the wolves get loose."

"Oh, I'm sure Lobo will be careful, Uncle George," Judith replied gravely. But she got into the wagon and sat down beside Lannigan. Sessions glared for a moment before disappearing into the house. Judith waited until Lannigan set the team in motion before she asked, "Would you really have turned the wolves loose, Lobo?"

"I don't know. But your uncle didn't, either."

"You really outmatched Uncle George that time," Judith smiled. "And I'm glad."

"You are?" Lannigan was genuinely surprised. He'd never been part of a family. It hadn't occurred to him that relatives didn't always agree about everything.

"I certainly am. He might be my uncle, but he's a pompous, mean, overbearing man. And I know he cheated you out of money you had coming."

"You heard about that?"

"I've heard about it every time there's been company for dinner this winter, and sometimes when there wasn't." She turned in the wagon seat to face him. "Lobo, why didn't you stop and tell me what had happened, instead of leaving in such a hurry?"

"I guess I was just too mad to think real straight."

"I thought perhaps it was something I'd said or done that made you push me away that day you left."

"Now, you oughta know better'n that. I—" He struggled for the words he needed. "It was about the nicest thing ever happened to me, being here, talking with you, going out that time we did."

"Would you have come back if you hadn't wanted to get even with Uncle? Would you have come back just to see me, after you'd read the note I left for you?"

"I thought a lot about that note, and about you, too, during the wintertime up in Kansas."

"I've thought a lot about you, too, Lobo. I'm glad you did come back, whatever your reason was."

"It was mostly you, I guess," he told her, and was about to struggle on when Sessions came up.

He handed Lannigan the draft, saying, "There're some skid timbers in the stable that we can use to get that cage off the wagon. I want to see it unloaded and you on your way out of here."

It took the combined efforts of Sessions, Lannigan, and Judith to slide the cage down the skid timbers from the wagon bed to the ground. The wolves growled uneasily and made a few snaps at them, but by now the animals had gotten used to being around humans and made no real difficulty. The job finished, Sessions told Lobo, "All right. You've got your money, and I've got four wolves I don't want or need. Get that wagon moving, and don't show your face on YL range again."

Lannigan was retying his pony's lead-rope to the tailgate. He replied tartly, "I don't want to stay here any more'n you want me to." He walked to the front of the wagon and was surprised to see that Judith had climbed up into the seat.

She said, "I'll just ride around to the front of the house with you, Lobo."

"You'll do no such thing!" Sessions rasped. "I don't want you to speak to this clodhopper again, or even look at him! Now, get off that wagon and let him be on his way."

Judith ignored her uncle. She turned to Lannigan and said in a quiet voice, "We won't stop at the house, then. I don't have enough there to bother about packing. Do as Uncle George says, Lobo. Just drive away."

Lannigan was bewildered. He began, "Now, will you tell me—"

Judith gave him no chance to finish. She grabbed the reins and slapped them sharply over the mules' backs. The wagon began moving. Sessions gaped, too amazed to start running after the wagon until it was impossible for him to catch up to it. Given their heads, the mules clomped smartly past the headquarters house and out onto the track that wound across the prairie.

Lannigan's surprise equaled Sessions's. It immobilized him until they were beyond the ranch buildings, then he turned to Judith and demanded, "You mind telling me what you think you're doing?"

"I'm going with you, of course." She looked at him, a plea in her eyes. "Unless you don't want me to."

"You mean, do I"—the word was strange on his lips, and he had trouble getting it out—"Do I love you? I reckon I sure do, only I never figured you'd want for me to tell you so."

"Would you have told me, if I hadn't spoken first?"

He said hesitantly, "I—I just don't know, Judith. I plain don't. I guess"—he looked for the answer in her eyes—"I guess maybe it's because I can't figure why a lady like you'd want a little sawed-off runt like me."

"Stop that," she commanded. Her voice was quiet but firm. "A man's not measured by size, Lobo. It's what's inside him that matters. You're all the man I'll ever want. I discovered that before you left, and all winter I've been praying you'd come back."

Lannigan saw in her eyes the truth he'd been seeking. "You mean, to marry and like all that?"

"Like all that. There's a minister in Tascosa. We'll stop there and—"

"No," he said quickly. "Tascosa's too close." He looked back. There was no one following them. "Your uncle's going to have every hand on the YL chasing after us when they come in from gathering. They'll go through Tascosa like a dose of hot salts." He clamped his lips together. "I got to mind the way I talk."

"Never mind that, it doesn't bother me. But where, Lobo?"

"Mobeetie, I reckon. We'll set a false trail west from Tascosa, then circle off it and head east. I got a friend in Mobeetie who'll help us, if we need any." Hesitantly, he added, "It'll be a hard trip."

"Whatever you say is best, that's what we'll do. I don't care whether we get married in Mobeetie or in Tascosa or on the moon. But—Lobo, don't you think it'd be nice if you kissed me now, and asked me to marry you the right way?"

CHAPTER 12

By midmorning of the day after they'd left Tascosa, the elopers began to relax. When no band of YL riders led by an angry Sessions appeared behind them, they agreed that the broad hints dropped by Lannigan in the Howard & McMasters' store had been effective. He'd mentioned New Mexico Territory more than once, had inquired about trail landmarks and watering stops, and the elopers had actually started west from Tascosa, then had left the trail at the first rocky stretch along the road and reversed their direction.

Until they could reach Mobeetie safely, though, they wasted no time in making plans for the future. They were too enraptured with discovering one another, whether squeezed together on the jouncing wagon seat or snuggled into the buffalo robe's folds under the wagon during the hours of soft spring darkness. For the first time in his life, Lannigan felt he had a home; not a house of boards with walls and floors, but a home in Judith, whose solemn sweetness and unabashed love as she opened herself to him was beyond anything he'd ever imagined.

"How come you just jumped in the wagon without a by-your-leave to your uncle?" he asked her in the quiet hours of their first night, while they lay relaxed and spent, waiting for sleep to find them.

Judith took her time answering. "I simply made up my mind I wouldn't let you ride off to heaven-knows-where without me. I knew you weren't coming back to the YL, after the way Uncle George acted."

"Well, you was right enough about that. Any man like him, I feel like crossing a street to keep from getting close to."

"I'd just about given up, when you didn't answer my note, the one I left at the line shack. I rode out there, you know, and found you'd gone. Why didn't you leave a note for me, Lobo?"

Lannigan frowned into the darkness. "Because I didn't figure it'd make much difference to you whether I stayed or left. You never did let on—"

"I was sure I did," she broke in. "I tried to, without letting anybody notice. I guess you didn't notice, either, did you?"

"I kept figuring it was something I was imagining to myself, Judith. A girl like you, a lady and all, and me just a little pigwidgeon of a wolfer?" It didn't occur to Lannigan that his description of himself was a measure of how much he'd gained in self-confidence during the months when he'd worked as an equal beside China Slim, the months when he'd met the challenges of a prairie winter from his own inner resources.

Judith said seriously, "I don't want you to talk like that about yourself anymore, Lobo. A man doesn't have to stand seven feet tall for a woman to love him, and for other men to respect him. And I guess there isn't any reason either one of us will ever come up with why I fell in love with you, or you with me. But there doesn't have to be a reason, does there?"

"No," he replied slowly. "I don't suppose so. From what I've seen, love's one of them things that just happens to folks."

When they could see Mobeetie looming on the prairie ahead of them, silhouetted against a low morning sun, on the fourth day after leaving Tascosa, Lannigan suddenly grew serious. "We better get ourselves married and move on quick," he said. "It ain't that I'm scared of standing up to your uncle, it's just I don't want him to upset you and maybe make you change your mind."

"Lobo, he couldn't change me," she assured him, equally serious. "You're the only one who could do that now."

"Which I sure don't aim to."

"Still," Judith went on, frowning, "if Uncle George did show up with a bunch of YL hands, there'd be trouble."

When they'd explained the situation to Coogan, he'd agreed. "And that's the kind of trouble we can do without," he told them. "Seeing as I'm the only law around here, I'd say the smart thing is to get hitched and move along fast."

"Soon as the minister's finished," Lannigan promised. "Guess it's all right if I leave my pony with you, Bert? I'll pay his feed."

"You're going to come back, later on?" Coogan frowned.

"Even if it's just passing through. We got no plans on where we'll settle. Maybe here, maybe further south. But I got to go to Fredericksburg and pick up some money the trader there's holding for me and China Slim, only Slim passed his half to me when he died. I imagine there'll be ranches along the way where we can stop, where I can stir up some wolfing jobs. I don't guess all of 'em has gone to using poison yet."

With a little help from Bert Coogan, Judith and Lobo were married less than two hours after they arrived in Mobeetie, and within another hour were on their way south.

Not all of the ranchers had started using poison, Lannigan discovered as they traveled on southward, but he could see the day when strychnine would put him out of business. The powdered poison was cheap, readily available, and could be used by ranch hands who lacked the skill for trapping. Any of them, from jinglebob boy up to foreman, could dump a bottle of poison into the wolf-killed carcass of a steer or horse or sheep. If the strychnine took toll of kit foxes, skunks, raccoons, and other scavenger animals as well as of hawks, eagles, and owls, or if an occasional steer grazed on grass poisoned by wolf-slobber and died, that was a small price to pay for getting rid of wolves.

"There's enough that won't use it, though," Lobo assured Judith. "I hope so, anyways. I got to set up to work regular now, not just go by guess and by God no more. I aim to take care of you right, get you a house or build you one, and fill it up with pretty things."

"I don't need a house, Lobo. I'll be happy just to go along with you. I could cook, keep camp, do things like that."

"No, sir. I mean, no ma'am. My wife ain't going to work like that. No other kind of work, either, except what's proper for a married lady, at home. We'll live proper, just like everybody else does. Once I get that money from old Helmut, we can figure it all out and get set up somewheres."

In Fredericksburg, though, there was no money. Georg Helmut's sign was gone from above his shop, its door was padlocked, its windows shuttered. Lannigan inquired at a neighboring store. Ach, he was told, too badt old Georg was three months ago deadt yet, undt die Frau had to Chermany gone back, her last years to live. Vere? The storekeeper shrugged and shook his head.

At Judith's suggestion they inquired at the bank, and at the bank manager's suggestion, went on to look for information at the courthouse. It was effort wasted. Frau Helmut's destination in the old country was not known, and in any case, the clerk told them, the legal period during which a claim could be filed against Helmut's estate had lapsed.

Judith felt the loss less keenly than did Lannigan. "It's not as though you're broke," she reminded him. "There's the money you got from Uncle George, and what you made in Kansas during the winter. Isn't that enough for us to start with?"

"It'll get us by, I guess. Except that I don't aim for you to do without the kind of house you were used to, back East. But I ain't all that worried. Tom Morrison at the Baby Doll said I was to stop by on the way back to Mobeetie and dicker out a wolfing job. We'll cut it, all right."

Without either hurrying or dallying, they started back north. If the return journey lacked the heady excitement that had ridden along with them on the way to Fredericksburg, it was because they'd begun to get over feeling that they were fugitives, as well as the feeling that everyone was watching them. Both Lobo and Judith were innocent enough to be unaware that all newly married couples, regardless of the similarity or disparity of their backgrounds, are positive that their joining in wedlock is an event unique in history, that all eyes are watching them, and that the feeling will persist until they have adjusted to one another and are at ease in their married lives.

At the Baby Doll Ranch, a long day's ride southwest of Mobeetie, they stopped while Lannigan came to an agreement with the owner to begin wolfing his range as soon as he could return. Mobeetie itself was quieter than Lannigan remembered. The community had the sort of hangdog atmosphere that prevails in a schoolroom where a number of students have joined to perpetrate some act of mischief and have been punished as a group. Bert Coogan told them why.

"Had elections while you was gone. Got us a new sheriff, he come up from Wheeler and cleaned up the town. Got rid of the crooked gamblers and their shills, and—if you'll excuse me, Miz Lannigan—all the fancy women, too. They'll some of them drift back after a while, but we got us a nice quiet town here right now."

"Did my uncle come looking for us?" Judith asked.

"Oh, sure, just like you and Lobo figured he would. Him and a bunch of YL boys blowed in about a week after you'd left. They asked around; come in and talked to me, acourse. I didn't let on, and the preacher was out riding circuit, so they missed him. We was the only ones that could've spilled anything, so I guess you two can rest easy now. Ain't likely they'll be back; the YL hands was talking about how you give 'em the slip over in New Mexico Territory."

"If you've run a bunch of people out of town," Lannigan said thoughtfully, "I'd guess we might find a house we can rent."

"You aiming to stay here, then?" Coogan asked.

"For a while. It'll take me a good two months to clear off at the Baby Doll. After that, I'll likely get another one close by. I'd feel better if Judith was here, where you can sorta keep an eye out if them YL yahoos come back."

"Go see Miz Brent," Coogan advised. "She's the one runs the boardinghouse over by the town well, you know?" Lannigan didn't know, but he nodded to encourage the deputy. Coogan went on: "She told me the other day she's got a house that's vacant."

Mrs. Brent was pudgy, from too-frequent tasting of the meals she prepared daily for her boardinghouse tenants; and pugnacious, as boardinghouse landladies learn to be in self-defense. The house she offered for rent was a square house, the dominant architectural style of the prairie frontier because it provided the largest amount of living area with the smallest use of scarce and costly lumber. Inside, the house was divided into three rectangular rooms: a long, narrow one across the back was kitchen, dining room, and storage pantry, and two in the front served as sitting room and bedroom.

"It ain't got but a few sticks and pieces of furniture in it," Mrs. Brent said briskly. "That's why the rent's only eight dollars a month. Now, if you was willing to go as high as ten dollars on the rent, I'd bring in whatever other pieces you need from my boardinghouse."

Lannigan questioned his bride with a look, and Judith said, "We'd rather buy whatever we need, I think."

"As you please. It's a handy house; town well's just up the street a few steps. I just had a new seat put in the outhouse and had it cleaned out. If you want to use the boardinghouse laundry-shed, it's right next door, boilers and tubs and all. Fifteen cents—a dime if you tote your own water. I guess you'll be wanting to move in right away?"

"Today," Lannigan said. He fished out a double eagle and four silver cartwheels. "We'll pay three months ahead, if it's all right with you."

Mrs. Brent softened visibly. "That'll be just fine, Mr. Lannigan." She looked around the dusty room, unswept and uncarpeted, and volunteered to Judith,

"You want some help cleaning up. I got a boy twelve years old. Bobby helps me, so he knows what to do. He goes to school of Miz Windham mornings, but afternoons after he's finished my chores, he's got time, if you need him."

"I'll remember," Judith promised.

"Well, then. I'll be getting along," Mrs. Brent said. "Keys are in the door. I hope you folks like it here."

When their landlady had departed, Lobo told Judith, "It ain't exactly what I had in mind for you, but it's walls and a floor and a roof. I guess it'll do until we find something better."

"It'll do very well, after I get some curtains up and carpets on the floor, and we get a few things of our own," she assured him. "But you know I'd just as soon be with you, where you're going. Rather, even."

"Now, we settled that, Judith. Wolfer's camp's no place for a lady, even when the only man in it's her husband. You'll be safer in town, too. Hands move around; somebody from the YL might stop off at the Baby Doll and see you."

"That wouldn't bother me. If you can face down Uncle George, I suppose I can, too."

"We'll face him, when the time comes. But I'll feel better if you're here, with Bert making sure nobody's going to bother you. Now, let's see what we got to do to make this house fit for you to live in."

Lannigan had no idea how much work was involved in setting up housekeeping. He did not know how many unfamiliar jobs a wife could find for a husband, or how important it was that curtains be hung just so, that carpets be stretched tight and tacked, that the perfect spot be found for each piece of furniture. From start to finish, it took four days of daylight-to-dark activity, with a few odd jobs completed by lamplight after supper, before Judith declared herself satisfied.

"At least, until the new furniture gets here from Dodge City," she amended. "That probably won't be until you're through at the Baby Doll. Then we can really get settled in."

"If it took as much time for me to get a new camp fixed up, I'd never get any sets out," Lannigan observed. "But I got to admit, it's a lot more comfortable indoors than out."

He looked at Judith, her sleeves rolled up, arms streaked with grime, her head swathed in a cloth to protect her hair from the dust that had settled on her face, and counted himself a lucky man. He still was not sure that he believed his good fortune.

"Now that you've got a home to think about while you're out on the prairie, maybe you'll finish your jobs faster and hurry back to it," she said, smiling.

"I'd be sorta afraid to think too much of the time about you waiting here. Might make me just leave the sets and come running."

"Any time you run home, I'll be waiting," she promised. "And if you're going to start for the Baby Doll tomorrow, I'd better get supper on the table. We'll want to get to bed early so you'll have a good night's sleep."

"Guess you're right. You're sure there ain't no more things you want me to help you with, now?"

"No. But there'll be a lot of jobs waiting when you get back."

Wolfing was wolfing, and just about the same anyplace you did it, except that some places meant harder work than others, Lannigan told himself as he started unloading the mule after getting back to the Baby Doll line shack that was his temporary headquarters. He'd left this section of the ranch until last because it was very rough country, sliced by ravines and dry creekbeds, and the wolf-runs on it had shown the least activity when he'd scouted the range at the beginning of the job.

On the three sides of the ranch he'd already trapped, the sets had been good. He'd delivered nearly three hundred scalps to the ranch headquarters and had the skins stored in a shed there. Even if this last line of sets didn't take more than fifty or sixty wolves, it'd still be a good job, he thought as he tossed the day's pelts down to be scraped and stretched. And the minute the daily take dropped off, he was ready to call it a job and head for home. He had an awful itching to be back with Judith.

"It's funny," he said to himself. "Man gets married, how he feels like he ain't all there unless his wife's along with him."

A chunking of hoofbeats coming up behind the butte against which the line shack nestled broke his thought of home. He put aside the stretcher and skin he was working on and stepped into the shack for his rifle. With Indian Territory only a dozen miles from the Baby Doll's eastern range, there was always a chance that some feisty Comanche or Kiowa had strayed off their reservation and gone out to look for trouble. As soon as the rider topped the butte and started down its steep bank, and he could see it was a white man, Lannigan relaxed. He still held the rifle, just in case.

"Looking for a man name of Lannigan," the stranger called when he came within earshot.

"You found him," Lobo replied. The man was close enough now for his deputy sheriff's badge to be seen. "But I can't recall that I've busted any laws."

"Didn't say you had." The deputy swung out of his

saddle. "I'm Wade Coulter, from the Wheeler County sheriff's office. Bert Coogan give me a note to hand you when he found out I was coming down this way." He groped in his shirt pocket and pulled out a creased and battered envelope and handed it to Lannigan.

"Trouble in Mobeetie?" Lannigan was frowning as he ripped the envelope open.

"None I know of. I was up there to pick up a prisoner and Bert asked me to swing by and give you this. If it'd been trouble, he'd prob'ly have told me."

Lannigan was reading the note. "Dear Lobo," it said. "Figured you ought to know a fellow was nosying around here askeing about you. Might be one of her uncle's hands. He dident come to see me. He was tall and hard looking, I heard, and wanted to know about you and your missus both. I been keeping a special watch on your house sence he was here. Dident want to tell your missus about it and spook her up. I put out strings so somebody will tell me if he comes back and if he does I'll ask him some questions. Your friend, Bert."

Looking up from the note, Lannigan saw the deputy staring at him curiously. The man asked, "Wasn't bad news, I hope?"

"Just something Bert wanted me to know about. Appreciate you bringing it. If you want to stay for supper, I'll be starting to cook it up in a few minutes. Be right glad to have your company."

"Thanks." Coulter looked at the sun, which was sliding toward the horizon. "If I leave now, I'll be home a little after dark. You want to send any word back to Bert? Might be a few days before I'd get it to him. . . ."

"Don't think so. Nothing I could tell him except thanks. If you run into him, tell him I'll be coming in

pretty soon, day or two, a week at most. I'm just
about finished here."

"Wolfing good?"

"Pretty fair, so far. Getting the range cleared, day
at a time."

"Well, from what I seen of wolves, no matter how
many you trap, there's always more where they came
from." The deputy swung into his saddle. "I'll pass
your message on when I see Bert."

"I'll be obliged." Lannigan returned the deputy's
wave as the man rode off.

Back at work on the wolfskins, his hands did what
they were supposed to do automatically while his
mind worked over Bert Coogan's message. The description of the stranger inquiring about him and Judith was so vague that it could have fitted a half-dozen
YL hands, or almost anybody else, for that matter.
Most of the hands on the ranches Lannigan had visited were lean; long hours in the saddle and hard
work when out of it didn't produce chubby men.
Days on the range, with faces exposed to sun, rain,
sleet, snow, or icy winds, gave most hands what could
be described as a hard look, though weather-beaten
might be better, he thought. He discounted the iden-
tity of the curious stranger as being unimportant; the
thing that mattered was that anybody should be
asking questions. It was obvious George Sessions
wasn't giving up.

By the time he'd finished scraping the three skins
he'd brought from the sets and putting them on
stretchers, Lannigan had made up his mind. He
tossed through a restless, worried night, was on his
trap line as soon as there was enough light to see by,
and was actually happy that none of his traps held
wolves, though two of them had been sprung. He
loaded his gear and camp equipment and was at the

Baby Doll headquarters house while the morning was still young. Two hours after sundown he pulled up in front of the sheriff's office in Mobeetie. Through the open door he saw Bert Coogan leaning back in his chair, feet on desk, eyes half closed. He went in.

"Lobo!" Coogan sat erect. "Didn't look for you back so soon." His forehead wrinkled in a frown. "That letter I sent didn't spook you off the Baby Doll, did it?"

"A mite. I don't want nothing to happen to Judith, Bert."

"No more do I. She's too nice of a lady. I've been keeping watch on your house, swinging by that way when I walk my rounds. She's all right, or was less'n an hour ago."

"That fellow you wrote about, he ever come back?"

"Not as I've heard. And I got everybody primed to tip me off if he does."

"You find out anything about him?"

"Couldn't find nothing to find out," Coogan replied. "Nobody heard him say who he was or where from. Just that you was an old friend of his, and he'd heard you got married and settled hereabouts."

"Old friend?" Lannigan shook his head. "I've run into a lot of men while I was cowboying, before I went to wolfing, Bert. Wasn't none of 'em I'd call a friend good enough to come looking for me in a strange town."

"You think he was sent?"

"Maybe. Didn't claim he knew Judith, too, did he?"

"Not as I heard. But he had you pegged real good; must've knowed you from someplace, Lobo. If you don't mind my saying so, there ain't too many men your size knocking around these parts."

"I don't mind." Strangely, Lannigan found that he really didn't mind. It dawned on him that it'd been a while since his small stature had bothered him, and wondered why he'd been so irritated in the past when somebody had referred to it. He said, "Well, I'm going to be around for a while now. I haven't got a job lined up yet. If you hear about that fellow coming back, be sure you let me know."

"Sure, Lobo. But I bet we've seen the last of him. Far as I know, the only places he asked was in the saloons. I don't see he could've found out much."

Lannigan nodded. He said, "Thanks for sending word to me, Bert. Guess I better be getting on home, now. Judith's not looking for me back so soon; she's in for a surprise."

Judith was surprised, and pleased as well, and her greeting left no doubt in Lannigan's mind of her pleasure. Even her scolding him for failing to let her know when he'd be back expressed her love. Lannigan glowed gently as he watched her scurry around, fixing him a bite of supper, after he'd confessed he hadn't eaten since breakfast. A man didn't know what he was missing, he told himself, until he had a home and a wife like his.

After supper there were new things Judith had to show him, little improvements: cushions sewed to fit a chair that had been bare and uncomfortable, a new tablecloth, a curtain stretched across open shelves in the kitchen, "so we don't have to look at a clutter of pots and pans while we're eating, Lobo. And the store's gotten in some Aladdin lamps, I think we ought to get one, perhaps even two. One for in here, the other for the parlor. They're so much brighter and more cheerful than the old kind."

"Looks like you've found enough to keep busy with. That's a lot of work to do all by yourself."

"Oh, I had help. A very nice young man."

"Now, wait a minute—" he began.

"A very, very young man. Mrs. Brent's boy, Bobby.

You don't have to start getting jealous, he's only twelve. But he's a good worker, and very bright. He's been taking care of the woodpile and the outhouse, and that's given me time to work inside."

"If I'd known somebody was cutting in on me, maybe I'd've got home quicker."

"Now, stop making fun of me, Lobo. You know how lonesome it is by yourself." She stopped, giggled, and said, "But I do think Bobby's got a bad case of puppy love."

"Now you really got me worried." Then, seriously, he went on: "I don't like to leave you by yourself, Judith. You know that."

"Of course I do. But you won't take me with you." Before he could say anything, she hurried on. "And I'm not complaining. I just miss you when you're gone."

"Glad you do. And you ain't the only one missing somebody. But I'll be home a while, it looks like." Keeping his voice carefully casual, he asked, "Anybody come asking for me while I was gone?"

"No. Were you expecting somebody? You didn't say anything about having a job waiting after you finished at the Baby Doll."

"No, no," Lannigan answered quickly. "But when we was traveling down to Fredericksburg and back, we stopped at an awful lot of spreads. I just thought one of 'em might've decided they wanted a wolfing job."

"Well, there hasn't been anybody. And I hope there won't be for a while. I want you at home with me, Lobo."

"I want to be here, honey. And I'm not aiming to start out looking for a fresh job. Not for a while."

Later, after Judith had gone to sleep, her head resting on his chest, his arm cradling her gently to him, Lannigan lay awake trying to decide the best course to follow. He didn't want to alarm Judith by telling her somebody had been asking about them, but he wanted her to be warned and alert to the possibility that her uncle might be closing on their trail. Just before he dozed away, he decided there wasn't any need to get Judith all stirred up and edgy, as long as he was there to see that nothing happened to her. Then he slept, better and more soundly than he had for weeks.

Absorbed in the strange and totally new world of domesticity he'd entered, Lannigan grew less worried about the inquisitive stranger as the days rolled by and the man did not reappear. It was his reluctance to leave home rather than any fear of danger that caused him to hesitate when Crede Stevens of the Bottle Brand came looking for him to do a special, urgent job.

"I got a renegade on my place," he told Lannigan, worry and anger balanced in his voice. "Showed up about the start of summer. None of my boys has seen the damned thing but we've sure seen his tracks and what he's doing to my herd."

"You sure it's just one? Lots of times renegades gets blamed for what a whole pack kills, just because its tracks are easy to spot."

"Oh, there's more than one wolf on my spread," Stevens admitted. "Not many—we keep putting out poison, and that keeps 'em down. But there's not any doubt about this fellow. Got a chopped-up front paw that even a greenhorn could see from his saddle."

Lannigan rubbed his chin thoughtfully. Renegade wolves, those that had felt the steel jaws of a trap snap shut and had managed to escape with a crippled leg, or a lost or mangled paw, were a cattleman's special bane. While all wolves were looked on as out-law, the renegade earned the title that had come to set it apart from its fellow. It seemed to acquire a seventh sense, perhaps no more than a magnified caution, that made the renegade almost impossible to trap, poison, or shoot. China Slim had told Lannigan tales of some famous renegade wolves—Pegleg, Bigfoot, Old Lefty, Three Toes, and others—that had survived for six, eight, even ten years, in spite of special efforts to kill them.

In addition to a reinforced sense of survival, renegades had other traits. They became loners; did not join packs; confined themselves to a territory that was normally only a dozen square miles in area. They also became killers more wanton than other wolves. Stockmen hated them, because in a single night a renegade would kill as many steers or horses as would a sizable wolf pack. A renegade seemed unable to stop killing; one might slaughter fifteen or twenty animals in one night, taking only a bite or two from each carcass before moving to kill another.

"Looks like you've got yourself a problem, Stevens. If you're certain it's a renegade, that is," Lannigan said.

"Yep. And it's a problem I can't afford right now. I got an Army contract to trail steers up to the Northern Territories to feed the Indians on them big reservations up there. I need every head of cattle I can roust," Stevens said. "And I know I got a renegade. No way to mistake the tracks it leaves. Got two long-claw toes on its left front foot; makes a deep hole when it steps down on that leg."

"I guess you got one, all right," Lannigan agreed.

"Look here, that damned wolf's killing about fifteen steers a night on me. I got one set of hands trailing a herd north and another set rounding up another herd to start off next month. The bunch on the ranch've been trying to get that renegade, nights, till they're not much use in the daytime. I want you to kill me that wolf."

"I'd have to think about it."

"Why? You're a wolfer, that's your business."

"Grant you that. But I'm the only wolfer in these parts, and the Bottle Brand's not the only spread that's having troubles."

"Maybe not. But I've got more'n most. Even if you're supposed to take on a job for somebody else, they'd likely stand aside so you could take care of me first. You want me to ask whoever it is?"

"No, thanks, Stevens. I can set up my own jobs." Lannigan stood up. "If you'll just sit a minute and enjoy your coffee, I'll be right back." He went into the kitchen, where Judith had retired to leave the two men to discuss their business. He explained the situation to her in a few quick words.

"So that's the way of it," he concluded. "Bottle Brand's only a little ways from town. I might luck out and get that renegade in a week or so—might take me a month. I didn't plan to go back out so soon. I hate to leave you by yourself so much."

"Don't worry about me, Lobo. If Mr. Stevens is in really bad trouble, I think you ought to help him."

Back in the living room, Lannigan sat down across from the Bottle Brand owner. "Say I was to decide to get you shed of that renegade, it'd cost you."

"I'd expect it to. How much?"

"We got to dicker on that. At six dollars a head, you're losing a hundred dollars worth of steers a night. How much you think that makes me worth a day to you?"

"You mean you'd expect me to pay you a hundred dollars a day just to trap one damned wolf?"

"Now, I didn't say that. Even if it might be worth it to pay me that much."

"Lannigan, I've got fifteen hands and a cook and a foreman on the Bottle Brand right now, another twelve hands with the herd trailing north, and my whole payroll's not that much a day."

"I know. You got twenty-five-a-month hands and forty-dollar foremen, and a thirty-dollar cook. But your twenty-five dollar hands can't get you rid of that renegade wolf. I can."

"All right," Stevens said. There was exasperated finalty in his voice. "Let's stop dickering. How much? If it's reasonable, I'll meet your price."

"I'll be fair. Five hundred dollars if it takes me more than a month. Seven-fifty if I do it in less."

After thinking this over for a moment, the rancher nodded. "If you do your job quick, it's worth it to me in the critters I'll save. We've got a deal, then. When'll you be out to the place?"

"Tomorrow morning. No use wasting time."

Stevens smiled at last. "I guess you're a reasonable man, at that. And I'll say this, when you take on a job, you sure get right after it. I hope you earn your seven-fifty, Lannigan."

When the rancher had gone, Lobo told Judith, "I'll get an early start. If I'm lucky, I won't be gone longer than two weeks. You sure you don't mind?"

"There's plenty to keep me busy. It's not that I won't miss you, but maybe if you catch the renegade, we'll have a longer time together afterwards. Now, stop worrying about me and start getting ready to go to the Bottle Brand tomorrow."

CHAPTER 13

During the first days following his arrival at the Bottle Brand, Lannigan did nothing but scout the range, looking for the routes most often followed by the renegade. He could read no pattern in the animal's movements. The night before Lannigan had started scouting, the wolf had killed eleven steers in an area close to the headquarters buildings and south of them, after approaching the herd from the west. On the next night, the renegade came in from the north, circled the bunkhouse at a distance of less than a hundred yards, and tore the throats out of seven brood mares in the remuda pasture beyond the stable. It then went on to the holding corral and killed three horses outright in addition to hamstringing four more, which had to be shot. The following night the predator came in from the east and angled across the range to a herd where it killed nineteen steers.

Never did the wolf follow the same path coming or going. Lannigan found runs in several places on the Bottle Brand's range, but none of them bore the unmistakable pointed left front paw-print of the killer. The renegade's den, if indeed it had one, might have been anywhere around the ranch's perimeter, or within a short distance from the headquarters itself. Never did it strike two nights in succession in the same area.

On the fifth day Lannigan began to set traps in a random pattern, choosing places the renegade had not visited recently. Some of the traps took other wolves, but on the ground he'd swept clean around the sets there were no prints of the one he was after. Lannigan did not remove the sets, but kept adding to them. Soon he had more than thirty traps scattered over the ranch, no two of them in the same vicinity, most of them a mile or more apart.

At the end of two weeks he almost admired the wiliness of the renegade. Tracks began to show in the vicinity of some of the sets; the familiar mangled left forepaw with its two unusually long claws made a deep impression even in the hardest soil. The tracks always stopped short of the traps. By now Lannigan could read the wolf's movements as if he'd been watching the animal itself on its forays. Invariably, it would circle around the set, sometimes more, more often twice, before going on to its bloody nighttime slaughter. He began making double and triple sets, spacing the extra traps around the circle the wolf usually made when inspecting the center trap. The wolf merely increased the size of its circle. It was as though it had been watching while Lannigan made the sets.

"Damned wolf's got to be getting some smell of me," he muttered after inspecting a fresh set that the renegade had approached to within a yard before backing off.

A few at a time, Lannigan removed the traps; boiled them again, to remove any trace of the oil he'd put on them after finishing his work at the Baby Doll. He buried his wolfing clothes in the manure pile once more, and used extra care in handling each garment, each shoe, each glove, the setting cloth. From the anal glands and urine of some of the other wolves he'd taken, he mixed fresh scent. It was no more effective than the old had been.

To take the renegade within the month had now become a challenge, a matter of personal pride. Lannigan had learned enough of wolves to know that each time the renegade was successful in avoiding a trap, the beast noticed some fresh detail of identifying a set that would make it easier for it to evade others. He dug into his brain for bits of half-forgotten conversations he'd had around their supper fires with China Slim when he'd been learning the wolfing trade. A nagging feeling grew that somewhere buried in his memory lay a method of trapping that might work. Whether because of or in spite of his efforts to prod his memory, the method finally surfaced. More, Lannigan recalled a place where it might be successful. He set about getting his equipment together.

Crede Stevens came into the cookshack while Lannigan was begging some slices of liver out of a freshly butchered steer from the cook. Stevens shook his head. "We've tried liver-bait with poison in it, Lannigan. The renegade don't notice it. Save your time."

"I tried it too, Stevens. Double-baited my sets with liver and kidney and fresh meat, guts, calf sweetbreads, everything I could think of. But this ain't for my traps, it's for fishing-bait."

"You're taking time off to go fishing while that damned wolf is still free? What's got into you?"

"I won't be fishing just for fun. It'd take too long to go into the whole thing now. Just leave me to do my job. I'll get your wolf, just like I said I would."

"You've got about nine more days to make that seven-fifty. I guess you been keeping track of the time, though."

"Just like you have. Now, I got to get over to Elm

Creek, so if it's all the same to you, I'll be on my way."

At Elm Creek, Lannigan put out set-lines ten feet apart along the big hole he'd noticed while scouting. He'd seen catfish in the hole at that time, and counted on their still being there. They were, and were hungry for liver. Within an hour he had six good-size fish. Back at the headquarters, he chopped the catfish into mush, cutting up skin, bones, heads, meat, and intestines into a fine mince. He scraped this into jars, topped off each jar with his regular trapping scent, and set the jars outside the bunkhouse where the hot sun would do its work. Then he waited impatiently during the two days required for the mixture to ripen before loading the jars into his wagon and setting out for the spot he'd selected as the site of his desperation effort.

A full mile from the place where he hoped to trap the renegade, Lannigan stopped and hitched the wagon to a mesquite-bush. He'd known that what he must do next would be unpleasant, but his imagination had fallen far short of just how bad it really was. Stripping naked, he opened one of the jars. The odor that rose from it gagged him even with the jar held at arm's length; it was infinitely more potent than his regular scent and fifty times more penetratingly nauseous. Gritting his teeth, he tried not to breathe while he rubbed the stinking stuff on his body, covering every square inch of skin from hair to toes, including the soles of his feet.

Taking only his ax, his sheath-knife, a hank of rawhide thong, and the remaining jars of scent, he set out after rubbing the scent over all the items he was carrying. His destination was a dry creekbed that had become a narrow-bottomed ravine after the creek gave up. Where water had once run, a few trees were rooted: a dozen cottonwoods, a few stunted salt cedars, and three or four hackberries. The trees were now all dead, and several had been toppled by the wind. The renegade used the ravine occasionally when he came onto Bottle Brand range, Lannigan knew; he'd seen the deep-pointed forepaw track there. He had no choice, really; the ravine offered the only combination of a narrow passageway with trees on the entire ranch.

As Lannigan walked toward the ravine, the prairie that seemed so smooth under his boot soles turned to needles and nails. His bare feet found every pebble, every rough-edged clump of sun-dried dirt, and he was limping by the time he reached his destination. He hobbled into the grove and stopped to rest for a moment in the scanty shade. While he rested, he renewed the putrid oily coating on his feet; then, after starting to work, he paused from time to time to rub more of the pasty stuff on hands, arms, legs, and feet.

From the wind-felled trees, Lannigan selected a hackberry about thirty feet long. By the time he'd cleared it of limbs with the ax, he was surrounded by a swarm of flies and buffalo gnats, and when he'd begun chopping he'd also begun sweating. The heat amplified the stench of his smeared body; between the smell, the insects, and the trickling drops of sweat, he was thoroughly miserable.

When the last branch had been removed from the tree trunk, he chopped the bole into three sections. Two of these were between six and seven feet long, and using a big limb as a lever, Lannigan moved these pieces until they lay parallel, a foot apart. He stopped to rest, to fight off insects that still swarmed around him in a buzzing, stinging cloud, and to renew his body coating. He'd almost gotten used to the way he smelled by now, he told himself wryly.

Next, he tackled the big section of tree trunk, twenty feet long and twice his weight, straining on his lever until he had its butt end lying next to the two smaller logs, the bole sections now lying parallel with each other. He drove stakes along the sides of the two short pieces and levered the long section into the hollow between the short pieces, resting on them. Using the thinnest, flattest stones he could find along the bottom of the ravine, he pried up the long length of tree-bole repeatedly, slipping a stone under it each time he raised it, until he'd formed a small tower of rocks on which the long section of tree trunk balanced at a precarious slant from the top of the cairn of rocks to the ground, above the short sections. The raised end resting on the stones was at the height of his chest.

It had been a long, hard job, and Lannigan rested for a while, studying what he'd done. After renewing the viscous fish-scent on his body, he selected the straightest and stoutest of the limbs he'd cleared from the tree trunk and lopped off its twigs. Sharpening one end with his ax, he drove it deeply into the ground a few inches from the base of the stone cairn, at the end of one of the short logs. A foot down from the top of the long stake he used his knife to whittle out a notch like an inverted figure seven, the bottom of the notch parallel to the ground. Heaving a sigh of relief, Lannigan told himself that the hardest part of the job was now done.

From the tree-trimmings, he selected a straight branch as thick as his wrist and from it cut two pieces, one as long as his forearm, the other twice that length. He whittled one end of the short piece to flatten it smoothly on one side, and in line with the flattened portion, scooped out a shallow conical depression at the other end. When the flattened end of the branch was fitted into the notch in the stake, it formed a horizontal crossarm, with one end free. To support this end, Lannigan trimmed the long section of branch to a length that he determined by measuring with the rawhide thong, and sharpened each end. Now, when he rested one end of the long section of limb on the top of the log at the bottom of the stake and put the upper end in the depression he'd made in the crossarm, he had a support that looked like an inverted figure four.

He rested again, and swathed another coating of the fish-scent on himself, paying special attention to his hands and feet. He no longer was conscious of his stench; it had become part of him. The final stage of his trap building began. After he'd cut a crotched limb to steady the crossarm and its support, he used his lever to raise the butt of the long, slanting treetrunk just high enough to enable him to slip the topmost rock off the stone cairn. When he gingerly lowered the tree-butt, it came down on the crossarm of the upside-down four, barely touching it. He removed another stone and the tree-butt settled firmly on the crossarm. The supporting branch quivered, but settled down as the pointed ends dug into place.

Stepping back, Lannigan studied his construction, holding his breath for fear that the delicately balanced upper log might fall. When it stood immobile, he removed the cairn stone by stone, tossing the rocks haphazardly behind him. The most dangerous part of the job lay ahead. Holding his breath and moving with slow deliberation, he tied one end of the rawhide thong around the vertical brace and ran the end between the two bottom legs. He drove a short stake cut from a limb into the ground between the logs and tied the thong to it, carefully drawing it taut as he formed the knot. Then he dumped an entire bottle of the fish-scent over the foundation logs and the thong and sprinkled the last few dribbles on the ground at the center of the deadfall.

He'd been so absorbed, trying to remember the description China Slim had once given him of a deadfall's construction, that he had almost forgotten the cloud of bugs surrounding him. Opening a fresh jar of scent brought reinforcements to the swarm, and amplified the stench of the scent until Lannigan thought he could not only smell it, but see and hear it as well.

Picking up his ax and the freshly opened jar, he started out of the grove, dribbling the scent as he went. He left from the end opposite that by which he'd entered, walking on bruised and smarting feet along the ravine, dropping small dollops of the scent. He carried the scent-trail up the side of the gully to the level prairie, and when the jar was empty, tossed it as far as he could. Back at the wagon at last, he rubbed as much of the slimy stuff as possible off his naked body. A residue still clung to him. He decided not to put on his clothes and ruin them. Naked on the wagon seat, he drove back to the Bottle Brand headquarters.

A bath in cold water in the horsetrough, followed by two more in hot water begged from the cook and soft soap cadged with the water, took away most of the odor, but Lannigan did not need the cook's upturned nose to tell him that he was a long way from being socially acceptable. He knew that; he still could not stand his own smell when he was indoors. He ate supper on the bench outside the cookshack, and to avoid the remarks he knew would be aimed at him in the bunkhouse, slept that night on the ground outside, under his wagon.

Lannigan was not a superstitious man, but he'd promised himself good luck would be his if he stayed away from the deadfall for two days. He knew that luck, much more than his care and skill in setting the primitive trap, would determine his success. He went over the possibilities in his mind. Another wolf might trigger the trap; this was not too much of a risk, for the Bottle Brand's poisoning and his own trapping had almost cleared the range of all but the renegade. The renegade, with its unpredictable movements, might not go near the ravine for days, even weeks. When and if the crippled killer did get close to the ravine, the scent might spook the wolf instead of attracting it; not a great possibility, Lannigan thought—the new, strange odor would more likely draw it to the trap. Strongest of all the favorable factors was that the deadfall was a kind of trap the renegade had not encountered before, one that would not arouse its suspicions.

While he waited for his self-imposed time limit to pass, Lannigan removed his sets. Scattered as they were around the Bottle Brand range, this was a full day's job. He took it as a good omen that there were only two wolves caught in the thirty traps, and that only four others had been sprung. At none of the thirty did he see the distinctive tracks of the renegade.

When he finally went to the deadfall, Lannigan tried to leave hope behind him. He did not take the wagon, but rode his mustang. He started out at a sedate walk, but as he neared the ravine and his eagerness to see if he'd been lucky mounted, he urged the pony to a canter. He reined in at the ravine, where he could look down through the trunks of the dead standing trees and see the trap. Had he been a religious man, he'd have offered a prayer of thanks. The top log had fallen, and he could see the head and

forepaws of a great gray wolf sticking out from
beneath it.

He did not take time to ride to the mouth of the
gully, but kicked his pony forward, rearing back to
keep his balance while the mustang slid down the
steep bank on its hindquarters. He swung to the
ground and hurried to look at the trapped wolf. From
several paces distant he could see the maimed paw.
Though he'd expected to be elated, Lannigan only
felt relieved. He stood gazing at the wolf, the rawhide
trigger-thong still grasped in its yellowed fangs. The
wolf, he thought, must have been excited by the
strange scent and snapped at the thong when it
stepped onto the base of the trap.

Even then, the renegade must have had a belated
premonition of danger, for its forepaws were beyond
the dislodged tree trunk that had crashed down on its
spine. The wolf's leap had not been fast enough or
soon enough to carry it through the trap. The deadfall
log had dropped, catching the animal's body between
it and the two short bottom logs, snapping the wolf's
spine and killing it instantly.

After Lannigan had levered the deadly tree trunk
off the carcass of the renegade and dragged the limp
form out, he looked at the dead wolf. Its crushed
chest and midsection were mute witnesses to the effi-
ciency of the trap. He led the pony over to the carcass, quieting the mustang's rearing when it got close
to the wolf and caught its scent over the fishy aroma
that still hung in the grove. Lannigan tried to lift the
carcass to the pony's rump, but its limp, unwieldy
weight was more than he could manage; he took his
lariat off its saddle-string and knotted it around the
wolf's forepaws, then looped the free end over a tree
limb and let the mustang lift the load. Once more the
pony balked when it felt the carcass swing against its

rump and got the strange scent in its nostrils, but Lannigan finally got the horse to accept the load, knotted the carcass in place, and started back. The odor that surrounded him as he rode to the Bottle Brand headquarters did nothing to diminish his inner satisfaction.

"Well, you made it, and just in time," Crede Stevens grinned as he inspected the carcass that Lannigan had dumped in front of the headquarters house. "And I ain't changed my mind about being glad to pay you the seven-fifty instead of five hundred."

"I didn't imagine you would. This old fellow's cost you a lot more than you're paying to get rid of him."

"Did you have to stink the hide up like this?" Stevens asked, his nose wrinkling as a draft of breeze swirled the scent-stench around them. "I wanted to make a rug out of it for my office."

"It's a mite high," Lannigan admitted. "I'll stretch it for you, and you let it stand outside a while, till the smell wears off."

"Think I'll settle for that crippled front leg instead. If you'll chop it off and bring it in, I'll have your money ready for you." He went into the headquarters house.

Lannigan was squatting beside the carcass, taking off the wolf's leg, when Bert Coogan rode up. He waved and went on sawing at the tough leg-tendons while the deputy dismounted and walked over.

"Godamighty! What's that stink?" were Coogan's first words. "I never smelled anything so awful in my life!"

"That stink's from the bait I had to use to get this renegade," Lannigan replied. He stopped work and looked at Coogan with a worried frown. "Nothing happened to Judith, has there?"

"Not a thing. She's just fine, or was when I rode out this morning." He looked around. "Lobo, let's get away from this smell so we can talk without me wanting to puke."

Lannigan put the knife down and they walked to the shade of the headquarters house. He asked Coogan, "What brings you out here, then? Some of the Bottle's boys in trouble? Or did you just close down Mobeetie and take the day off?"

"Had some papers to deliver to the Diamond Tail; it wasn't but a little bit outa my way to stop by. Reason I saw Miz Lannigan this morning was because I went by your house to show you something. She told me there wasn't any telling when you'd be back, and I thought you oughta see this." Coogan pulled a folded square of thick paper out of his pocket and handed it to Lannigan. "Deputy from Wheeler brought this up with some other stuff last night."

Lannigan unfolded the paper and stared at it with widening eyes. He could not quite believe what he was reading.

"WANTED!" the poster proclaimed. "For the Abduction of Miss Judith Sessions from the YL Ranch near Tascosa, Texas! $1000 REWARD for the capture of LOBO LANNIGAN!" Below, smaller type gave a less than complimentary description of Lannigan, stressing his small stature. There followed a description of Judith, with a caution that she might be using Lannigan's name and "posing as his wife." In a second outburst of large type beneath the descriptions, the text read, "$1000 REWARD for the return of Miss Sessions, well and unharmed! $500 REWARD for information as to Miss Sessions's whereabouts!" At the bottom of the handbill, smaller type gave its source: "George Sessions, Manager, YL Ranch, Oldham County, Texas, near Tascosa."

Boiling indignation burst through Lannigan's first stunned silence after he'd finished reading. "That damned Sessions! He knows me and Judith got married. She sent him a letter when we was down at Fredericksburg." He thought a moment and added, "But I don't think she remembered to tell him where we aimed to go from there." Then, with a worried wrinkle forming on his forehead: "How long's this damn thing been going around, Bert?"

"Hard to say. Might be quite a while."

"Hell, me and Judith been married now going on six months." Indignation took over again. "That damned blatherskite! Bert, this handbill ain't legal, is it? Far as I know, Sessions hasn't made no charges against me in court. And Judith come off the YL with me of her own free will. You know that."

"Sure I do. I guess Sessions does, too, Lobo. But you still don't see what's got me worried. That thing's a wide-open bid for bounty hunters to take after you. And that kind plays rough. They don't give a damn whether it's the law wants you or somebody else. Far as I know, though, there's not any law against putting out a handbill like that. Hell, Wells Fargo, the stage lines, banks that've been robbed, railroads, they do it all the time."

Lannigan had been thinking, only half listening to the deputy. He asked, "You think that whoever it was asking around while I was off at the Baby Doll last month might've seen one of these?"

"I'd say it's a pretty good bet he did. Which is why I brought it out here to show you."

"All right, I've seen it. And I'm leaving to go home just as soon as I can load up. I got my traps all collected, and it won't take me long to throw my gear in the wagon."

"Now, simmer down, Lobo. You don't have to go

off half-cocked. I told you, Miz Lannigan's all right."

"I ain't arguing that, Bert. I'm finished up here, that wolf hulk over there's all I had to deliver. I'll collect my money and be started in about an hour. You might stop by and tell Judith to be looking for me. You'll travel faster. Them mules don't have trot in 'em."

"Sure. Glad to. And I'll keep an extra-careful lookout, too. But you don't need to worry. If anything was going to happen, it'd've been right after that fellow come looking for you."

"And that's been more'n a month," Lannigan said thoughtfully. "I guess you're right. If there was going to be trouble, it'd've caught up with us by now. But that's not going to hold me back from moving out tonight, even if it is the dark of the moon. It's a fair to middling trail, I can follow it without any trouble. You tell her I'll be home about midnight."

Judith was not waiting for Lannigan when he got home, an hour later than he'd planned. Instead, Coogan was sitting in the parlor, staring glumly at nothing. When Lannigan came in, the deputy looked up and said in a flat voice, "She's gone, Lobo."

"Judith? What do you mean? Where'd she go?"

"I don't know. I headed here first thing when I got into town. There wasn't any light in the house, the door was unlocked. She just plain wasn't here."

"Didn't you look for her?"

"Now, Lobo, you know I did. I went all through the house, out to the yard in back, even went next door to Miz Brent's and asked. She said she hadn't seen Miz Lannigan all day."

Fighting down the sick feeling that was sweeping over him, Lannigan said, "We got to go ask somewheres else, then. Bound to be somebody seen her."

"Lobo, it's past one in the morning. Who're we going to find up and around to ask about anything, this time of night?"

"Saloons are open. And I was going to rouse up old Pete at the livery stable, anyhow. He takes care of my critters."

"All right. We'll see what we can find out. But I don't guess we're going to turn up much of anything."

They roused Pete, made the rounds of the saloons, but learned nothing. All the barkeeps remembered strangers having dropped in, but recalled nothing helpful about any of them. The liveryman hadn't been at the stables during the day, and had no way of knowing who might have left horses or teams to be cared for earlier.

"Maybe if we knew what we was looking for, we'd've had better luck," Coogan said unhappily just before they gave up. "But we'll start out fresh tomorrow; see if we can turn up something."

Lannigan nodded dully. He was feeling the effects of his long day, which had started before dawn on the Bottle Brand; for almost twenty-four hours he'd been working without rest, and the added strain of Judith's disappearance compounded his exhaustion. He said, "You come by the house as soon as you get up, Bert. I've got to rest a while. It's getting so I can't think straight."

He went home, but sleep came slowly. The dark, lonely bedroom was beginning to gray with morning when he finally slipped away to sleep, only to be awakened—almost, he thought, before he'd closed his eyes—by thuds and clatter outside the kitchen door. He jumped from bed and went to investigate. In the yard, a boy was tumbling chunks of wood off the woodpile.

"What're you doing, messing around my house at

this time of day?" Lannigan demanded. He still was not fully awake.

"Well, I asked Ma, Mr. Lannigan. She's got chores for me to do after school. She thought Mrs. Lannigan wouldn't mind if I did my work here this morning."

"Oh." Lannigan realized who the youngster must be. "You're Mrs. Brent's boy. Billy? No, Bobby. That right?"

"Yessir. This is my regular day to split stovewood for Miss Judith. I thought she'd be back by now, and she always gets up early, so I didn't think she'd mind if I came this morning instead of later."

"Wait a minute." Lannigan was late in interpreting what the youth had said. "You say you thought Judith'd be back. Back from where?"

"Whillikers, Mr. Lannigan, I don't know where. I just saw her leave yesterday morning, about the time I was starting for school. I don't know where she was going."

"By herself, was she?"

"Nossir. There was two men with her."

"You know them? Men from town here?"

"I never saw either one of them before. I don't know who they were. Never saw the brands on their horses before, either."

"But you got a good look at them?"

"Pretty good, I guess."

"What'd they look like?"

"Well—" Bobby hesitated. "They looked about like anybody else."

"They have whiskers? Mustaches? Old men or young ones? Come on, Bobby, you must've noticed something."

"I guess I was mostly looking at Miss Judith."

"Why? Did she look different from always?"

"Well, I waved at her and she didn't wave back.

She was looking right at me, too. Then they went on past, and I noticed the horses."

"What about the horses? Was it the one she was riding?"

"Nossir. The one that one of the men rode. It had a brand like the other two, and I couldn't make it out. And it was limping."

"What'd the brand look like?"

"They were all the same, like a W or two Vs, only it wasn't really either of those. The brands had funny curleycue marks all through the straight lines."

Lannigan let that go by. He knew what overbranding usually meant, and didn't have time to explain it to the boy. He asked, "All right, how were the men dressed?"

"Like any of the hands you see riding in from the ranches. I wasn't watching them all that close, honest, Mr. Lannigan. I was watching Miss Judith."

It was obvious to Lannigan that he was going to get no more information that would help him identify the two strangers. He asked the boy, "Did you see which way they headed out?"

"Oh, yessir. North. I looked back before I got to school and saw them turning onto the Canadian River trail."

"Toward the fort?" Lannigan had expected a different reply. "You sure they didn't head for the Tascosa trail?"

"I'm sure. They went north, all right. I was watching."

"Um. Well, thanks, Bobby. You've been real helpful. Go on and split that wood, now. I'll square up with you when I get back."

"Is Miss Judith coming back with you?"

"That's one thing you can bet on, Bobby. I'm going to bring her back."

Lannigan pulled on his clothes and hurried to the jail. Bert Coogan was still asleep on the cot in the office; he'd turned in fully dressed except for his boots. While he was listening to Lannigan's story, he started coffee boiling and bacon frying, then began to split leftover biscuits to fry in the bacon fat. When Lannigan had finished, the deputy said, "Two strangers on horses that got strange brands. Overbrands, you figure?"

"Bound to be. Rustled stock, most likely."

"Or so nobody could tell real quick where the nags come from. I've known bounty hunters to use the same trick," Coogan said.

"If that's so, why didn't they wait and take me, too? I'm worth a thousand dollars, that's twice what Judith'd bring from Sessions."

"Likely they're planning to come back. If there was just the two of 'em, they might've figured they couldn't handle you both."

"And why'd they head north? The YL's west."

"I'd bet they got a hideout along the Canadian. There's a hundred box canyons and caves and such that outlaws use up there on the river. Prob'ly going to leave Miz Lannigan there until they can come collect you."

"And deliver us both at once?" Lannigan stood up. "Well, I don't aim to wait for that, Bert. I'll be on my way. A horse with a lame leg leaves a trail that's easy to follow."

"Damn it, Lobo, ain't you going to eat and give me time to get my boots on? Or don't you want me along?"

"If you got the time and feel like it. Be nice to have the law on my side."

"Then sit back down and eat breakfast. I don't

travel so good on an empty stomach, and right now my belly's yelling for help."

Between Mobeetie and Fort Elliott the road was used so much that it was impossible to find any tracks of the limping horse. They'd covered about half the six miles to the fort when a congregation of birds a quarter mile off the road caught Lannigan's eye. The birds were swooping and wheeling in a small area, only a few feet above the ground, a mixture of black-birds and hawks. It was a sight the wolfer had seen often before, birds hovering over a wolf hulk, swooping down to feed on it. What the scavenger animals, coyotes, and foxes and their like did not tear off a carcass at night, the birds finished by day.

"Something dead over there," he told Coogan.

"Likely a sick yearling some rancher cut out of a herd he was delivering to the fort." The deputy studied the fluttering birds for a moment and said, "Maybe it ain't, though. Look right there on the ground between us and the birds, Lobo."

Lannigan squinted into the early sun. In the short-grass he saw a blur of blue and a glint of sunlight reflected from yellow metal. "Looks like an Army cap to me."

"Does to me, too. Let's go take a look."

There was not much left of the face of one of the dead men who lay in a little buffalo wallow beyond the Army forage cap. His body had been lying faceup. Enough remained for Coogan to say at once, "That's Tobias." He dismounted and leaned over the body. "He was shot. Guess him and this other one had some kind of fracas."

They turned the second corpse over and looked at its face. Lannigan frowned. There was something familiar about the features. He was still studying the dead man, trying to jog his memory, when Coogan said, "This one's been shot, too. I don't know him, though. Likely it's one of Tobias's outlaw friends."

"Sure." Lannigan's memory meshed. "I know him, Bert. Leastways, I've seen him before. In Tascosa, with two other fellows. His name's either Slane or Whiteside. There was three of 'em I had a brush with in a saloon there. The other one I knew from down south; we worked on the same spread for a little while. His name's Harris. They call him Hardcase."

"You certain?"

"Certain-sure. I fought Harris a couple of times; he was always poking fun at me. Then, when I first come up here, I had that run-in at Tascosa. Stood 'em off with this old fuke that's hanging right here on my saddle-strings. Barkeep told me later that this fellow here used to run with Billy the Kid's gang.

Coogan nodded slowly. "That'd hang together, from what we suspicioned about Tobias, him having come from the Territory. Guess they got into a wrangle and it wound up with him and Tobias dead. The two that was left dragged the bodies off the road."

"You think Tobias was mixed up with them taking Judith?"

"No," Coogan answered positively. "These bodies been here a day or more before yesterday. Now, I'll tell you how it looks to me. The three of them you know was coming after you and Miz Lannigan. They might've had some loot they wanted to sell Tobias, long as they were here anyhow."

"And fought, and this one and Tobias was killed, the other two went on to town and got Judith?"

"About like that," Coogan agreed. "They was in a hurry, or they wouldn't've set off with a lame horse. Well, I guess this cuts me outa your trip, Lobo. I got to take care of these two and start asking questions, seeing what I can find out."

"Sure. You got a lawman's job, and I can't help you with that. So I'll push on." Lannigan was swinging into his saddle while he spoke. Coogan nodded agreement. Lannigan reined his mustang toward the road. As he turned away, he called to the deputy, "You get finished quick, you might catch up with me; but I'm not going to stop or turn aside till I catch up with them two that's got Judith. Especially now I'm pretty sure one of 'em is Hardcase Harris!"

CHAPTER 14

North of Fort Elliott, Lannigan found the first tracks of the horse that favored its right hind leg. There was less travel beyond the fort than between it and Mobeetie, though the road was still a patchwork of wagon-ruts, horse and mule hoofprints, and occasionally all tracks on the road were lost in a confusion of cattle-tracks where a herd had crossed it. But the lame horse's prints were unmistakable: three shoes cleanly marked, the fourth faint and imperfect. Only the front portion of the shoe on the animal's right hind hoof touched the ground. It left a crescent-shaped imprint, deeper than most others, that stood out like a quarter moon.

Fifteen miles past the fort, Lannigan suddenly woke to the fact that he'd been thinking instead of looking. The crescent hoof-mark had vanished somewhere behind him. He backtracked until he picked up the place where Judith and her captors had left the road to cut across the open prairie in a long westward arc that roughly paralleled the sweep of the Canadian River. Forcing all other thought, all worry, from his mind, he set off on the trail again.

Why the men who'd taken Judith had chosen the route was plain. The wagon road connecting Mobeetie and Tascosa was too well traveled to be risked. Tempting as was the idea to ride in a straight line

toward Tascosa and risk cutting across the trail later,
Lannigan discarded it. The prairie was simply too immense. If he'd guessed wrong about Tascosa being
the destination of his quarry, he might spend days
zigzagging across the huge expanse of empty land in
search of the crescent print.

Though Lannigan had been able to move faster
once he was on the single trail left by the trio after
they'd left the road, backtracking and his earlier slow
progress had reduced the distance he was able to
cover before darkness overtook him. He stopped reluctantly, though he'd been forcing himself to stay
awake for an hour or more, swaying in the saddle,
half asleep with open eyes. He had barely enough en-
ergy left to stake his horse and spread his hotroll before crawling in. Hunger woke him in the gray
hushlight of dawn. He ate the bacon and fried biscuits left over from the breakfast Coogan had prepared the morning before, topping them off with a
small airtight of peaches he'd found in Judith's pantry. The tracks were easy to see by the time he was in
the saddle, and he resumed the same steady pace he'd
forced himself to adopt after the mistake he'd made
the day before.

That delay had brought sharply to Lannigan a
lesson he'd learned from wolfing: when a tracker
overruns a trail and loses it, locating the place where
the tracks changed direction can wipe out all the time
gained by moving fast. He held to a deliberate pace,
stopping at every one of the rare small rills he came
to and letting his mustang drink, drinking himself as
the sun mounted higher and started baking his back,
and refilling his canteen against the dryness that he
knew he'd encounter later. At noon he did not stop,
but ate in the saddle, chewing parched corn and buf-

falo jerky from his saddlebag while the pony continued to cover ground.

In the early afternoon he came upon the ashes of a
buffalo-chip fire beside the trail. He dismounted long
enough to search the ground around it, finding a
woman's shoe-print mixed with those of two booted
men. From the dryness of the horse-droppings where
the party's animals had been tethered, he learned that
he was gaining a little bit on the trio, but they were
still almost a full day ahead of him.

Tracking into the sun was easier than when the
light was behind him or directly overhead, even
though the brassy glare of the two hours preceding
sunset left Lannigan sun-blinded when twilight came.
He could see well enough to stake his horse where
the animal could drink from the tiny trickling creek
by which he made camp. It was not until the next
morning that he saw the fresh burned-out fire marking the night camp where Judith's abductors had
stopped the previous evening. They were obviously
traveling faster than he was; they had no need to
move slowly, following tracks. He speeded up when
he was on his way again, in a hurry to catch up
quickly.

It was late afternoon, nearly an hour left to go until
sunset, when Lannigan saw the line shack ahead of
him, square against a thin line of green that marked a
creek's course. He reined in, his eyes squinted against
the blinding rays of the low-hanging sun, and studied
the area around the little shanty, as well as the shack
itself.

There was no cover between him and the shack, no
brush, not even a gully through which he could approach it. Yet, no smoke came from the stovepipe that
elbowed out of one side of the structure, and no
horses stood outside it. Lannigan did not remember it

as a YL building, though it might have been. It might
equally well, he thought, belong to the Box X or the
Pickaxe, both of whose ranges adjoined that of the YL
on the east and north. He bent low to sight along the
ground into the sun. As nearly as he could tell, the
line of tracks he was following led directly to the
shack.

"If I can see it, they can see me," Lannigan muttered to himself. "But if they're in there, where's their
horses? And if they see me, why ain't they shooting?"

He decided the odds were on his side that the
shanty was unoccupied and started toward it in a
direct line. He took the precaution of drawing his rifle
from its saddle scabbard and slipping his feet part-
way out of his stirrups so that if necessary he could
roll out of his saddle and hit the ground shooting.

As he drew closer to the shack, Lannigan could see
that the little building was a hide-house, a relic of an
earlier day, when shelters on the barren prairie were
made by setting tree limbs into the ground and
nailing untanned dried buffalo hides between them.
The hides, stiff as boards and almost as thick, put on
the poles hair-side out, turned wind and snow almost
as well as a soddie and could be erected in a fraction
of the time digging sods required. This one had almost outlived its day. It was leaning south from the
pressure of the prevailing north wind; it had only one
opening, made by sawing out a rectangle from another hide to serve as a door.

A dozen yards from the shack, Lannigan felt safe
enough to ride right up to it before dismounting. He
pushed the hide-flap open. His eyes were slow in ad-
justing to the dim light of the shack's interior after
he'd stared into the sun for so many hours. It was a
full minute before he could see Judith, tied in a chair
and gagged, in the middle of the shanty.

"Judith!" he called. "It's me, Lobo! I'll have you out of those ropes in a minute, now!"

Lannigan fumbled with the knotted gag, his attention focused on Judith's pleading eyes. The dirt-streaked cloth fell away. He asked her, "Are you all right, honey?"

Judith's lips worked, but the incoherent jumble of sounds she formed in her throat came from her mouth in a whisper so faint that Lannigan was unable to hear much more than the gusts of her breath. He said, "Sure. Your mouth's all dried out. I'll get you some water."

He ran outside and brought back his canteen, held it to her lips. She drank a few sips before shaking her head vigorously. Lannigan put the canteen on the dirt floor beside the chair and drew his sheath knife. Judith flinched when she saw the blade. Tears flooded her eyes and she tried again to say something, but could only produce the unintelligible whisperings in her throat that had marked her first efforts at speech. Lannigan slashed away the rope that held her in the chair. He reached out a hand to help her to her feet, but when he tried to put his arms around her, to kiss her, she twisted out of his embrace and turned her back on him.

Lannigan was bewildered. He asked her, "What's the matter, Judith? Why don't you talk to me?"

She stepped away and turned to face him; tried to say something and failed again. She buried her head in her hands and her body began shaking with soundless sobs.

"Judith, honey, you're all right now," Lannigan assured her, his voice a plea. "Nobody's going to hurt you as long as I'm here to look after you. Now, get hold of yourself and tell me where the men are and when they'll be back."

Lifting her tearstained face, her eyes still flowing, she made another effort to form words, but with no more success than before. She looked at the open door and started toward it, but Lannigan caught and held her.

"Judith, Judith!" he pleaded. "Talk to me, won't you? Everything that scared you's all over. You're safe, now."

She seemed unable to understand. Lannigan thought it might help her to get outside the hut, and led her through the sagging door. She tried to pull back, but he gently forced her to go with him.

In the light outside, he could see her clearly for the first time. Anger bubbled through him hotly as he looked at her face, red and swollen, with the marks of bruises that were to come beginning to show beneath her fair skin. He saw a stain on the collar of her dress and lifted her chin, pulled away the dress, and revealed red scabs that had formed over the fresh cut. He could tell they had been made by the tip of a knife.

"Them two men, they abused you, didn't they?" he asked her. She did not try to reply, but attempted to free her chin from his hand so that she could lower her head. He repeated, fierce rage in his voice, "They abused you, didn't they?" Judith's tears began to flow again. She nodded her head as best she could.

Lannigan's anger was swept away by pity. He embraced Judith in spite of her efforts to push him away, and gave her the best comfort he knew. "It don't matter. You don't need to talk about it or even think about it, ever again," he told her in a half whisper. "You're my wife, Judith, and I love you so much I can't tell you how much. There ain't nothing could happen that'd stop me from loving you. You hear me? You understand what I'm saying to you?"

Bit by bit, Judith's trembling eased. Slowly she raised her head and nodded. But when Lannigan tightened his embrace and tried to kiss her bruised and swollen lips, she turned her head aside.

"It's all right," he assured her. "I guess I don't really know how you feel, but maybe I do, a little bit. And you hold on to what I'm trying to tell you. You're my wife, and I love you, and you're the only woman I want for my wife. No matter what. You understand me?"

Still trembling, Judith nodded. She made another effort to talk, but Lannigan's assurances had not broken through the trauma that stopped her voice. She was calmer, though her eyes were still wide and troubled. Her trembling was not now constant, but she was seized by recurring fits of quivering that shook her body.

"Now you listen to me," Lannigan said. He subdued his returning anger and kept his voice soft and gentle. "Them two men, are they coming back here?" Judith nodded. "All right. Now, I don't want you to be in the shack when they get back. I'm going to put you on my pony and lead you off a ways, where they won't see you. And I want you to promise that whatever happens, you won't ride off. You promise me that?"

After she'd studied her husband's face for a moment, Judith nodded again. Lannigan said, "You remember, we said we'd always keep a promise we made each other. Now, let's go."

He helped her into the saddle and led the horse to the creek. The trees that grew along its banks were far-spaced and their growth scanty, but they were the only cover the prairie offered, though the slope of the land toward the stream provided some concealment. He helped Judith down, tethered the mustang to a tree, and as an added precaution, hobbled the animal, while Judith was bending over the creek, washing her hands and face.

Lannigan walked to the stream and hunkered down beside Judith. With the grime removed, the red and ugly splotches on her face and the scabs on her neck, the bruised and swollen lips, showed even more plainly. Lannigan's face grew grim, his eyes hard. Judith misread his expression. She began to shudder again, and tried to move away from him.

He forced his features to soften and said softly, "I'm thinking about them fellows that mistreated you, Judith. Now, when they come back, don't be scared. I want you to stay right here by the pony. No matter what you hear, shooting or anything else, don't come up to the shack. Don't run away, either. Now, you promised me you'll stay here, and I'm promising you I'll be back to take care of you, soon as it's safe."

Judith nodded, but when her throat pulsed in an effort to reply, only a faint, incoherent jumble of sound passed her lips. Lannigan told her, "It's all right. You just got the talk scared out of you for a while. It'll come back." He hoped he was telling her the truth.

He took his hotroll from the pony and spread it on the sloping bank; when she lay down she'd be invisible from the shack, even if it was still daylight when Harris and his companion returned.

"Crawl in here, now," he instructed her. "And don't crawl out of these soogans till I come back."

Judith nodded. Lannigan did not try to touch her, this time. The way she shrank back from his hand hurt him more than he could admit, and led him to imagine things he didn't like to think about. When Judith was settled into the bedroll, Lannigan took his fuke and saddlebags off the horse and went back to the shack. It was dark inside, and though the stub of a candle stood stuck in its grease on the small table, he did not light it, but stepped outside in the twilight to check his rifle and pistol. He filled his coat pocket with shells from the saddlebag.

Back in the shack, he rolled up a blanket from the bunk and tied it in the chair. He fastened the white cloth of the gag around the top of the blanket, where it would show at the place Judith's head had been. He didn't expect the crude dummy to fool anybody for more than a few seconds after they'd entered the dark shack from outside, but those few seconds were all he wanted. When he'd set his trap, he sat on the edge of the bunk and waited.

Darkness moved into the shack, imperceptibly at first, then in a swift plunge to totality, as was the way of night's coming to the prairie. Lannigan waited; he'd learned patience. The hours passed, but he did not know how many of them, before he heard the clump of hoofbeats begin as a distant ghostlike echo and grow steadily louder until horses stopped outside the shack. He was sure he counted three sets of hoofbeats, and wondered if Harris and his partner had recruited a third man to replace the one killed by Tobias at Mobeetie. Then he understood what was happening, when they started talking.

"Get your money in your hand, Sessions. The woman's in the shack, and like we told you, she ain't hurt."

Lannigan did not recognize the speaker's voice, but he knew Sessions's when the ranch manager spoke. "I believe what I see, I told you that at the ranch. And I don't pass money on promises."

"We deliver." This was Harris's voice. "Go bring her out, Slane. Then we can get our payoff and go back after Lannigan."

Before Slane opened the door, Lannigan dropped to one knee at the corner of the bunk. He saw the man's figure outlined in the door opening, black against a starred purple sky. A match sputtered. He had a glimpse of the outlaw's face when the match caught. Slane's eyes were blinking in the sudden light. He may have seen the dummy, may have spotted Lannigan, for he dropped the match as he clawed for his gun. Lannigan fired one barrel of the fuke and Slane's dying reflex pulled his pistol's trigger. The gunflashes blinded Lannigan, but he sensed rather than saw another figure at the door. He fired again, the figure crumpled. He dropped the fuke and picked up his rifle.

"Slane?" Harris called. "Is that Lannigan in there? Did you get him?" A momentary pause, then, urgently, "Slane!"

In the instant before he began pumping rifle slugs, Lannigan called back, "It's me, Harris!" Then he was shooting and Harris's answering slugs were whistling by him, the lead splatting when it struck the buffalo hide above his head.

Lannigan pumped shells through his rifle until the magazine was empty, and drew his Colt. Harris had stopped shooting. Lannigan wondered if he was dead, started for the door to find out, and got his answer when hooves drummed on the baked soil and faded into the distance.

Steadying his hands, shaking now in delayed reaction, Lannigan lighted the candle-stub. Slane was lying dead on the floor beside the table. In the doorway, Sessions was stirring, trying to sit up.

"You hurt bad, Sessions?" Lannigan asked, going to stand over him.

"I'm dying, damn you! And you're responsible!"

"You sound pretty lively to me. Don't look any

worse than you generally do, either." Lannigan examined Sessions's torso; Judith's uncle was sitting up by now. His shirt was bloodstained on one side, but all his limbs were moving. Lannigan did not offer to help him sit up. He said, "Get on your feet and I'll fix you up. You're not hurt all that bad." Then he went to look at Slane. He prodded the outlaw's body with a toe and wondered that he felt no emotion whatever at having killed a man. The body might have been a wolf hulk for all the feeling it created in him.

Sessions, on his feet now, whined. "You said you'd fix me up. I'm in bad shape, Lannigan. I'm bleeding to death!"

"You're lucky you ain't already dead." There was no sympathy in Lannigan's voice; he was thinking, though, that he'd rather have shot Harris than Sessions.

For the first time, Sessions saw the dummy in the chair. He exclaimed, "Those men lied to me! They said they had Judith here, but all they wanted to do was to get me here and rob me!"

"They had her, all right," Lannigan said curtly. "I got her hid outside. Now, let's see how bad you're hurt." He ripped Sessions's shirt open. Two buckshot had hit him; one had grazed his ribs, the other was buried in the fleshy part of his upper arm, just below the shoulder.

"Am I hurt badly?" Sessions gasped, craning to see his wounds.

"You'll live. Get out of that shirt, I need some clean cloth to bandage you up with." He tore Sessions's shirt into strips and bandaged the rancher's side and arm, using what was left of the shirt to make a sling that kept the wounded arm from dangling. Sessions started to speak several times while Lannigan worked, but the look on the small man's face stopped him.

"That'll do," Lannigan announced when he'd tied the last knot in the improvised sling. "You'll need a doctor to dig out that buck slug you got in your shoulder. How far is it to anyplace from here?"

Sessions was eager to help. "It's about thirty miles to Tascosa. Twelve or fifteen to YL headquarters. This a Box X shack we're in."

"All right. I guess I can stand you around long enough to ride to Tascosa. I'll bring Judith up."

Belatedly, Sessions forgot his own troubles and asked, "How is she, Lannigan? I'd never forgive myself if she's been hurt."

"Time to've thought about that was before you put out them reward handbills. She ain't shot or wounded, but she's hurt. In ways I don't guess you'd understand. Now, you leave her alone. Don't get close to her when I bring her up here, you understand? Because I got no give at all where you're concerned, Sessions."

During the flurry of activity after Lannigan returned from the creek, leading the pony with Judith riding it, Sessions stayed silent. He said only one thing as Lannigan motioned for him to mount. "That man." He motioned toward Slane's body. "What about him?"

"Leave him lay, for all I care," Lannigan snapped. "You can stay and bury him if you want, or send some hands to do it. He's no concern of mine. That's your trash laying there, Sessions, and I'll leave it for you to clean up. Now, let's get on to Tascosa."

"You sure it's all right for you to go off, with Miz Lannigan the way she is?" Bert Coogan asked. His face showed his concern.

"I can't help her by staying, Bert. The doctor here and the one in Tascosa said about the same thing. It's not like Judith's got something medicine can cure. She's just got to have time to get over what happened to her." Lannigan did not want to talk about the explanations the doctors had given him. He grew angry every time he thought about his wife's condition, and the cause of it. He went on: "Mrs. Brent and her boy, Bobby, they'll look after her. The doctors said it might even help her if she was left alone, so that's what I aim to do, for a while."

"How long you figure to be gone?"

"Till I run Harris to earth."

"Might take a while, Lobo. He's just one outlaw with a lot of country to hide in. Texas, New Mexico, Colorado, Indian Territory. How you going to find him?"

"I'm not. I'm going to let him find me. I've got Harris figured, Bert. He's like a wolf, and wolves have got regular runs, one over here, another one over there, and another one someplace else. Thing is, they don't like to get away from them runs. They use 'em over and over, stick with the ones they know."

Coogan frowned. "How's that going to help you any?"

"Harris's pals was with Billy the Kid. I figure they used the same hidey-holes right along, and Harris learned 'em. The gang mostly worked from Tascosa into New Mexico Territory; that's likely the way he run. After that killing in Mobeetie, he wouldn't hardly head east. He's someplace west of Tascosa, I figure."

"Makes sense. But I still don't see it's helping you. Awful lot of country there."

"Now, Bert, when I'm working at wolfing, I don't go chasing wolves all over the prairie. I find their runs and make my sets and put out my scent to draw 'em to the traps. So this time, I'm going to be the scent. Harris wants to get rid of me. I know he figures I'll be after him the rest of his life if he don't."

"Risky, Lobo. Mighty risky, being bait. You be careful."

"Sure. I'm not forgetting." Lannigan stood up. "So I'll pull out around sunup. Sorta keep an eye out, Bert, Judith's going to stay at Mrs. Brent's."

"You know I will, without you even having to ask."

"I know. Well. I guess I'll see you when I get back."

Lannigan had spent long hours planning, during the two weeks since he'd brought Judith home. He set out the next morning to see if the plans would work. He traveled as though he was going on a wolfing job, though he left all but a few of his steel traps behind. This was part of his plan. He could move faster on horseback, but a man riding a mustang, even a man of small stature, was no novelty in cattle country. People would remember and talk about a man who was not only small, but who was traveling in a mule-drawn wagon with a saddle horse on a lead rope.

At Tascosa he started trying to locate the runs. He waited out an afternoon at Garrity's Saloon until the proprietor was alone, and carried his empty stein up to the bar for a refill. Garrity had been too busy to notice Lannigan before, but as he studied him while waiting for the stein to fill, recognition grew in his eyes.

"I know you, sure," he said, sliding the stein over the bar. "Been a while, though. A year like, wasn't it? You faced down Slane and Whiteside and that other fellow with an empty fuke."

Lannigan nodded. "That's right. Like you said, it's been a while. Those three still hanging around Tascosa? I'd just as soon not run into them again. Except Harris. Him, I'd like to see."

"Harris," Garrity repeated. "Couldn't call his name right off. But they were all three here a month or so back. Afterwards, I heard Whiteside got shot and killed over to Mobeetie."

"That so? Leaves just Slane and Harris, then." Lannigan sipped his beer slowly. "You said Slane used to run with Billy the Kid. Any more of his old gang around?"

"What's your interest?"

"Nothing special. Just curious."

Garrity studied Lannigan with narrowing eyes. "You on the prod to find Harris? The way you talk, you got something to settle with him."

"If that was the way of it, I wouldn't be bragging about it, now, would I?"

"That depends." The saloonkeeper puckered his lips thoughtfully. "Some men talk a lot, others don't. I'm beginning to place you better now. You're that wolfer who stirred up a ruckus on the YL this summer. Had Sessions running backwards on a greased skid. Which didn't make me too sorry to see."

Lannigan waited a moment, then reminded Garrity, "You never did say whether there was any more of the Kid's old gang still around."

It was Garrity's turn to measure silence before replying. At last he said, "There never was more than a dozen riding with Billy. After he broke jail and had to run, most of 'em drifted off. Slane tried to hold the gang together, I heard, but when Pat Garrett shot the Kid over at Fort Sumner, it was sort of good-night, Miss Lucy." When Lannigan waited without pressing for details, Garrity added, "I guess Cruz Padilla's the only one left around here from Billy's old bunch."

"He still lives in Tascosa?"

"Oh, sure. He cut away early. He's got one of those little 'dobe shacks north of town. But far as I know, he never went on with Slane, so he might not even have run into this Harris fellow."

Lannigan made an obvious show of trying to hide his interest. He told Garrity, "Well, like I said, I was just curious." He put down his empty stein. "Got a long way to travel, over to New Mexico Territory. Want to cut the trip a few miles before dark."

Cruz Padilla was younger than Lannigan had thought he'd be, and quite a bit more suspicious. He parried Lannigan's first questions with shrugs and silence until convinced by repeated assurances that he was not being asked to betray a former outlaw comrade and that he'd be well paid for the information Lannigan wanted.

"In gold?" Padilla asked, indicating that he was at least ready to talk after nearly an hour of parleying.

Gold figured prominently in Lannigan's later plans; he was well-prepared. He pulled a double eagle from his pocket and held it in front of Padilla's face. "One of these for every one of the hideouts Billy used. He must've had a lot of holes he could duck into when things got too hot for him."

Padilla smiled thinly. "Many, *señor*. From here to the west, you ask?" He brought a hand up, palm spread. "Ten, fifteen. Perhaps new ones that he used after I rode with him no longer."

"But you heard?" Lannigan cocked his head questioningly. Padilla smiled and nodded. Lannigan went on: "I won't grudge paying for as many as you remember. But the ones I really want to know about are the ones close to a town, like around Tascosa, where a bunch of men holed up might get supplies easy."

"There are a few such," Padilla admitted thoughtfully. He was still weighing Lannigan's offer. He shrugged. "It can do no harm if I tell you. I will take your gold pieces, *señor*."

Dusk was creeping over the prairie when Lannigan left the little adobe house and headed north, for a fork of Rabbit Ear Creek and the first of the hideouts Padilla had described. He camped on the prairie long before he reached his destination, and lay awake most of the night going over Padilla's directions and descriptions of miles and landmarks, rock formations, canyons, trails, creeks, springs, and ponds that watered groves of trees. Before sleeping, he'd imprinted on his mind a map of each of the outlaw sanctuaries. Lannigan had succeeded in learning where to find the runs of the human wolf he was trying to follow on a trail already cold.

Most of the hideouts were within a short distance of the sinuous Canadian River or the creeks that fed it. Some were dry camps, isolated in box canyons; these and the spots on the tributaries took time to find and check, so Lannigan's progress was slow. He had visited four or five without finding any traces that they'd been used recently and was worrying that he might have miscalculated Harris's reactions as resembling those of a wolf hesitating to leave familiar territory, when he found the first encouraging sign. At a backdraw off Rita Blanca Creek, thirty miles north of the Canadian, he discovered ashes and embers that had not been crusted by either rain or snow, and the gnawed bones of a rabbit to which some shreds of meat and soft gristle were still clinging.

"Two weeks, maybe three," he muttered after examining what he'd found. "Got this far before he run out of whatever grub he was packing in his saddlebag. He'll have to stop and buy stuff someplace before he can hole up or move on."

Someplace proved to be Trujillo, an all but dead

sheep station just short of a day's ride from the hideout on the Rita Blanca. The town was only eight or nine houses large, the dwellings scattered haphazardly between mounds of brown earth that showed where other adobe houses had stood, but it still had a store and a saloon. The store's stock was limited to a few bags of parched corn and dried beans, boxes of salt and *penuche*, strips of jerky, and some strings of purple chili peppers. The saloon offered Taos Lightning and *aguardiente* poured from jugs.

"Not like the old days, I guess," Lannigan remarked to the aged survivor of an earlier era who was tending bar. He took another sip of the raw, sweet *aguardiente* and tried to look as though he enjoyed it. "I'll bet I'm the first customer you've had from outside the town here in a month."

"Ah, you are wrong by two weeks," the old man cackled. "There was another, an Anglo like yourself, that short a time ago."

"You don't say," Lannigan replied. "Going west, like I am?"

"He left in that direction, *sí*," the saloonkeeper agreed. "A big man, tall, not like you." He chuckled. "*Tu es enano.*"

"I guess." Lannigan thought he knew what the ancient had said, but it did not worry him. He put money on the bar and left. There was a trail to follow now, not yet warm, but a better one than he'd had before. He had no doubt that it was Harris who'd gone through Trujillo. The old sheep station stood on the abandoned river road that paralleled the tortuous windings of the Canadian, and most travelers now preferred the straighter Army road south of the river. Lannigan climbed on the wagon and geed his mules. Somehow, the vastness of the country ahead had diminished.

"Not a lot more places to look now," he told the rumps of his team as the mules plodded up the long rise that led to the broken mesa land of New Mexico Territory, only a half-dozen miles ahead. "Two between here and that big creek, Ute Creek, Padilla called it. One place north on the creek, and then we hit that town where the Kid's outfit used to go funning. Gallegos. But I'd say we're on the right track and getting close."

If anyone had stopped at either of the two hideouts along the river, he'd left no signs that Lannigan could find. The third outlaw refuge was a camping spot rather than a place of concealment. It lay north of the river, two hundred yards off the seldom used road that ran beside Ute Creek; the creek was almost a river itself at the spot Padilla had described, ten miles from the Canadian, in a large grove of trees. Lannigan examined the ground carefully. It was moist, shaded by the trees which were still heavy with summer foliage, and kept soft by a spring that formed a small pool near the glade's center. The pool's outlet, no more than a handspan wide, trickled through a rocky channel into Ute Creek.

Because of the moist ground, Lannigan could not tell how old the droppings were that he found in the glade. There was no evidence of a recent fire, though the earth bore scars of many old ones. The soft ground held the prints of scores of horses and the booted feet of many men, and its softness defied all of Lannigan's efforts to judge whether they were old or new. But Lannigan's confidence was restored; it had begun to wane after he'd drawn blanks at the two hideouts he'd examined after leaving the sheep station. He felt better as he started for the town, a dozen miles north of the glade.

Gallegos had escaped the fate of Trujillo; it remained a town, one almost the size of Tascosa, Lannigan observed as his wagon rolled down the gentle slope leading to it. He counted houses until he'd tallied thirty, estimated there were another ten or so that he could not see and found his estimate confirmed when the wagon reached the little plaza that was the town's heart. The buildings that faced the square housed two stores, four saloons, a barbershop, a hotel, and, just off the plaza, a livery stable. Hitching posts were spaced around the plaza's inner perimeter. He tied up at one and set out on foot.

Although he'd never used himself for bait until now, Lannigan had spent many hours since leaving Tascosa in planning how to go about doing so. He circled the plaza, moving slowly, studying the faces of the men he passed until he was sure they'd remember his searching gaze. As he walked around the square, he spotted the saloon Padilla had mentioned as being one of the Kid's gang's hangouts and returned to it after he'd completed his circuit.

Inside, El Pajarito Azul was dim and moist-smelling and empty except for a barkeeper. At one time the place must have been busy, Lannigan thought, judging by the condition of its scarred wooden floor and the battered upright piano that stood in one corner. He ordered beer and when served made a business of hauling out a fistful of mony and picking through the gold coins in search of a silver dollar to put on the bar. When the barkeep brought change, Lannigan remarked, "Quieter in town than I'd thought it'd be. I always heard Gallegos was pretty lively."

"With a disinterested shrug the man replied, *"Com' si, com' sa,* quiet today, lively tomorrow.""

"That ain't what a friend of mine told me. He made out like Gallegos is always bustling." When the barkeep failed to ask the anticipated question, Lannigan said, "You might know this fellow I'm talking about. Name's Harris, most folks call him Hardcase."

Again the barkeep shrugged. "I know the names of few I serve."

"Too bad. I was sorta hoping I'd run into him when I got up this way." His second effort drew no more interest than had the first. Lannigan finished his beer and left.

He repeated the gambit with minor variations as he circled the plaza, buying a beer in each of the other saloons, making small purchases at the stores, inquiring about rats at the hotel, buying a sack of oats for his horse at the livery stable. It might, he told himself, have been imagination, but in more than one of the places he'd visited, he was sure there'd been flickers of recognition when he mentioned Harris's name. But when he left Gallegos in the late afternoon, he still was not positive that he hadn't been following a false trail and had now come to its dead end.

"Almost ain't quite as good as sure," he told the mules' rumps as the wagon rattled over the rutted road to the grove where he'd slept the night before. "But this is all the trail I got, so I better play it on out, win, lose, or draw."

Back at the glade, Lannigan let the team stand hitched for nearly an hour while he walked between the trees, studying the ground inch by inch. The little motte was an almost perfect circle, about three hundred feet in diameter, with the pond a score of paces north of its center. The trees grew thickest in the half-circle south of the pond; on the north they were more widely spaced, and the ground between them showed that this was the area favored by most of those who'd camped within its shelter. Over the years the campers had cleared the north half of wind-felled trees and limbs, while the south half was strewn with the trunks of trees and tangled branches.

Satisfied at last, Lannigan ended his tour. He climbed on the wagon, opened the sack of oats, and dumped half of the grain where the wagon stood, midway between the pond and the grove's outer edge. He drove the wagon around to the other side and dumped the remaining oats, then wheeled it back to the center of the grove and unhitched. He led the mules to the pile of oats on the east side, tethered them, and led his horse to the second oat-pile and tethered it. The wagon he left where he unhitched. Then he made camp a short distance from the pond, placing his bedroll at the foot of a massive cottonwood with a three-foot trunk that shielded him from the south.

Squatting beside the bedroll, he studied the bastions he'd erected: animals on both flanks, wagon in the center, to shield him from the north. Anyone seeking to sneak up on him would be forced to approach from the south. There was but an hour of daylight left. Lannigan used it to gather firewood, and while doing so, to move many of the twig-laden dry branches south of the pond. His rearrangement was not obvious, but he moved the tinder-dry limbs to form a wide vee, a corridor with its apex at the pond. When it grew too dark to work, he cooked a meager supper and crawled into his soogans. The day had been long, and it was too early to expect Harris to show up, if indeed he would show up at all. Lannigan slept soundly.

After breakfast the next morning he built the deadfall. It was almost identical with the one in which he'd taken the renegade wolf on the Bottle Brand. He placed it across the narrow opening he'd created by shifting the dry limbs the night before, and raised the trap-log to a height that would invite a sniper, shoot-

ing at night or in the dim light of pre-sunrise, to use
the log as a rifle rest. He ran the trigger-thong the
length of the trap-log, testing its position to be sure
that a man with a rifle would have to go beyond the
rawhide strap to rest his gun on the inviting trap-log.

Most of the remainder of the day, Lannigan spent
concealing the evidence of his work. It was a job akin
to hiding a set. He smoothed the ground that had
been disturbed when he'd positioned the deadfall's
logs and the branches that made his corridor. His last
move was to conceal a bottle of wolf-scent close to
the deadfall.

He finished his job by sunset, and in the failing
light Lannigan walked through the grove, inspecting
his work. There were few signs, he decided, that
would be observed by a back-shooter approaching his
camp even by daylight. He did not look for his expected visitor to try to penetrate the grove until after
dark, or before sunrise. With the wagon cutting off
certain sniping from the north, the pony and mules
posted to give warning snorts if he was approached
from either side, he was certain that any attack would
come from the south.

That night, Lannigan slept fitfully, and dozed during much of the long day of waiting that followed.
The only sounds he'd heard were those made by his
stock moving on their tethers, and the yowls of a distant pack of coyotes. The short catnaps robbed him
of the need for sleep on the second night, and it,
too, was uncomfortable. He swept sleep away deter-
minedly during the boring, dragging hours of his
third day in the grove, but even so, the darkness was
uncomfortable. He sweated in spite of the cooling
breeze and squirmed under his covering. Then, when
he threw off the tarpaulin and blankets of his hotroll,
he was too cold.

Nights are times when men worry, lying awake, and all three nights brought Lannigan his share. He worried about Judith, and the knowledge that she was being well cared for did nothing to blunt his concern. He thought of the agonizing hours she'd had, the acts that had taken her from him, and anger rising hotly renewed gave him fresh resolution to carry on his vigil. He wondered if Harris was really in the vicinity, or if the outlaw had never gone to Gallegos. In the early dawn of the fourth morning he dozed when the sky was just tinged with the new dawn's gray, but woke with a start when the mules stamped and snorted uneasily.

Holding himself motionless in the tangled hotroll, Lannigan strained to hear. The hush was unbroken except for the now leisured clopping of the mules moving at the ends of their tethers. There was not enough light by which to see, day was a bright streak on the jagged eastern horizon, but light had not trickled into the sky overhead. The burgeoning day was windless, and the glade's silence unreal. Lannigan began to feel clammy again, his booted feet moist and in need of airing, and his stomach was reminding him that for the past few days he'd eaten scantily and irregularly.

He put aside the alarm as imagination; perhaps some small animal had disturbed the mules and caused them to rouse him. He was reaching for the edge of the blankets, to throw them back, get up, cook breakfast, wait out another day, when he heard the noises. It was all but inaudible, just a brushing of disturbed twigs, but it came from the corridor he'd arranged beyond the pond. He stayed motionless.

Seconds stretched from heartbeats to minutes to infinity before the noise was repeated, the same faint twitching of disturbed dry brush. Silence returned, and all that Lannigan could hear was the faint shush of his own breathing and the pounding of his heart. He wanted to move, to look, but light was replacing darkness overhead. He could see the branches of the cottonwood above his bedroll as a dark tracery against the now starless sky, and on the ground a few yards away the dark coals of last night's supper fire could be distinguished from the black outlines of the coffeepot and skillet sitting beside them.

Suddenly it happened. There was a muffled crash from beyond the pond, followed at once by the sharp ringing cry of a man in pain. Lannigan threw back the blankets, grabbed the fuke that lay beside the soogans, and hurried to the deadfall.

Harris was lying on the ground, his left leg trapped below the knee by the top log. He'd brought up his free leg and planted his foot on the trap-log; was trying to push it aside. The log was too heavy to be moved without a lever; in any case, the awkward position into which the trapped leg forced Harris kept him from exerting any effective pressure. The log lay solidly in place, resisting all his efforts. He was so engrossed in trying to free himself that at first he didn't notice Lobo.

During the hours he'd waited, Lannigan had wondered more than a few times if he'd be able to hold back from shooting Harris on sight. From the first time the two men had met, hostility had flared between them almost spontaneously. At the saloon in Chispos, in the S Bar T bunkhouse, and in Garrity's place in Tascosa, Lannigan had reacted instantly to Harris's gibes. Now, carrying a hurt so much bigger than words could ever create, Lobo hadn't been at all certain he'd be able to stop his finger from pressing the fuke's trigger, if he had Harris looking into the muzzle of the ancient sawed-off double-barrel.

Facing Harris now, seeing his enemy trapped and helpless, Lannigan was surprised to discover that he could let reason overrule emotion. The urge to press the fuke's trigger was strong, but he was strong enough to hold it in check. He'd learned, in the months that had lapsed since his first encounter with the trapped Harris, to think and plan instead of rushing in with fists swinging. The success of his plan brought him a feeling of victory, but it was not a victory to be celebrated in hot anger. This time his anger was deep, cold, and restrained—not a quickly flaring flash that demanded instant action, immediate satisfaction.

From some deep well of memory an almost forgotten line of the lessons he'd learned at the orphanage came back to him. I guess them old prophets was right, Lannigan thought, I've put by being a young wild tad now, and growed up to be a man.

Harris finally saw Lannigan and twisted as though to draw his holstered pistol, but his position made the effort awkward and slow. Lannigan did not have to speak. He merely lifted the shotgun to cover Harris, and the threat stopped Harris's hand before it touched the gun-butt.

Lannigan kept all emotion from his voice. "I was wondering when you'd come calling."

"Damn you, Lannigan!" Harris snarled. "You and your wolfing tricks! I oughta know you'd pull something sly and sneaky!"

"You oughta know better than to lay a hand on my wife." Lannigan's voice was still carefully flat. When Harris made no response he went on. "I'll feel better when you're rid of that Colt. Take off your cartridge belt and throw it over here. And don't get no ideas. If you even look like you want to touch the butt of that pistol, you're a dead man."

Harris glared, but he knew men and weapons. He respected the authority of the shotgun. Grimacing with pain as he moved, he unbuckled the gunbelt and tossed it to land at Lannigan's feet. His movement drew Lannigan's attention to the rifle that lay partly concealed by Harris's torso. Letting the pistol belt lie where it fell, he stepped up quickly and slid the rifle free, kicked it out of Harris's reach.

"All right, little man," Harris grated. "You got my guns. Now get me out from under this damned log. I'm hurting."

"Not near as much as you hurt my Judith," Lannigan told him dispassionately. "You got a lot more hurt coming for what you and your friend did to her."

"Save your sermon, runt. I'll take my medicine from a judge. If you don't get me outa here pretty quick, my leg's going to be ruined. I can feel blood running in my boot right now."

"That don't surprise me," Lannigan said coldly. "Likely your leg bones has poked through your hide. You're bleeding some, and your boot's going to fill up and run over in a little while."

"In a little while? To hell with that! Get me out of here now! There's a doctor in Gallegos; he'll fix me up when you take me in to turn me over to the sheriff."

"Where'd you get the idea that the law was going to come into this?" Lannigan hunkered down and took the jar of wolf-scent from the tree-root crevice where he'd put it.

Harris had stopped paying attention when Lannigan walked over to the tree where the jar of scent was hidden. He'd gone back to trying to push the trap-log away with his free leg. The pain of the crushed leg was too great. He stopped straining and looked up to see Lannigan taking the lid off the jar of scent.

"What's that?" Harris asked.

"It's what wolfers use to toll wolves to a trap," Lannigan replied in a casually conversational tone. "Ever smell it, Harris?" He moved close enough to let the trapped outlaw get a whiff of the scent. "This stuff draws wolves from fifty miles away." He began dribbling the jar's contents on the ground around the deadfall.

"Oh, now, wait a minute!" Harris protested. For the first time anger was absent from his voice and fear tinged it instead. "You can't leave me for the wolves. You got to take me to town and turn me in to the law!"

"It might take the wolves a day or two to get here," Lannigan went on, as though Harris hadn't spoken. "But if there's any close around, they'll smell it and come running, sooner or later." He emptied the jar and tossed it aside. "That'll give you a while to think about things while you're waiting."

"That's the same as murder!" Now, Harris was almost openly pleading. "I got a right to have the law handle me!"

"All the right you got is what I decide to give you," Lannigan responded. "And there's not a law can make you pay for what you done to my wife. Not if you was in jail a thousand years. Wolf-law's what you lived by, Harris, and I'm giving you wolf-law to die by."

Lannigan picked up Harris's gunbelt. Removing the revolver, holding it where Harris could watch, he took out all but one cartridge. He said, "But I'll make it easy for you. I'll put this where you can reach it if you strain real hard. I figure there's three ways that you can use that shot. You can try for me, but if I see you go for this gun, I'll cut you to pieces with my fuke. You can hope to hear somebody going by on the road and try to signal 'em, but there hasn't been anybody pass for three days, and nobody's going to pay any mind to just one shot. Or, you can save the shell until the wolves get here."

Harris looked searchingly into Lannigan's eyes and saw no mercy, only the grimness of death. He did not speak when Lannigan placed the revolver where by long and painful stretching he could grasp it. He did not try to reach for it after Lannigan stepped back.

Walking the short distance to the wagon, Lannigan carried in his mind a picture of Harris's face, a mixture of hatred, fear, and pleading. He tried to summon up some pity for the man he was leaving in a trap, but could find none in his heart. Strangely, he found no pleasure or satisfaction, either.

He made a fast job of throwing his bedroll and cooking utensils into the wagon, hitching the mules, and tying the mustang to its lead-rope. The sun was rising as he pulled onto the road after leaving the grove. He geed the team to a bit more speed. The glare would be bad after an hour or so, when he'd reached the Canadian and turned east, but that didn't matter.

Lannigan was already thinking about Mobeetie. There he had a wounded mind to heal, a hurt body to mend with gentle care, and a wife to make into a whole woman again.

AN ENVIRONMENTAL FOOTNOTE

A great deal of natural history as well as national history is being revised by motion pictures and television. The so-called "real life" outdoor productions that purport to show the relationship between Western explorers and settlers and the animals of the area succeed in misrepresenting and saccarinizing reality.

It started with *Bambi*, which was a cartoon fable, but which is now taken seriously by the ignorant and uninformed. Sadly, urbanization of the United States has removed a majority of its citizens from any contact with or personal knowledge of nature. City-dwellers take the most improbable fables seriously.

Slick commercial presentations dealing with human/animal relationships are usually as phony as the well-known three-dollar bill, and so-called ecologists and environmentalists use them as propaganda in their efforts to prove the unprovable and the unreal. I do not question the sincerity of the uninformed, but cannot excuse them for failing to do their homework and dig out some facts. Nor can they be excused for ignoring what most of them choose to ignore: that Nature grants no "rights" to any animal, including man, except to survive through its own efforts. Individuals in any species live to reproduce only if they are strong enough, skillful enough, agile enough, and intelligent enough to do so. Nature is neither kind nor cruel. Nature simply is. We do ourselves no favors when we ignore this.

On a television program, a news broadcast, in February 1977, the statement was made that "there are fewer than six hundred wild wolves in the United States today." This is arrant, uninformed nonsense. There are that many wolves in many counties of a number of western and southwestern states. There are uncounted numbers of wild wolves in Alaska and Canada, and these still behave as wild wolves always have. Their habits do not include being friendly with other animals or with humans.

This book has presented the war of settler versus wolf realistically. To give the wolf credit: it is a highly intelligent animal, but it is a wanton killer and a savage adversary. Consider a few facts taken from documents of the period 1837–1915. Remember, these are records set down by men who had no interest in lying to posterity, men who were simply recording facts of their daily lives.

Item: Attacks on trail oxen, mules, and horses along the Santa Fe Trail in the 1840–1870 period often stranded parties for weeks. The wolves did not generally kill the draft animals, but hamstrung them.

Item: From 1890–93, the LX Ranch in the Texas Panhandle kept a hundred breeding mares but did not brand a single colt from them during this period; wolves killed a hundred percent of the foals.

Item: On the Rocking Chair Ranch in the same area as the LX, wolves in 1880 killed 3770 head of cattle, five percent of the entire ranch herd. Ten percent of the cattle killed were yearlings.

Item: In Walla Walla, Washington, in 1887, a pack of about 18 wolves herded 120 head of cattle for several miles to a cliff and by repeated attacks stampeded them over the edge. All died.

Item: On the Galisteo range in New Mexico in 1879, one renegade wolf in one night killed seventy-three sheep, fourteen lambs, one horse, and three mules.

Item: Renegade wolves, identifiable by their tracks, were fearsome slaughterers. The Aguila Wolf in Arizona killed sixty-five sheep in one night, forty the next night. Three Toes, a South Dakota renegade, killed sixty-six sheep in two nights. Old Lefty, in Montana, killed 1348 head of cattle in an eight-year period of depredations.

These are a few of over one hundred documented cases I found in researching *Lannigan's Revenge*. If the ranchers who pioneered the West had not matched the wolf in mercilessness, there would be little beef on United States tables today.

M.M.

DELL'S ACTION-PACKED WESTERNS

Selected Titles